Methodical Agenda

Methodical Agenda

Rebekah Roth

Methodical Agenda is a work of fiction based on historical facts. Some names, characters, places, events, and incidents may be either the product of the author's imagination or a compilation of persons the author has met. Any resemblance to actual events, locales, organizations, or person, living or dead, may be pure coincidence and beyond the intent of either the author or the publisher.

ISBN 978-0-9976457-6-7

Library of Congress Catalog-in-Publication Data
Roth, Rebekah
Methodical Agenda
Fiction
2021916873
ISBN 978-0-9976457-6-7
Library of Congress Number: 2021916873

To contact Rebekah Roth:
www.readroth.com

KTYS media
www.ktysmedia.com

This QR code will take you to Rebekah's store where you can purchase personalized and autographed books from the author.

Printed in the United States of America

Dedicated To:
To my fellow flight attendants, both active and retired,
for their patience, support, and help.

You know who you are.
This one's for you!

FROM THE AUTHOR

I never dreamed I would write a book, let alone write a series of books. When I first began to look closely at the 9/11 event, I questioned the official story but had no replacement theory. Some specifics of the official story simply did not jive with my professional airline career. I have never been one to question the government or its involvement in nefarious dealings. However, once I researched 9/11 with a genuine desire to find the truth; magical, some might say mystical, things began to happen. Upon discovering that several of the accused hijackers were still alive long after they supposedly died on those four planes, I met a retired special forces soldier who was at the

Pentagon that day. Many of us remember the chorus line of men searching for 757 parts on the lawn and questioned what they were looking for. A fuse? A contact lens? Certainly not something from a 757! My friend reassured me that no 757 crashed into the Pentagon; he knew because he was there. That chance meeting encouraged me to open both eyes and not stop until I completely understood the historical episode.

Methodical Agenda is now the fifth book in the series, so it would be best to read them all to know the characters. When I wrote the first book, I never dreamed anyone would read it, let alone see it climb into the top ten on Amazon books. However, that book and an interview on Coast to Coast brought me so many fellow airline employees, pilots, flight attendants, and others that the books practically wrote themselves.

Since the fourth book, Methodical Exposure, I have read through thousands of books, manuals, documents, news articles, and magazine stories to discover who was behind this operation, how they pulled it off, and why. Many government officials have written books about their whereabouts on September 11th, 2001, and what they did or remembered doing that day; luckily, they have gone down in history telling their stories. Unfortunately, many of those accounts are contradictory at best and condemning to say the least. I guess none of the actual perpetrators ever thought anyone with inside knowledge would read and remember all the details and meticulously put every word together to uncover the crime of the century.

In researching, I recognized a pattern that intelligence agencies use for various types of operations. They train and work together often in unison to provide each agency with plausible deniability if their crimes are closely examined. Throughout our history, we have been warned of the dangers of the military-industrial complex and the international globalists that make money from endless wars. Unfortunately, history will continue to repeat itself.

Many people have asked me to put all my information and documentation into a non-fiction book. I have given that a great deal of thought. But I realize now how dangerous that would be for myself, my family, and my friends. So, I am sticking with the novel series, so my grandchildren have a grandmother for a few more years. This book exposes the how, who, and why of 9/11. All the puzzle pieces are now in place to show you a clear picture of the intelligence operation that changed the world forever.

THE MAIN CHARACTERS

Vera Hanson: A senior flight attendant and international purser for decades who doubted the official government story about 9/11. She eventually meets up with Jim Bowman, a friend of her deceased husband, and together they begin researching the events of 9/11. She marries the President of the United States, Joel Sherman, and together they continue their quest for truth.

Joel Sherman: **A** Boeing Aircraft executive turned Congressman then becomes Speaker of the House. He becomes the President when the President and Vice President are simultaneously impeached. No sooner does he take up residence in the White House than his wife Mica is killed in an airplane accident in Las Vegas.

Jim Bowman: A Retired airline captain turned 9/11 researcher. Jim is connected to research teams across the country. President Sherman engages Jim, who then persuades Vera to join him in getting to the bottom of 9/11.

Max Hager: A Vietnam veteran, independent 9/11 researcher, and a friend of Jim Bowman. His smarts and cunning have kept him alive through many dangerous adventures. He joins Jim working in the White House and, together with the rest of their team, continue to uncover facts about September 11th that lead to the revelation of a plan for worldwide global communism.

Ruth Ann Lowey: An original member of Max's investigation team who shares a traumatic experience with the First Lady, Vera Sherman. Ruth Ann meets Rosslyn at a spa and, when she discovers Rosslyn's airline career, invites her to join the 9/11 research team.

Rosslyn Langley: A retired flight attendant with American Airlines who becomes fast friends with Ruth Ann. She joins Ruth Ann on her quest to discover the truth about 9/11. She utilizes her website and blog to gather input from other airline employees who have begun to question the official government story about 9/11. She has a dramatic run-in with a pilot she recognizes while visiting Vancouver, Canada. She brings to the research team the missing piece of the 9/11 puzzle.

Jerry Reitz: The head of the NSA throughout Joel's administration. He brings experience and knowledge to all the investigations and is a loyal supporter of Joel.

Tom: A retired air traffic controller for the Los Angeles area.

Chip: An air traffic controller at Edwards Air Force Base with connections to Area 51. Chip began helping his friend Tom, and together they joined the White House investigation team in book 3, Methodical Conclusion.

Kelli: Vera's intuitive golden retriever who ends up living in the White House when Joel and Vera marry.

FLIGHTS

American Airlines Flight 11

Scheduled to depart Boston Logan International Airport at 07:45 am, this Boeing 767-233ER aircraft carried a crew of 11, consisting of 2 pilots and 9 flight attendants. It carried 76 passengers. Aircraft capacity: 158. Destination: Los Angeles, California. The flight took off at 07:49 am. Air traffic controllers at Boston Center lost radio contact by 08:13 am. By approximately 08:18 am, a flight attendant made a phone call to a reservations line. She reported mace or pepper spray was sprayed, but it only affected the forward cabin. The other flight attendant called her supervisor and reported the hijacker was in 9B, later she said that there were four other hijackers but listed seat locations that did not exist on that configuration. Neither crew member followed the FAA hijack protocol in place at that time. Official claim: It struck the North Tower at 08:46 am.

United Airlines Flight 175

Scheduled to depart Boston's Logan International Airport at 08:00 am, this Boeing 767-200 aircraft carried a crew of 9, consisting of 2 pilots and 7 flight attendants. It carried 51 passengers. Aircraft capacity: 168. Destination: Los Angeles, California. The flight took off at 08:14 am. Officials estimate a hijacking occurred between 08:42 am (last transmission from the cockpit) and 08:46 am. Two passengers called multiple times using their cell phones. One passenger reported mace or pepper spray was sprayed, and everyone around him was vomiting. He said that the hijackers stated that they were going to Chicago and fly into a building. The other caller claimed he and others were going to take back control of the cockpit. He thought they were over Ohio. No crew members phoned from the aircraft. Official claim: It struck the South Tower at 09:03 am.

American Airlines Flight 77

Scheduled to depart Washington Dulles International Airport at 08:10 am, this Boeing 757-223 aircraft carried a crew of 6, consisting of 2 pilots and 4 flight attendants. It carried 53 passengers. Aircraft capacity: 188. Destination: Los Angeles, California. The flight took off at 08:20 am. Phone calls from the aircraft began at 09:12 am. Calls were made from cell phones. One call was placed by a flight attendant who phoned her parents. A passenger made a call to her husband's office. Both callers gave conflicting information. Neither reported the number of hijackers correctly. This aircraft did not have working air-phones. Official claim: It struck the Pentagon at 09:37 am.

United Airlines Flight 93

Scheduled to depart Newark Liberty International Airport at 08:00 am, this Boeing 757-222 aircraft carried a crew of 7, consisting of 2 pilots and 5 flight attendants. It carried 33 passengers. Aircraft capacity: 182. Destination: San Francisco, California. The flight took off at 08:42 am. Several phone calls were made from this flight by numerous passengers and two flight attendants. The first phone call was placed at 09:27 am, moments before the official hijacking supposedly started. His cell phone number was displayed on his home phone caller ID. After that, numerous calls were placed, most with conflicting information about what was happening onboard. Neither flight attendant followed FAA hijack protocols in place at that time. Official claim: It struck the ground near Shanksville, PA., at 10:03 am, 10:06 am, or 10:10 am.

We cannot abandon this rabbit hole for fear
of a traumatic encounter with our own culture.
~ Elif Safak

one

The airline captain steered his yacht slowly into the Vancouver Harbor to not draw attention to himself or his frantic escape from the Yacht club. He set a heading north-northwest toward the Lions Gate Bridge, which would lead him past Stanley Park and into the Burrard Inlet. His destination was Horseshoe Bay, where he had moored several summers ago. He knew he could refuel and buy all the provisions he would need. His hands were shaking, and his heart was pounding. How in the world could he have been recognized?

First things first, he thought to himself as he pulled back on the throttles of the twin engines. He knew he had to make a phone call. He poured himself a cold beer and took a long gulp. The stress of the encounter at the Yacht Club left him parched. He took another swallow, this time letting the brew fill his mouth while he paused to reflect on the woman that tapped his shoulder moments earlier. He took a deep breath. This was a call he dreaded and feared making for two decades.

He unlocked the side compartment near the captain's chair and pulled out a special cell phone he needed to contact his handlers. He tapped the contacts icon and hit the letter C; the only number listed activated. *Calling,* scrolled across the screen.

"Yeah," The voice answered. "Go."

"This is one, one, niner, November, Victor, Charlie, Bravo," the captain replied.

"Stand by," the voice commanded.

Moments later, a gravelly voice came on the line. "What's up?"

The captain cleared his throat. "I'm afraid I have been compromised. I have been recognized," he continued. "A woman, I must have flown with years ago," he paused.

"She looked familiar, but I can't put a name to her face. It's been a long time. She knew who I was. There was no doubt she recognized me." He cleared his throat again; his words became more difficult to form. "I, I panicked, I hit her, knocked her out cold."

The voice on the other end interrupted, "We always knew this was a possibility when we set up the arrangement. Do you think she was a flight attendant based with you in D.C.?"

"I honestly don't know. I usually flew with a crew of five or six flight attendants, most of whom I didn't know. So, I have no idea where our paths could have crossed," the captain admitted.

"Those damn flight attendants, don't they ever stay at home?" His handler grumbled. "Where are you now?" He asked coldly as he began taking notes.

"Right now, at this moment, I am on my boat, headed out of Vancouver Harbor. I waited until the fire department, and ambulance arrived at the club before I motored away."

"The fire department?" The voice asked, interrupting the captain.

"Yes, I pulled the fire alarm as I ran out of the club that set off the sprinkler system and must have notified them. The police were right behind the fire trucks."

The captain realized that he was nervously rambling at this point. He no longer trusted the Agency to keep him protected. He always feared his identity might somehow be exposed. He could feel a combination of fear and adrenaline surge through his veins. He had not felt this degree of anxiety since the day his old life ended and his new life began. His mind quickly replayed flashes of scenes from that busy September morning inside the military hangar. He recalled the mistrust he felt of the Agency as he watched those whom he thought were part of the team lose their lives. That same panic and distrust began to overcome his normally calm demeanor.

"Good God, man, you *did* panic. Are you certain nobody saw you board your yacht?"

"Sir, I am not completely one hundred percent positive, but I'm pretty sure."

As he spoke, his mind tried to review the incident inside the Yacht club. He recalled where the woman who recognized him was seated. He closed his eyes tightly and remembered the details of the scene.

"Are you certain you don't remember this woman's name? The gal that recognized you, do you remember anything about her, like where she lived? Anything?" The handler asked him.

"I could have met her on a layover when I was flying to South America. We always went out for dinner with the entire crew. I could have flown with her; I must have," the captain shook his head slowly as he spoke. "I'm not certain, but there was another woman seated at her table. I bolted out of there pretty fast; I'm just not sure of anything," the captain admitted. "I have to say, I was shocked to be addressed as 'Captain.' I want to say I recognized her voice, but I know most flight attendants go through voice training, and so many of them sound alike."

"Ok, get yourself up to Horseshoe Bay, moor in there until you hear back from us. Keep this phone charged and with you at all times," the voice firmly ordered.

The captain acknowledged, "will do, sir."

As he ended the call, the captain changed the ringer adjustment to loud. He reached for his beer and finished it off as he pushed the throttles forward and gained speed.

"We've got one hell of a huge problem up in North Vancouver," the handler reported to a team member. "We need a staff meeting in the conference room on the seventh floor set up as soon as possible," he commanded.

two

Just as Ruth Ann turned to see who Rosslyn recognized, the man stood up and coldcocked Rosslyn, knocking her on her back. Before Ruth Ann could push her chair away from the table, the man ran past her so fast that all she could make out was his khaki pants and navy-blue polo shirt. As she stood up, sprinklers began spraying water from the ceiling. He must have pulled the fire alarm; she thought as she rushed toward Rosslyn, who was not moving.

"Rosslyn, are you okay?" Ruth Ann tapped on Rosslyn's shoulder firmly. "Rosslyn? Can you hear me?" She repeated her questioning, tapping her friend harder with each word.

Rosslyn did not move.

After several minutes, Ruth Ann noticed they were both soaking wet. A young medic came and knelt beside her. "What's her name?" He asked. Before Ruth Ann could answer, he asked another question, "What happened? Did you see what happened to her?"

"Some guy came in whom she must have recognized from her career at American Airlines. I heard her say, 'Captain,' he must have hauled off and hit her, then he ran out of the club. He pulled the fire alarm as he fled. There isn't a fire in here, is there?"

"No, Ma'am, no fire that I'm aware of," the medic answered as he checked Rosslyn's pulse. Another paramedic came in carrying two large duffle bags of equipment. "Is she okay?" He asked.

"She got coldcocked by some guy," the first medic answered. "Her heart rate seems strong and normal. Grab her blood pressure, and I'm assuming she's on the floor from the blow she took and not for some other reason."

"One sixteen over seventy-four," the second medic called out. "You want to try an ammonia inhalant on her?" He asked.

"First, can you go tell the battalion chief to turn off these sprinklers? Then check in the parking lot to see if anyone witnessed someone running away from here. Toss me one of those ammonia inhalants before you go."

Ruth Ann began to tremble. She was soaking wet and frightened for Rosslyn. "Is she okay? Can you find anything wrong with her?" She asked.

"Looks like she took a pretty hard blow to the head, but I think she'll be okay. The local police will be here any moment. I'm sure they will want to speak with you about what happened."

"All I saw was a tall, dark-haired man; he ran by so fast. I did not get a good look. Everyone started running out of here. I was afraid Rosslyn might drown with all that water spraying. I was afraid to move her."

"You did the right thing," the medic reassured Ruth Ann. "Larry, we need to get this patient out of here and into the ambulance. Bring a backboard and a gurney. Take," he stopped and looked at Ruth Ann, "I'm sorry, ma'am, I didn't catch your name."

"Ruth Ann"

"Take Ruth Ann with you; give her a set of scrubs; she can change in the rig."

"Larry, you don't think she'll have to go to the hospital, do you?" Ruth Ann asked. "We aren't Canadians, and I'd like to get her to the American side of the border for any medical treatment she might need."

"You're Americans?" Larry asked. "We can release her if you want to sign the forms. If she does not come around to answer questions, you can refuse medical treatment on her behalf. If she is not talking soon, have her see a doctor," he said as he placed a stack of towels and a set of blue scrubs next to her. "Dry off, don't worry about the scrubs; you've earned them. We will be right back with your friend."

"Thanks, I'll hurry." Ruth Ann said. "I think I'll run over to our car and get some dry clothes for Rosslyn. I don't want the border agents to think we are two medical doctors fleeing Canada for some reason."

"Good that you have extra clothes in your car for her; you got our only extra set of scrubs until we get back to our station," Larry laughed. "Be right back."

Ruth Ann changed into the scrubs and ran to the rental car to gather a set of dry clothes for Rosslyn. She was back at the ambulance by the time the medics returned.

"She is still not coming around to answer questions. She may have a concussion," Larry explained as they lifted the gurney into the aid unit and locked it firmly into position. "Her vitals are fine, she either has a concussion, or she is in shock. She appears to be in a catatonic state. Does she have any adverse medical history?"

"I can't imagine she does, she was a flight attendant for many years, and I would think she had to be healthy to do that job." Ruth Ann continued to ask about Rosslyn's condition. "Do you think this is from the combination of seeing someone that traumatized her combined with an unexpected blow to the head?"

"Anything is possible," the senior medic answered. "One thing we learn in emergency medicine is that nothing is constant, and anything can happen. Emergency medicine is sometimes like Murphy's law on steroids. What can go wrong will go wrong. Everybody reacts differently to situations. But you might be on the right track; if there was something about that man that confused her mind when he smacked her, that could very well be the case. The combination of an emotional and a physical trauma could certainly do that."

"We're staying in Seattle. Would it be safe for her to travel there this evening?" Ruth Ann asked.

"If you can manage to keep her upright and not allow her to move much, she should be fine. She might seem confused when she comes back around," he continued, "if you want to sign this release form, we can help you put her into your car."

"That would be great; why don't you let me put these dry clothes on her," Ruth Ann suggested.

"Sure, we will wait in the front of the rig," the senior medic agreed.

The two men transferred Rosslyn to the rental car. They secured her seat belt, reclined her seat back, and padded her with small pillows for her head.

"I went to Seattle a few months ago to visit friends and do some shopping. If you have problems with her for any reason, there are several hospitals along the way. Good luck with her. Have a safe journey," Larry said.

"Thanks, guys, you were great. Thanks for the towels and the set of scrubs," Ruth Ann said as she slowly began to drive away.

Ruth Ann felt relieved as she drove toward the border.

It was too late in the evening to call Max in Washington D.C.; she decided to wait until morning. By then, she hoped to have more information about Rosslyn and the man who hit her. She called Jenny to let her know what happened and that she would be arriving back at Vera's house sometime in the late evening.

"Jenny, it's Ruth Ann. I'm on my way back to Seattle; we have been involved in a rather strange incident in Vancouver. A man struck Rosslyn, and she is in a catatonic state; that is what the medics said. I have her in the car with me now. To be honest, I'm not certain what to do at this point."

Jenny was shocked, "My brother's a physician on the eastside, I'll call him. So, she was hit in the head, and now she's not responding?"

"Yes, we were having dinner, a man she thought she recognized came in and sat down across the room, she walked over to say hello, and he hauled off and smacked her. I had my back to his table, but I heard the commotion," Ruth Ann explained.

"Give me ten minutes; I'll call you right back. Let me get a referral from my brother," Jenny said.

Ruth Ann set the cruise control and tuned the radio to a station that would relax her but keep her from falling asleep. She felt a strange nervousness as she drove. Could he have been one of the American captains involved in 9/11? She felt her heart race. Oh my, she thought to herself, could that be? And if it *were* one of those pilots, how would they ever find him again? She checked the digital clock on the dash. She wished she could call Max, but she knew he would be sound asleep. Just then, her cell phone rang.

"Ruth Ann, Jenny," the voice said. "Listen, my brother said to take her to Harborview Hospital in Seattle. They have a great neurological center there. He went to school with

Dr. David Cohen, who is the department head. Take her to the emergency room, tell the on-call doctor that Dr. Cohen will see her in the morning, they will book her into a room. My brother will have spoken to Dr. Cohen by the time you arrive. Ask the nurses what time Dr. Cohen does his rounds in the morning. I am sure you will want to be there. The address is 325, 9th Avenue, Seattle."

"325, 9th Avenue, got it. Expect me to roll into Vera's house sometime later tonight. If you happen to see any of those secret service guys on watch, let them know."

"Text me in the morning when you wake up, and I will bring coffee over," Jenny offered.

three

Ruth Ann pulled off the I-5 Freeway at the James Street exit and followed the guidance of Siri on her iPhone to Harborview Hospital. She pulled the car under the emergency entrance canopy and spotted a wheelchair next to the door. She parked close to the curb and quickly ran into the lobby. A young man dressed in pale green scrubs was standing inside the glass doors and offered to help.

"I need to get my friend some help; she's in the car just outside," Ruth Ann explained.

Ruth Ann held the wheelchair steady as the orderly lifted Rosslyn out of the car and placed her into the wheelchair.

"What happened to her?" The young orderly inquired.

"She was struck in the head and is unconscious," Ruth Ann explained. "We were in Canada for the day." She heard herself nervously offering useless information.

"No problem," the orderly smiled. "Ma'am, does she have a purse or anything you think she might need?"

"I'll bring her purse in," Ruth Ann said as she tried to calm herself. "Will my car be okay parked right here while I get her checked in to the emergency room?"

"Your car will be fine there. The ER is on the second floor, and the elevator is to your right," he pointed toward the stainless-steel doors. "Are you a doctor or a nurse? I can't help but notice you're wearing scrubs."

"Oh no, I'm not a medical person at all, my clothes got wet, and the ambulance team was kind enough to give these to me," Ruth Ann explained. "Thank you; you have been most helpful."

"That's what I'm here for."

Ruth Ann pushed the red number two button for the emergency room. As the elevator opened, she turned right toward the reception area.

"Hello, my friend was hit in the head and is not able to speak." She explained to the receptionist.

"Name?" The receptionist asked coldly, not looking up at Ruth Ann.

"Rosslyn," Ruth Ann answered. "Rosslyn Langley."

"One 's' or two?" The woman asked.

"I believe two," Ruth Ann answered, not sure if it was correct. "Someone called, and she is to be seen by a Doctor Cohen, David Cohen, in neurology."

"I see she was entered into the computer system. We are so busy tonight with the usual drug overdoses and shootings; I'll send you right up to the seventh floor. No need to hang around here if she's going to be Doc Cohen's patient," she handed Ruth Ann a plastic wrist band, "Will you wrap this around her wrist and lock it in place for me, please?"

"No problem," Ruth Ann smiled, "does she need any other paperwork?"

"Everything's already in the computer, ma'am. Push her to the elevators over there and up to the 7th floor, or I can call an orderly to do it for you."

"Thanks, I can take it from here," Ruth Ann reconfirmed as she pushed Rosslyn down the hall.

"Good evening," the administrator greeted, "this must be Rosslyn Langley." She lifted from her chair to see Rosslyn's face. "She will be down the hall in room 747. Her nurse is there now. If you would like to wheel her over there, we can get her situated for the evening."

"Thanks. Oh, by the way, my name is Ruth Ann, and I'll be coming to see her regularly," she offered.

"Oh, thank you, I'll note that in her file. You'll want to check in with us whenever you visit," the woman explained. "My name is Kay, and if you call into the seventh floor after five, I will answer the phone. I'm always at my desk here."

Ruth Ann pushed the wheelchair toward Rosslyn's room.

"Let me call for another nurse to help lift her into the bed," the nurse explained as she finished filling a large plastic mug with ice water.

After the nurses positioned Rosslyn in bed and supported her head with pillows, the first nurse asked, "how long has she been like this?"

Ruth Ann looked at the large clock on the wall and quickly guessed, "probably about five hours, maybe a little longer. We were in Vancouver when she was hit. I found her on the floor; the paramedics that looked at her said something about a concussion and catatonic something or other."

The nurse was taking down notes as Ruth Ann talked.

"Had she had much alcohol to drink?" The nurse asked her.

"No, we had just ordered a glass of wine and were eating; she had iced tea before that," Ruth Ann explained.

"Did you see if whoever hit her used an object or a fist?" The nurse asked her. "Sorry to ask so many questions, but the doctor will want to have these answers, and you probably don't want to sleep all night in this uncomfortable old chair. The doctor gets in early, and it would be best to come in for his afternoon rounds unless you like to fight the most miserable Seattle traffic imaginable. I know, if it is that early in the morning, the traffic should be light, but that is just not true. You'd be shocked at how many commuters think they'll beat the rush and become the rush before there should even be a rush," the nurse laughed.

Ruth Ann finished answering all the questions watching Rosslyn for any sign of movement while she spoke. "Do you think she'll be okay alone for the night?" She asked.

"Oh, she won't be alone. We will keep a close eye on her. This is one of the busiest and most exciting floors in the hospital, after the emergency room. We pay close attention to every patient up here," the nurse explained. "By the way, my name is Sylvie, and I will be here every night for the next seven nights in a row."

Ruth Ann offered her hand, "Ruth Ann is mine."

"Ruth Ann, I suggest you get yourself a good night's sleep. Do not worry about

Rosslyn, and if you have left your cell number with us, you can expect a call from the doctor between nine and ten in the morning. He is one of the best in his field, and he is a routine kind of guy, a Sagittarius, very predictable. If you spend time around here, you will see what I mean," Sylvie explained as she continued hooking up monitors and noting Rosslyn's vitals.

Ruth Ann collected Rosslyn's purse and said good night to Sylvie. She stopped at the receptionist's desk near the elevator. "Here's my cell phone number, Kay. If she wakes up and starts talking, would you give me a call, no matter what time?"

"Sure, I can do that, Ruth Ann," Kay replied. "Have a good rest. We'll probably see you tomorrow night. Situations like hers often take a few days before they begin to show progress."

Ruth Ann entered Vera's house address into her iPhone. Jenny's lights were all off by the time she pulled into Vera's driveway. She was exhausted but decided to unload their suitcases before she went to bed. Even though the property had secret service protection, she did not want the car broken into.

As she set Rosslyn's tote bag on the floor, a small book covered with a delicate Asian brocade fell out as the bag tipped over. Ruth Ann picked it up and noticed the unique fabric print of the cover. She opened the book to discover that it appeared to be a diary. What is this? Her curiosity got the best of her. She sat down and opened the book to a random page somewhere halfway through and began to read.

four

President Joel Sherman tossed and turned all night. The day before, as the First Lady was preparing to visit the Walter Reed Hospital in Bethesda, an astute secret service agent noticed a mechanic with an open engine cowling on Marine One. He alerted the suspicious circumstance to the crew chief. Upon investigation, they discovered a severed hydraulic line, which would have resulted in a catastrophic accident. When the president was notified of the potential threat, he immediately canceled the event at the hospital. Joel was distraught. The thought of losing Vera after the loss of his first wife was more than he could bear.

"Coffee, sir?" Mike lightly tapped on the door of the residence.

Joel replied as he headed toward the door, "Thank you, Mike. I don't know how you knew I was up so early, but I could use some coffee about now."

"Yes, sir." Mike filled the porcelain cup. "Is there anything else I can do for you, sir?"

"Mike, this is all I need right now," Joel took a sip of coffee then continued. "Give me another hour, and I'll be ready to get on with my normal day."

Two hours later, Joel was at the resolute desk in the Oval Office. He hated to call this meeting to order, but he knew this discussion had to happen. Within minutes, there was a tap on his door, "Are you, ready sir?" A voice asked.

"Yes, thank you. Please show everyone in."

As the group filed into the Oval Office and began to position themselves on the opposing sofas, Joel asked Vera if she would take one of the chairs next to him.

Joel began, "as you all know by now, yesterday we had a security breach involving Marine One. Thankfully, we had a very perceptive agent that immediately remedied the situation. Unfortunately, we must interrogate the mechanic to find out how serious and deep this breach may go. After the recent incident at the Congressional gym, we are reassessing several aspects of our security, both at the Capitol and now at the White House. I cannot express to you how disturbing this is. Because of the rabid media that has attacked me with their biased version of what they think I said, it is impossible to present the truth to the citizens of this country. I am sure they have convinced their readers or viewers that I am the devil incarnate. Now that I think about it, they might like me better if I was the devil." Joel shook his head slowly, "I realize that last sentence might sound crazy, but considering what most of these people in the press support, it might not have been embellished. Their constant attacks on Vera for everything from her shoes to her hair, let alone anything she may say or do, are disgraceful. As a Congressman, I was aware of unfair reporting toward members of my political party, and at the time, I had my doubts about these so-called journalists that cover the White House. But I had no idea how hate-filled and destructive they could be."

As Joel spoke, he noticed everyone in the room was nodding in agreement. He turned to Vera, then back to the group. "As you might imagine following the incident with Marine One, Vera and I are contemplating how to proceed and what is best not only for us but for the country. I realize that a decision will have to be made soon, and I wanted you to know two things: one, we are working on a decision, and two, to inform you of this security breach so that you can reassess your personal protection. I tossed and turned last night, going over how this security breach could have happened. Has an unseen enemy infiltrated our intelligence agencies? Is this a coup d'état? Is this the action of a crazed person or a much larger hidden danger from a more complicated plan? Until these questions are answered, the First Lady and I will not be traveling for any reason. The White House press corps will no doubt spin some crazy conspiracy once they figure it out."

The President sat quietly, waiting for any comments.

Jim spoke up first, "when do you expect to know more about this person?"

"I know that he is being interrogated now, and they are surely asking if he was connected to the death of the two congressmen. If that is the case, then we are in a much more serious situation as a nation than we have ever been," Joel answered.

"Thank you for letting us know about this, and we hope it doesn't affect your decision on running in the next election," Jerry Reitz said.

"Thank you, Jerry, and I want to thank all of you for your understanding and for keeping this and future meetings confidential. We must be diligent and work together to allow those investigating this event to do their jobs while all of us continue to keep our eyes open and our ears to the ground. Worst case scenario is that our own intelligence network is compromised, and in that case, we will find ourselves back here drawing up a new set of plans on how to proceed."

Max spoke up, "sir, do you think this could be related to our 9/11 investigation? Might we have uncovered something meant to remain secret? Could this incident be a diversion from the path we were on?"

"Anything is possible at the moment, Max," Joel answered as he stood up. "Until we know more, consider every possible scenario as you reassess your situations. Take nothing for granted and trust no one. That's the best advice I can give at this point. So, let's adjourn this meeting. We will release nothing to the press unless it is an old-fashioned canary trap by releasing false intelligence to a specific reporter then waiting for it to appear in print. If we suspect that there is a conspiracy and need to identify the players, that's probably the best way to uncover it."

five

Max thought to himself; it had been quite some time since he heard from Tom. So, he decided to make a phone call to check in.

"Tom, my friend, how's everything going? Were you able to gather any information about Chip's death at the funeral?"

"I spent a few hours with Chip's wife. His death is still a mystery, Max. I asked her if Chip had any enemies that might want to harm him, you know, a typical detective question. She couldn't think of anyone but reminded me that Chip had a top security clearance at Edwards Air Force Base, and there were many of his associates that she had never met and that he never spoke about. He was the military liaison between the base and Area 51. She knew that, but she had not ever asked about what went on there. She knew he was not allowed to discuss his work, and Edwards has always been a secret base where high-tech weaponry and experimental aircraft are tested."

"Do you have any idea what could have happened to him?" Max asked.

"No, I don't, Max, but before I left, his wife gave me a file. She was positive this was what he was most recently working on. It is a good-sized file, Max. When I asked about the Star of David on the outside, she said she had no idea but told me she was Jewish, so it did not concern her. She said Chip spent hours on his computer late at night."

"Have you had a chance to look at the file yet?" Max asked.

"No, I thought it best to see if you wanted to look through them first. I have the encrypted laptop, and I can scan and email everything to you this afternoon," Tom suggested.

"That would be great. I'd love to see what all old Chip was up to. He did remarkedly interesting research last we met. He also seemed healthy for his age. I'll be interested to learn the outcome of his autopsy," Max said.

"Great, Max, it'll take some time to scan and email all of this to you; expect it to come in most of today and maybe some tomorrow."

"Thanks, Tom; I'm looking forward to an informative read and to discover what the old Chipster discovered," Max replied. "Tom, Jim's on the other line; I've got to catch this call."

"Max?" Jim asked as the phone switched calls.

"Jimbo, I was on the other line with Tom. He has a file of Chip's he is scanning over to me in the next day. What's up?"

"I made it to that ticket agent's house in St. Louis. I saw the real passenger manifests from those two American flights. Not one Arab name was on either one. She printed off the final passenger lists from both flights the moment the flight numbers were announced. She told me that the FBI was all over the airport. They checked everyone's purse and bags as they left the terminal. She received a heads up, so she stuffed the printed manifests up her blouse and said nothing. She was suspicious of the FBI for being at her airport. I had to agree with her. That did seem strange but what was really odd was how they treated her fellow airline employees. It seems the FBI did not want the names on the manifests exposed to the public," Jim explained.

"I can see why, Jimbo," Max exclaimed, "this is the kind of information that would blow the official story right out of the water!"

"Indeed, it would, Max," Jim agreed.

"What's next on your schedule?" Max asked.

"I've got one more place to visit; that shouldn't take long. If I can arrange a quick meet-up, I will be back in D.C. late tonight," Jim offered.

"Swell," Max agreed, "Let us plan on breakfast at that coffee joint I like so much, say about eight-thirty?"

"See you then," Jim replied.

"Jimbo, I have another call waiting. Tomorrow, eight-thirty, my man."

"Max?" Ruth Ann asked when Max had switched lines.

"What's up, Ruth Ann? How did it go in North Vancouver?" Max asked, excited to hear the details.

"Max, you won't believe what happened!" Ruth Ann continued to fill Max in on the situation with Rosslyn and explained that she would know more after the doctor called.

"Well, that sure isn't what I expected to hear," Max said. "Any idea who that guy was?"

"I have a hunch, but I won't say a word until she comes around and tells me exactly who it was and what she said to create the reaction she did," Ruth Ann said.

"Give me a call back the minute she starts talking," Max instructed her. "You keep your radar on high alert woman, I can't go into details now, but just take this as a warning to be extra cautious. Vera's house on the beach is still under secret service protection, isn't it?"

"Yes, it is. There are at least two agents somewhere around her property at all times," Ruth Ann informed Max.

"Okay, try to record her statements on your iPhone if you can," Max informed her.

"Will do, Max," Ruth Ann answered.

Just as she said goodbye to Max, the back door opened. Jenny was carrying a large tray with a pot of coffee and coffee cakes from Starbucks. "Hope you're awake," she hollered into the house, not knowing where Ruth Ann might be.

Ruth Ann was making her way downstairs, "I was upstairs, on my way. Pour me a cup!"

Jenny wanted all the details about what happened to Rosslyn on their trip to Canada.

Ruth Ann brought Jenny up to date and thanked her for the referral to the hospital and the doctor. She shared the details of her experience at Harborview and told Jenny that she was expecting the doctor to phone her at any moment. They decided they would wait for the doctor's recommendation to see if they should journey into the city to visit Rosslyn later in the day or wait for her to come around. The women agreed they would meet after the doctor phoned Ruth Ann.

As Jenny reached the backdoor, Ruth Ann's cell rang. "It must be the doctor. I'll be over to fill you in in a bit."

"This is Doctor Cohen from Harborview. Is this Ruth Ann?" The voice on the other end asked.

"Yes, this is she; thank you for calling doctor. Is Rosslyn doing any better?"

"Her vitals are stable, we have her on IV fluids, and we're hoping she wakes up and remembers what happened. So far, she is still in a catatonic state. I do not detect any concussion, but I have ordered a CT scan later today. I will have the results this afternoon. I will do my late rounds after five this evening. I should know much more by then," the doctor explained.

"Would you recommend I come in and sit with her, or will she even know I'm there?" Ruth Ann asked.

"In the state she is in now, it's questionable that she would be aware of your visit. We will only know of her degree of cognizance when she comes to. You can ask her then what her experience was like while in that state. It's your choice. If you have left instructions to be notified when she wakes up, the nurses will call you," the doctor's voice replied matter-of-factly.

Ruth Ann felt her confusion grow, "Dr. Cohen, how long does it usually take for a patient in this condition to come back around and begin talking and remembering?"

"That all depends on the patient. I have seen similar cases where the patient begins to come back to normal senses in a few days; rare cases can take much longer. And of course, her condition is the result of a physical blow along with emotional trauma. So, this is not a typical case of catatonia with which we are dealing. My advice would be to be patient and be supportive when you visit her with your encouragement and words. She could very possibly hear and understand what you are saying; she just cannot respond. This is a rather unusual case, that's for certain."

"Thank you, doctor; I will visit her this afternoon. I hope to meet you then," Ruth Ann confirmed.

"I'll likely be in to review her scans and talk with the physical therapist that should have completed an evaluation on her neurological responses by then," Dr. Cohen said.

"I'll be there," Ruth Ann said as she felt a level of anxiety build inside. What would she do if Rosslyn were in this state for weeks or months? What about her cat, Dizzy Bear, and her RV, left in California? The questions continued to swirl, especially about that man who reacted so violently toward her.

She called Jenny with the update from the doctor, and Jenny agreed to go with her and suggested while they were in the city, they plan to have dinner at one of her favorite restaurants.

six

Vera woke up to discover a note left on Joel's pillow: *I have cleared my schedule. When you wake up, I will be on the bench in the rose garden. Please join me. Love, Joel.*

"Hey, sleepyhead, are you finally ready to make an appearance? I should have told you, it's just me, no need to put on fancy shoes and get every detail to match," Joel laughed.

"I asked that someone bring coffee service for us; I hope you don't mind," Vera admitted as she joined Joel on the bench.

"That is a great idea," Joel agreed. "It's a beautiful morning, and I thought this was a good place and time to put our heads together and give some thought to our future. I know how hard this corporate media has been on both of us, and we really need to give this next election cycle a great deal of thought. I realize the unique way I came to this office and that the Constitution will only allow me to run in this next election. I am trying to figure out the best path forward for you, for me, for us, and for this country, and I need your help. While I was in congress, I knew something, some group or dark force, seemed to permeate through all the institutions in this town. I had often heard of politicians and judges that both foreign and domestic intelligence agencies blackmailed. I was made aware of these years ago; at the time, I thought this was a crazy conspiracy theory. Once I got into politics, I was acutely aware of this tactic and others. Forerunners like JFK tried to warn us about this. Kennedy said, '*The very word secrecy is repugnant in a free and open society; and we are as a people inherently and historically opposed to secret societies, to secret oaths, and to secret proceedings. Today no war has been declared – and however fierce the struggle may be, it may never be declared in the traditional fashion. Our way of life is under attack.*'"

"I remember reading about that speech," Vera commented.

"Did you know he gave that speech to the American Newspaper Publishers Association in the spring of 1961?" Joel asked.

"No, I only remember hearing segments of it and how it referenced some hidden force, like a secret society or something like that," Vera admitted.

"The view from the White House is a different view than from any other house in this country. It is clear from Kennedy's speech that he was aware of the infiltration of our country, our society, or even the entire government operation. It is interesting now that we have seen personally what the press can do, how they can listen to a speech or press conference and print complete and total lies about what was said. They mock and ridicule every hair on our heads and every word out our mouths every day. They are like rabid dogs eating their vomit, while what both you and I are fighting for is a free America, a better America, and a stronger America. Instead, they seem to want to see a weak and defenseless America, broke and hungry. It appears that the entire media in this country is infiltrated with a dark force that lives to destroy everything our forefathers fought and died for. If I plan a Fourth of July celebration on the mall here in Washington, they go apoplectic for two weeks, calling me a dictator and worse. Looking back at each attack as I have worked to make this country greater, stronger, and more prosperous, they have become more fanatical by the day. Could it be this very press that JFK was warning us about? Did you know that Karl Marx was a paid journalist for the New York Daily Tribune for a decade between 1851 and 1862? When the editors of the paper refused his continued demands for higher payment for his installments, he began devoting his talents full time to the cause that would bequeath the seeds of Leninism, Stalinism, revolution, and eventually the cold war. Considering the message in Kennedy's speech that spring, in conjunction with everything we know about Marxism and how deceptive our media is today, we can see that a secret society exists. It does not want America and her freedoms to survive and thrive," Joel stopped to consider his own words.

"Throughout my flying career, I would try to keep up with the news. In my youth, I believed the reporting was true; after all, it was 'news' right," Vera said. "As I gathered more experience, I began to see a clear political bias. I saw progressives be above the law and constantly flattered regardless of what they were doing. I remember growing up and hearing from the television and my parents what a great man John F. Kennedy was. That speech you referred to and others like the '*ask not what your country can do for you, but what you can do for your country*' speech today would be chewed up and spit out if it came out of your mouth. There has always been a negative political bias, especially toward conservatives. Now, to find me as a direct target of these fanatics that hate America, I can clearly see that they do indeed have an agenda. That agenda is not what most Americans want for their children and grandchildren. It is not the America my father fought for in two wars."

"I am not and never have considered myself to be a conspiracy theorist. However, sitting here in this position as our nation's leader, I can hear the words of warning from Kennedy and Eisenhower. They warned not only of secret societies but of the threat from the military-industrial complex. Eisenhower gave the nation a dire warning about what he described as a risk to our government. He referred to it as a formidable union of defense contractors and the armed forces. He was a retired five-star Army general that led the allies on D-Day. He made this warning in his final speech from the White House. He warned, '*In the councils of government, we must guard against the acquisition of unwarranted influence, whether sought or unsought, by the military-industrial complex. The potential for the disastrous rise of misplaced power exists and will persist,*'" Joel recited.

"That makes me remember how as a teenager I heard about the military-industrial complex being behind Kennedy's assassination, I never understood what that meant exactly, but those words have stuck with me all my life," Vera said.

"Vera, we are in the swamp, surrounded by people we can't trust. Some of them are undoubtedly involved in trafficking arms to hidden wars, and God only knows what else. They target and cancel anyone that tries to create peace with our perceived enemies. If it were not for the controlled media telling the public whom to hate, whom to distrust, and even whom to eliminate, the public wouldn't know who the enemy was supposed to be or even if there was an enemy," Joel was thinking aloud.

"Joel, we are their enemy, and all you and your administration are doing is trying to build this country up in every way. They hate you and everyone around you for promoting our great country and our flag. From our perspective, it is easy to see; I wonder how many Americans realize they are being lied to and manipulated. That manipulation from the media promotes foreign wars that only weaken us as a nation. Right now, Joel, they are manipulating their audiences to hate not just America but you, me, your administration, and every American that supports your efforts."

"We do have a much clearer picture from here, Vera. So, my question for you, my dear, is should we run for another four years and attempt to drain this evil swamp or do we cut and run and give it up to that dark force that we can feel lingering above the Capitol?" Joel asked.

"Joel, there were times in the past when I wished I were in a normal job with a more normal life but look where I am now. When my husband Jeff was killed, I thought there was no way I could stand at the boarding door and smile while welcoming passengers on board. I forced myself back to the flight line. I am sure others thought it was much too soon, but doing so made me stronger, and I knew Jeff would have wanted me back there. You know what they say, it takes pressure to make diamonds. Forcing ourselves to do things that are difficult only makes us stronger. You and I have had an unusual experience of leading the country from this position, and it sure has not been easy for either of us. I will take your question to heart, and I will give it a great deal of consideration over the coming days. I ask you to do the same, then let us meet again in the rose garden and make our decision together. If we do not stay, we may never be able to uncover the truth about 9/11, which is particularly important to me. I love this country. I want to expose the truth, and I want you to be able to restore the republic. We could, from this position, also expose the infiltrations and the enemies within. I think I know my decision, but I will take this next week to give you an answer."

seven

Ruth Ann and Jenny arrived at Harborview in the late afternoon. As the large stainless-steel elevator doors opened on the seventh floor, they were greeted by a nearby receptionist.

"Good afternoon, ladies. Are you here to see a patient?" She asked.

"Yes, we are here to see Rosslyn Langley in room 747. I am RuthAnn, and this is my friend Jenny. I hope it is okay to bring a friend. We are supposed to meet Dr. Cohen later this afternoon," Ruth Ann explained.

"I'll need to see your identification, Ruth Ann; just yours is fine," the receptionist asked.

"Sure," Ruth Ann agreed as she pulled her driver's license from her wallet.

"Thank you," the receptionist said, "please proceed to her room. I'll mention to the doctor that you are waiting."

Dr. Cohen arrived moments later. "It's a pleasure to meet you, Ruth Ann and Jenny. I am afraid I do not have any good news for you. However, on the other hand, I do not have any bad news either. Rosslyn's condition has not changed much, but that too can be a good sign. Nothing on her CT scan gives us any reason to worry. We'll need to keep her here until she regains consciousness, just to be certain her condition does not deteriorate."

"Of course, doctor," Ruth Ann agreed.

"One more thing, I'm on my way out of town this evening. I will be attending a medical conference in Las Vegas for three days. My colleague, Dr. Levine, will be tending to my patients until I return. I will leave him with your contact information, and of course, the receptionists have it in her computerized file. Should Rosslyn begin to wake up and remember what happened, Dr. Levine will contact you and me immediately."

Ruth Ann was taken back by the doctor's announcement of his planned absence. "This

Dr. Levine, are you comfortable leaving your patients with him? Is he qualified? I mean, you know, does he have experience?" Ruth Ann was beginning to embarrass herself. Before Dr. Cohen could explain that Dr. Levine was very qualified and second in charge of the neurology department, Ruth Ann nervously began to apologize, "I am so sorry, Doctor, of course, he's qualified."

"It's unfortunate for me because her case is quite rare. I would love to be here the very moment she awakens," Dr. Cohen admitted. "This conference has been scheduled for months; it is being presented by a colleague of mine from Harvard. He is quite well known for his credentials."

"Then you will be checking in with Dr. Levine, and you will be back four days from now?" Ruth Ann confirmed.

"Exactly! I will check in with Dr. Levine every evening after the conference and before dinner," Dr. Cohen added. "If you would like to meet Dr. Levine, I suggest you stop by in the morning. He does his rounds later in the morning than I do. If you are interested, the nurses or the receptionist can tell you what time he usually arrives."

Ruth Ann looked toward Jenny, then to poor Rosslyn laying propped up in her hospital bed. "Oh my, Rosslyn, what did I get you into?" She said aloud. "Thank you, doctor; I will be in tomorrow to meet with Dr. Levine."

Jenny could see that Ruth Ann was feeling responsible and guilty, that she brought Rosslyn into a situation that proved to be dangerous. "Let's take off and grab an early dinner. We might be lucky enough to catch the last offering of happy hour prices on a good glass of wine. It looks like you could use one," Jenny said as she touched Ruth Ann's shoulder.

"Good idea, Jenny. Yes, a glass of wine and dinner would hit the spot. I am buying. I owe you for everything you have done for us." Ruth Ann turned toward Rosslyn, "Rosslyn, my friend, I'm so sorry, dear. I do hope you are back on your feet, and we are chatting up a storm soon. Of course, I am dying for all the details, so please, please, remember everyone. See you tomorrow morning."

Ruth Ann stopped by the receptionist's desk to remind her to call should Rosslyn wake up and that she would be returning to meet Dr. Levine in the morning.

"He usually comes in between nine and ten," the receptionist reported.

"See you then," Ruth Ann said as they stepped into the elevator.

eight

It had been an uneventful flight, and it was late in the evening when Dr. Cohen arrived at the hotel in Las Vegas. His day began early at the hospital, followed by a full schedule of patients at the office, then his late rounds. The evening flight to Las Vegas left him exhausted. As he headed toward the elevators, he noticed a sign, 'Welcome Doctors!' He glanced at the board and the listed courses offered. He could barely focus his eyes to read. In the morning, he thought he would make those decisions. He intended to take in three full days of lectures and knew he would, unfortunately, have to miss some lectures due to time constraints.

Morning came quickly. The desert sun rose earlier than he was accustomed to. He quickly showered and dressed, grabbed his iPad, tucked it into his leather briefcase, and headed for the coffee shop in the lobby.

"David? David Cohen?" He heard a voice nearby. He turned around to see his old college friend Matt Johnson standing at the end of the ordering line.

"Matt, I was hoping to run into you this morning before the conference gets started. But unfortunately, I arrived way too late to call or even text you last night," Dr. Cohen explained. "Let me place my order, and I'll join you to chat."

"I'm glad you could make it, David," Matt said as the two men waited in line. "This should be an interesting conference. I am sure you will agree; we are all experiencing a huge paradigm shift in society thanks to the internet, social media, and how our patients are affected by the cancel culture. With your background in neurology and psychiatry, I am sure you will have some interesting stories to share at dinner. I hope you do not have any dinner plans while you are here. In fact, how about dinner tonight?" Matt continued before David could give more than a quick nod to the dinner invitation. "I know you will find this one of the most interesting conferences of the year. My assistants have outdone themselves this time. Some of the presenters I have known since our college days, and they are very connected to the movers, shakers, and money makers back in Washington D.C."

After picking up their coffees, the two men walked together toward a long registration table where the attendees picked up their programs, name tags, and lanyards for the event. "I'll catch up with you later, Matt. What time and where is that dinner you mentioned?" David asked.

"If I don't see you at lunch, we will meet in the lobby at 6 o'clock," Matt replied.

Matt was correct. From the looks of the program, this was going to be a highly informative conference. He was going to do his best to attend as many of the lectures as he could. Scanning the brochure, he noticed the program included guest speakers from government agencies, law enforcement, and world-renowned psychiatrists and psychologists. David decided on the first lecture and was happy to discover it was held directly across the hall and started in five minutes.

He juggled his briefcase in one hand and a large paper coffee cup in the other as he hurried into a row of seats near the front of the conference room. He was not familiar with the keynote speaker, but the subject matter grabbed his attention at first glance of the program. '*Trauma-based Mind Control*' with a tagline of '*Brainwashing via the Use of Trauma: Getting Your Message to Stick.*'

He set up his iPad to record notes as the other participants filled the room. He had placed his briefcase in the seat next to him to assure that it would remain empty. He was not particularly social and sure did not want someone sitting next to him that might have a cold or, heaven forbid, influenza. That thought reminded him of the alcohol wipes in his briefcase. He arranged his items in order, placed his coffee cup down next to the iPad and thoroughly wiped his hands with the alcohol wipe, then tucked it back into the tiny envelope and dropped it into his jacket pocket.

The speaker placed his notes on the podium, then adjusted the microphone. He spoke into the mic. "Can everyone hear me, okay?" He asked. Several people in the room applauded lightly, including David.

"Good afternoon, ladies and gentlemen, if I'm still allowed to use those terms. I am Dr. Justin Sherwood. I am a government consultant and have worked in my current position for twenty years. I guess I'll leave it at that," Justin paused. "This afternoon, I want to discuss how our changing world is managed and how we can recognize what we are dealing with because of those changes. Yes, I did say managed. I am not sure everyone understands how the Central Intelligence Agency has garnered so much control and why they did so, let me start there. First, a little history lesson to set the stage. As the radio found its way into every American's living room, some astute gentleman in the government realized that he could program the listener to believe what they were being told. You might recall reading about the 1938 Orson Welles radio broadcast called *The War of the Worlds*, a fake Martian invasion of New Jersey. The presentation was so realistic that it created nationwide hysteria, including suicides from sheer panic. Welles may not have known it at the time, but he set the stage for the art of fake news. As we refer to them, the manipulators of minds have studied the psychological effects of this type of trauma-based mind control ever since. With the help of colleagues and professionals in your field, we became experts at presenting material that would lead the public in the direction we wanted them to go mentally. Later, as media transitioned from radio to television, we evaluated the effectiveness of audio combined with video. Some of you might be old enough to remember the 1960's television show, The Outer Limits. The *control voice* narration was broadcasted over visuals of an oscilloscope at the show's beginning, telling the viewers, '*There is nothing wrong with your television set. Do not attempt to adjust the picture. We are controlling transmission. If we wish to make it louder, we will bring up the volume.*' "It continued," '*again, there is nothing wrong with your television set. You are about to participate in a great adventure. You are about to experience the awe and mystery which reached from the inner mind to... The Outer Limits.*' The show ended in a shorter monologue, '*We now return control of your television set to you, until next week at this same time, when the control voice will take you to... The Outer Limits.'"*

The audience nodded in recognition. An unusual way to begin a presentation, David thought to himself. He was not old enough to have watched the television show but had seen rerun episodes in college. He remembered the opening and closing control voice. The episodes he had seen were dealing with UFOs and spacemen. He recalled how as a college student, he wondered if this was a twisted way for the government to present the possibility of life on other planets. He chuckled to himself as the speaker continued.

"That is one of my favorite openers, but I ask that you do consider every aspect of what I just said because there is truth in that short, little story. Today, we have televisions in our living rooms and bedrooms, guest rooms, kitchens, and even in our pockets. We also have other forms of media that were not available fifty or sixty years ago. We have the internet with its social media platforms, online broadcasting channels, along with new formats that seem to sprout up monthly. Some of us have found it hard to keep up with these recent technologies.

Getting back to our subject title of trauma-based mind control, I believe everyone in this room is old enough to remember the first Gulf War of 1990. And one of the most popular and most memorable characters of that war was not a general or a politician. It was a young fifteen-year-old girl named Nayirah. You will remember the emotional plea of this young woman as she explained how she saw Iraqi soldiers removing babies from incubators in a Kuwaiti hospital, leaving the babies to die. Her story was presented to the Congressional Human Rights Caucus and was corroborated by Amnesty International, which also published independent reports about the killings along with testimonies from evacuees. After the war was over and Kuwait was liberated, reporters were given access to the hospital. What they discovered was, yes, babies died, but they died after doctors and nurses fled the hospital.

Furthermore, Iraqi soldiers had not stolen incubators at all. Amnesty International issued a correction and accused the Bush administration of opportunistic manipulation of the international human rights movement." Dr. Sherwood took a long drink of water.

"It was quite a memorable event, and most of us Americans were mortified by her story. But what was it all about? Several years later, it was exposed that Nayirah was not a witness to the atrocities she claimed. She was the daughter of the Kuwaiti Ambassador to the United States, and her story was created as a public relations campaign to promote the war with Iraq. The public relations company ended up being a renowned global consulting firm headquartered in New York City, which received ten million dollars from the coffers of an organization called Citizens for a Free Kuwait. Of course, the company denied that it was spreading false information, but they continued to expand and purchase smaller companies worldwide, growing larger and more powerful every year. Nayirah's testimony has come to be regarded as a classic example of modern-day atrocity propaganda," Dr. Sherwood paused.

David shifted in his chair. He remembered the young woman and her horrific story of babies being ripped from incubators. He never did understand why Iraqi soldiers needed infant incubators or why any hospital would have hundreds of them; it made no sense. He recalled how shocked he was to hear her testimony and how his own opinion of Iraqis changed. He also did not remember learning that her story was false and was used as disinformation to gain the support of the American public. So, that was a fake news story, he thought to himself. I wonder how I missed the explanation that it was not true. He felt a pain in his lower back as he adjusted himself in his chair. I'll be damned. He shook his head as he continued to grasp how the clever deception took him in.

Justin Sherwood continued, "over the years, her story has become employed as a learning tool. Atrocity propaganda is the spreading of both information and disinformation about a perceived crime committed by an enemy. It can be factual, but it often includes deliberate fabrications or gross exaggerations, commonly known as lies. The invention of atrocities often becomes the main staple of propaganda. It can involve photographs, illustrations, interviews, eyewitness statements, videos, and other forms of reporting. Patriotism combined with human concern is often not enough to make people hate an enemy, making such propaganda necessary. A great psychologist you are probably all familiar with, Harold Lasswell, wrote: '*So great are the psychological resistances to war in modern nations, that every war must appear to be a war of defense against a menacing, murderous aggressor. There must be no ambiguity about who the public is to hate.*' What we do know is that atrocity propaganda leads to real atrocities. It often incites the enemy to commit more mayhem, and conversely, it can stimulate revenge. Unfortunately, it can also cause the public to mistrust media reports. Now, I realize those were heavy words, so I will pause and set up some images on a PowerPoint to go with us as we proceed. You all might want to take a minute to stretch your legs, take in a breath of fresh air or make a short phone call. This will take me about ten minutes to get set up."

David jumped at the opportunity to stretch his back and quickly hit the pause button on his iPad before leaving the conference hall. He dashed for the men's room, then did a few quick stretches in the hallway before he returned to his seat.

"I think we are all back, so let's continue," Dr. Sherwood began. "By the establishment of a baseline lie and by painting the enemy as a monster, atrocity propaganda serves as an intelligence function, since it proves to help waste both time and resources of the enemy's counterintelligence. It begins to dampen how the enemy can defend itself. The goal is to influence perceptions, attitudes, opinions, and policies. This technique often targets officials at all levels of government. It is designed to dehumanize the enemy, making them easier to control or even eliminate. Often this strategy will paint the enemy as a fanatic. Again, Lasswell saw it as a handy tool for arousing hate and said that '*if at first, they do not enrage, use an atrocity*.' This technique has been used in every conflict known to man. In the run-up to the invasion of Iraq by the United States and NATO countries, there were press stories on both sides of the Atlantic describing how Saddam Hussein and his son Qusay used a woodchipper to eliminate their opponents. These stories gained worldwide attention and, as a result, boosted support for the military action. About a year later, it was determined that there was no evidence to support any aspect of the woodchipper story. Likewise, the accusations of weapons of mass destruction in Iraq were never proven to be true. However, these types of falsehoods did create monsters out of soldiers on both sides of the war. We often find that these stories of atrocities are later debunked, but that usually happens long after the battles have been fought and the damage has been done.

When terrible things happen, for instance, a terror attack, our natural human response is to find out who was responsible and how to retaliate in a similar fashion. When we are emotionally traumatized by seeing a horrific attack or other people being killed, our natural reaction is to seek revenge. We find the enemy, and we do not stop until we feel we have been justified. We know that the public can be manipulated to believe falsehoods and even the illogical or impossible. Let me give you an example of how vulnerable we all can be. We were told commercial aircraft were flown through two skyscrapers in New York City about twenty years ago. That morning, we were shown footage of office workers jumping to their deaths from hundred-plus stories. Then, we were told and shown by the media that a Boeing 767 flew straight through the South Tower, creating a massive explosion. We were, as a nation, emotionally traumatized. I do not think one adult watching those people jumping from the towers did not put themselves in the jumper's position. Do I jump or burn to death? How much fear filled those people suffering from intense heat until finally breaking out a window and jumping to their inevitable deaths? We were all there emotionally. We were in shock, traumatized, and vulnerable to being programmed, or as it's more commonly known, brainwashed.

I would like each of you to recall the details and the use of atrocity propaganda as I continue. Back to that September morning, remember the jumpers, the flames, the smoke, and the confusion. Firefighters and law enforcement told us bombs were going off inside the towers. Later, a television news broadcaster interviewed a random bystander on the street that explained how the building collapsed due to the jet fuel weakening the structure. Sometime later, we discovered that bystander was an actor and had been told what to say. We were hungry for an explanation of what we just experienced on television. We needed an explanation as to how those two towers could explode as they did after being hit by an aluminum aircraft. Most of us did not stop to question anything; we just listened and believed what the news people told us on the television. I would like a show of hands now if any of you remember that we were told of a police officer who had been handed a passport shortly after the planes crashed. It was from a foreigner; some recall hearing the name Mohammad Atta. We were told he must have been a hijacker. What would have caused anyone to believe that this passport belonged to someone involved in the hijacking? We were being set up. How many of you remember that?"

Several in the audience slowly raised their hands to acknowledge that they indeed did remember a passport of a hijacker being found that day. David was sure he remembered it.

Okay, now one more time, a show of hands. How many of you did *not* believe that a passport could have survived that crash, fire, and float to the ground?" Dr. Sherwood asked as he scanned the room for hands. None were lifted. "As I suspected. You all believed that a paper passport and only one paper passport was somehow ejected from a man's pocket, briefcase, or carry-on luggage and floated to the ground. Not one other passenger or crew member's wallet, passport, or purse found its way to the sidewalk, just this one passport from what we were told was a hijacker. Magical. Later, we were told that no office furniture or plane parts survived, no bodies of passengers or crew, just this one paper passport from an accused hijacker. Why did we believe that most incredible story? Because we needed to have an explanation and an enemy. We just witnessed an atrocity, had we not? As the day progressed, we were told that an aluminum airplane crashed into the Pentagon, and it completely vaporized. We were told it was flying over seven hundred miles per hour at ground level when it hit, which is indeed impossible. Then, we all heard a CNN news broadcaster at the Pentagon tell us there was no airplane crash, but there was an explosion. Nothing of the actual aircraft survived, but days later, we were informed that the plane captain carried with him a paper prayer card, and his prayer card was found among the wreckage. There was no sign of titanium engine parts, landing gear, luggage, or anything else you would expect, just this paper prayer card. Unbelievable, right?" He asked, stopping to change a PowerPoint image.

"Have I got you all thinking now?" the doctor smiled and paused before he continued. "Keep that atrocity propaganda front and center in your mind. Collectively, as a nation, we all wanted to know who did this to us, to our country. We woke up the next day to see huge American flags draped on the sides of every skyscraper and massive structure in New York, Washington, and other cities. We never questioned where those flags came from or when they were ordered. We saw New York firefighters interviewed, and they each had small American flags clamped to their fire helmets.

The head of the FBI told us cell phone calls were made from the flight attendants and passengers. There were eighteen hijackers or maybe nineteen; the FBI was not certain. But they had the passenger manifests and would let us know. That they did, they told us the passenger manifest listed eighteen men, but that soon changed to nineteen, and they stuck with that number, without explanation. Nobody asked logical questions. We were all still stunned as this information poured out. We were told these were radicalized fundamental Muslims that hated us for our freedom. Many of us had never met a Muslim or visited the Middle East. We didn't even question the FBI when they told us that the ringleader drank alcohol, gambled, snorted cocaine, and lived with a pink-haired stripper." Dr. Sherwood paused, looking around the conference hall at the attendees. "So, going back to how that atrocity propaganda works, we were so emotionally traumatized by the impact of that morning that we as a nation collectively stopped thinking logically. We believed the utterly impossible details that continued to flood the airwaves for months. All knowledge and understanding of basic physics were put aside to accommodate the impossible, improbable, and the unbelievable. We were being programmed to believe what we were told, and now, you can clearly see that we were told crazy things; aluminum planes can fly through buildings, and paper passports can withstand plane crashes, fires, and even building collapses. We saw Building 7 collapsed at near free-fall speed, having not been hit by an airplane or any debris from the other buildings, and that fact was never mentioned. If an entire population is emotionally traumatized, it will easily believe the impossible. At that moment, we just needed to know who to aim our weapons at. In his book *Mein Kampf*, Adolph Hitler referred to the use of a lie so 'colossal' that no one would believe that someone 'could have the impudence to distort the truth so infamously.' In other words, and as later quoted by Joseph Goebbels, in short: *'If you tell a lie big enough and keep repeating it, people will eventually believe it.'* The lie becomes a person's reality and personal history over time.

Now, here is where it gets interesting. Over the years and without the general public's knowledge or awareness, the media will use the terms *9/11* or *'September 11th attacks'* to trigger their audience's emotional reaction. It works much like a light switch to open or trigger someone back to the very moment of horror they felt that September day. If you recall the movie *The Manchurian Candidate*, you will remember how a voice on a phone call triggered the assassin into action. Today, a new target can be identified by a newscaster comparing events with the words' *9/11'*. The event could be in an African or Middle Eastern country, an Asian country, or even a political party. The atrocity could be any event that claims to kill people. Those familiar with hypnosis and may even use it in your practices recognize the method used here. This triggering can also be used against a politician or anyone the media manipulators aim to destroy. Anyone that is considered a threat to the status quo will be targeted using this same tactic. Another excellent example of how atrocity propaganda was used to trigger an audience is the JFK assassination. If you question that event, you will become the target of hate and much worse. This is compounded in the age of social media, but more on that in a different lecture.

Getting back on track, our understanding of historical events such as wars and propaganda leading up to conflicts is the accumulation of news broadcasts telling us what we are to believe. But what if we discover that over decades, we have not been told the truth? What if we learn that an agenda behind the curtain has been calling the shots all along? Let us stop for a moment and consider what you are learning because what comes next could be helpful in your practices, and you may have already experienced what I am going to discuss. So, take a ten-minute break, and when I see all the chairs are filled again, we will continue," Dr. Sherwood said.

David used the time to text his colleague to check on his new patient: ANY CHANGES IN MY NEW PATIENT, ROSSLYN LANGLEY?

Dr. Levine replied: NOTHING SO FAR.

The conference room was nearly full when David returned to his seat.

Dr. Sherwood cleared his throat into the microphone to quiet the hall and began to speak, "Why is all of this important? You will no doubt one day come across a patient that has had a truth encounter. This experience is often such a shock to a person's psyche that it shorts their circuits. For all their lives, they have been told a particular version of what should be considered reality by positions of authority. When they encounter the opposite direction and expose what they thought was real and true, the mind can rebel. If one rejects that opposing reality, their mind will often shut down completely. Therefore, as doctors, you will not be able to diagnose what caused this condition unless your patient was with someone who can explain the details of their trauma.

As you know, the mind is a fascinating machine. It can be programmed, but un-programing it can be a tricky business. In closing, remember, things are not always as they seem. Consider this lecture to be your red pill. I have my business cards on the back table if you would like to contact me any time. I prefer an email before a phone call. Feel free to contact me with any thoughts or questions. Thank you all for your attention. Enjoy the rest of the conference. I know several of the speakers, and I am confident you will greatly benefit from time spent with all of them.

I recommend attending a lecture with Dr. Steve Peretz. If you did not choke on this red pill, he will surely take you deeper down the rabbit hole. Steve has worked with the government for fifty-five years combined with a thriving practice in the D.C. area. So, if you get an opportunity to share a luncheon or, better yet, a dinner, you will want to jump at the chance. Nobody can tell stories like he can, and he doesn't hold back!"

nine

"Barry?" Jim asked as the voice on the other end answered.

"Yes, this is he," Barry replied.

"This is Jim Bowman, special assistant to the President," Jim informed him. "I'm just about to land."

"Oh, I'm glad you could make it. I would like to meet you someplace other than my home. I always have my guard up when I meet with government officials."

"That's fine; where would you like to meet?" Jim asked.

"There's a small restaurant on 5th and Wall Street; it's called Mack's. There's an old neon sign out front; you can't miss it. I will be in the back booth on your right as you walk in, wearing a black cowboy shirt with white trim. I've become slightly larger in my retirement, so you won't miss me," Barry laughed.

"How long will it take me to get there from the airport?" Jim asked.

"It'll take you about five minutes longer than it'll take me. I'm ready to head out now; see you there," Barry replied as he hung up the phone.

Jim immediately recognized Barry as he walked into the restaurant. The moment he sat down, a young waitress brought a large thermos of coffee, two large mugs with fresh cream.

Barry thanked her, "We're just going to have coffee for now and lots of privacy. If we decide to add to that, I'll give you a shout-out."

"Sure thing," the waitress smiled and tipped her head in acknowledgment of Barry's message.

"So, Barry, you were DEA?" Jim asked, anxious to get the conversation started. "Would you mind if I record our chat?"

"No, I won't mind at all, record away," Barry continued. "I was with the Drug Enforcement Administration for about twenty-eight years. I worked mostly along the southern border after a couple of stints in Central America and a shorter tour of South America, mainly Columbia."

Jim asked, "You mentioned in your email that you had an interesting experience in the year 2000 with some foreign art students. Can you tell me more about that?"

"Yes, I have a copy of the report for you, but it was eventually leaked to the public, and it only tells a small part of the story." Barry reached into a well-worn leather briefcase, pulled out a manila envelope, and slid it toward Jim's side of the table. "The report is there along with a list of names and addresses of some of the so-called artists. A few of us at the DEA and several other federal employees had troubling encounters with some of these shady characters. These confrontations happened about a year, maybe a year and a half before the 9/11 terror attacks. We did not give it much thought until one of the U.S. Marshals, whose identity and home address were top secret, had a group of these art students show up at his front door. They addressed the marshal by name and explained that they were selling prints to pay for their art school back in Israel. This marshal was so tuned-in to deception; he picked up immediately on something suspicious. He inquired about the art school and its location; you know that type of thing. They rattled off the name of a school, thinking he would never check to see if it existed. But like I said, he was a very astute kind of guy. After they left, he did check. Oh, and they abandoned any further conversation the moment he inquired what type of visa they held. That spooked the artists right off his porch and into an awaiting van. He copied the license plate number and ran it the next morning. The vehicle traced back to an address the DEA had under surveillance. Nothing about these Israelis panned out to be true; most of them were on tourist visas that had expired. At the time, we had teams watching large active Israeli drug rings in Florida, California, and Texas. I don't want to bore you with too many details, but as I reflect upon that time, troubling elements pop up that should have been investigated." Barry took a drink of his coffee before continuing with his story. "Once we began receiving reports from government agents, we gathered and questioned these traveling art students. We discovered that they were spread out all over the country. They were reported on military bases from Virginia to Guam and all points in between. They were also found in possession of blueprint drawings of Federal offices and buildings. As a result, we were alerted to a possible national security threat. As you can imagine, many Americans have the impression that Israel is our biggest ally in the Middle East. Most people would never dream that Israel would spy on us or be in our country to do something malicious. Our media has failed to educate the public of historical figures like the Rosenbergs, Jonathan Pollard, and other Israelis that spied on our country. Americans have little recognition of those names or the information they shared with Russia, China, North Korea, and Iran. Our media never seems to want to discuss matters detrimental to Israel. Now, do not get me wrong, I am no anti-Semite or anything like that. It is just that this story of the Israeli art students became more convoluted as it evolved. I had a gut feeling, but I wasn't one hundred percent certain about what was transpiring."

Jim nodded, encouraging Barry to continue.

"So, the DEA began monitoring an Israeli drug ring in southern Florida. We deployed listening devices, then suddenly, they go silent. We tracked them down again, and as soon as we were about to bust them, they disappeared. We are communicating via our agency's email system all this time, so we assumed we had secure communications, but someone was reading our mail. We began eliminating some of our people to find who might be the mole, but we never figured it out. One day, several months into our investigation, we learned that our administrator was petitioning the government for a Boeing 767 extended-range aircraft. She wanted the ability to fly direct from D.C. to Tel Aviv, Israel."

Jim interrupted Barry, "Tel Aviv? Isn't that where the Israeli military intelligence agency Mossad is located?"

Barry smiled as he began to speak, "We were beginning to wonder if this particular administrator had more than one job, if you get my drift. Most of us suspected that an intelligence agency had gained access to our email system. The drug ring was an Israeli operation, and she was connected to Tel Aviv, alerted us to an unpleasant possibility. The security breach could have been our own FBI, CIA, or the Israelis tapping into our email. When I reevaluated these strange details, I started looking at pieces of the puzzle in a different light. Some art students were headed to New York City or New Jersey, and they could have been there about the time of the attacks. Looking back now, I distinctly remember that many of those art students were trained demolition and ordnance specialists. They all served at least two years in the Israeli Defense Forces, and several of them were officers. Those military and intelligence backgrounds did not seem to match what you would think an art student would be. It's hard to imagine a soldier who has been trained to use an Uzi machine gun, tap phone lines, and blow-up buildings would be inclined to pick up brushes and paint landscapes."

"I'd have to agree with that," Jim laughed. "From an Uzi to a paintbrush is quite the stretch."

"Jim, as part of my job at the DEA, I and a few others attended an OPSEC meeting in June of 2001. The meeting was held at a hotel in Tampa. We were told by top military brass and intelligence officers that there would be a terrorist attack on our soil in the coming months. They told us there would be six or eight 'targets' somewhere in the United States."

Jim interrupted, "Are you talking about operations security?"

"Hell yes, and nearly every intelligence and government agency were in attendance. The top brass briefed us from the Pentagon, the CIA, the FBI, and they all had foreknowledge that something big was on the horizon. They knew we were about to be attacked by terrorists, and there was not much we could do about it. Well, that was the feeling they left us with anyway."

"They predicted six or eight targets would be struck?" Jim asked.

"Yes, so when the Twin Towers were hit that morning, I was expecting several more strikes. The moment I heard about hijacked planes, I was certain there would be at least two or four more targets. Since we had been informed the terrorists would be Middle

Eastern, we had no reason to suspect anyone else. Years later, I started thinking about how that plane sliced through the tower like a hot knife through butter. I started to think about what aluminum planes do when they hit steel and concrete surfaces. I felt like I had been manipulated. I believed what I was shown on T.V. that morning. Looking back now, I think about the DEA's trouble at that time, not with Arabs but with Israelis. They were running drug rings all over this country, but especially in southern Florida. It was Israeli art students, not Arab art students, that federal employees were apprehending with blueprints of our buildings. After we started emailing about these art students, strange things began to happen. If we typed Israeli art students in the subject title of an email, those messages would never reach their destination. We eventually figured out that the only emails disappearing were those with that specific information in the subject title line, so we used the initials IAS instead. We were convinced that someone was not only spying on us, but they were good enough to reroute our email." Barry raised his eyebrows, "You ever have anything like that happen to your email?"

"No, I can't say that I have. Nor do I know of anyone else who has," Jim admitted.

"I don't remember exactly when it was that I started to question the administrator's possible involvement with the Israeli drug ring. Before that, suspecting the administrator would have been unheard of. Even more alarming was the arrest we made of a group of Israelis near the perimeter of Dallas Ft. Worth International Airport. They had a stash of surface-to-air missiles and intended to shoot down a jumbo jet as it took off!" Barry revealed.

"You are kidding; I never heard anything about that. It didn't make the news," Jim said.

"After I left the agency, I did contract work in Iraq. There were young Israeli's all over the place, not art students, mind you, but they were about that same age," Barry explained.

"What were they doing in Iraq?" Jim questioned.

"None of us ever figured that out. Mossad agents were all over that country; we assumed they were doing what spies and assassins do; tapping phones, intercepting emails, and keeping the Israeli military informed of every move the NATO troops made. They were young men and women that looked like they might be barely twenty years old. They stayed to themselves, which also created distrust between all of us. We were twenty years older than they were, so we had a much different perspective on everything. You must understand being in drug enforcement for so many years; I always had one eye open for suspicious activity. There were lots of drugs flowing around Baghdad. Drugs were there, but there were even more over in Afghanistan," Barry said.

"I had several co-workers in the airline whose sons came back from Afghanistan hooked on heroin; they suffered from PTSD and could not cope with life after their tours finished. It was incredibly sad," Jim added.

"Well, both those countries were hell on earth, Jim. I was lucky to be older, maybe a little wiser, and not in combat. But, still, I did my time in Viet Nam, got in at the very end of that mess, and please, do not get me started on that subject," Barry said.

"Gotcha," Jim agreed.

"Now, getting back to why I contacted you. I found it to be beyond coincidence that many of these art students, the drug dealers we were monitoring, and the accused 9/11 hijackers had addresses in the same cities, neighborhoods, and in some cases, the same apartment complexes. Jim, this might sound crazy but, I would not be shocked to learn that the art students or the drug characters were the same people as the accused hijackers. Hell, I would not be shocked to learn that these Israelis set a memorable footprint for the feds to expose when they were on a flight back to Israel. Call me an old dog, but at this stage of my life, nothing would surprise me."

Jim studied Barry's face as he spoke, "I hear you there, my friend."

The two men continued their discussion until Jim realized he had lost track of time. "Excuse me; I have to send a couple of quick texts." He quickly informed the pilot that he would like to fly back to D.C. as soon as the plane was ready. Then a quick text to Max: ON MY WAY TO THE PLANE, I WILL LAND LATE AND PLAN TO SEE YOU AT SET TIME.

RIGHT ON JIMBO, MEET ME AT THE BREAKFAST PLACE, Max replied.

"I'm sorry, Barry; I appreciate your spending time and sharing your information with me," Jim said as he reached for his jacket. "Here's my card; if you think of anything else that you can share, please feel free to phone or email me any time."

"One more detail before you head out, Jim. When these Israeli art students were detained, two Israeli companies located in Richardson, Texas, were bailed out. I researched them both, and they proved to be involved with all our telecommunications. What was more alarming than American telephone companies hiring foreign assets to monitor our phone calls was that both companies were associated with Israel's Unit 8200."

"Unit 8200, is that something I'm supposed to be aware of?" Jim asked as he leaned forward toward Barry.

"To put it more simply, they were spies that specialize in wiretapping and internet hacking," Barry explained.

"Now, that *is* interesting. Do you suppose they could have been involved with 9/11?" Jim asked.

"Considering American Airlines Headquarters and Operations center are located near Richardson, Texas, I'd think their espionage skills could have kept the flight loads light."

Jim interrupted, "In addition, they could have controlled crew scheduling. That type of skill would have been almost indispensable. That could explain a lot of things. I wonder if they have offices near Chicago?"

Barry responded, "That's a good question; let me look into that and get back to you."

"Barry, your information has been invaluable; I can't thank you enough. I realize it was not easy coming forward, but I am sure that this information will help solve this puzzle. But unfortunately, I have to get back to my plane before it takes off without me," said Jim as he zipped up his leather jacket, picked up his cell phone, and headed toward the door.

ten

Jim arrived at the prearranged breakfast location and waited several minutes for Max.

"Neither of us has much time, so let's just order coffee and a pastry and get to work," Max suggested.

"I'm cool with that. I got in too late last night to copy the interviews with the customer service and DEA agents I spoke with. So, I will head over to my office and copy those off for you."

"Sounds like a great idea. The website has been cooking with gas; it's all I can do to keep up. I need to get over to the office. I'm expecting an overnight package from Tom, and I'm still waiting to hear an update from Ruth Ann."

Max spent the rest of the morning answering emails from the 9/11 information website. No sooner had he responded to his last email when there was a knock on his office door.

"Max Hager?" A young man's voice asked as he cracked open the door.

"That would be me, sir, yes sir, last I checked," Max answered with a loud laugh. "Come on in. Whatcha got for me there?"

"An overnight express package looks like it came from California, sir," The young man answered. "I need you to put your signature on this line," He held a small electronic tablet toward Max.

"There you be, John Hancock," Max laughed again. "Thanks for your expedient work, young man. It looks like I have some serious reading material."

"You're welcome, sir. Have a great rest of your day," the young man said as he hurried out the door.

Max was expecting this package from Tom and knew what it contained. He decided to place it unopened into his office safe and read the electronic versions later that evening.

Later that morning, Jim stopped by Max's office with the promised copies. He briefly filled Max in on his conversations with the airline customer service agent and the retired DEA agent. The details of these conversations opened a lengthy discussion on the ramifications of their findings.

eleven

Dr. Cohen checked his watch; he agreed to meet Matt for dinner at six. He had ten minutes to freshen up. He quickly jumped to his feet, changed his shirt, and decided to forego a tie. One glance in the mirror as he headed out the door caused him to lick his fingers and try to tack down a few hairs that were wildly out of place. As he stood waiting for the elevator, he decided to text his colleague to check on his new patient: ANY IMPROVEMENT WITH ROSSLYN?

NOTHING SO FAR, the reply from Dr. Levine returned.

He texted back to Dr. Levine, TRY TO GATHER MORE INFORMATION FROM HER FRIEND AS TO EXACTLY WHAT HAPPENED.

WILL DO, Dr. Levine replied.

"David, over here," Matt Johnson called out as David entered the massive lobby.

He lifted his hand to acknowledge his friend.

Matt was standing with a small group of men. David recognized Justin Sherwood from the talk he had attended earlier in the day. He didn't recognize any of the others.

"David, I would like to introduce you to Justin Sherwood, Dr. Steve Peretz, and my assistant Jim Maxey. Gentlemen, Dr. David Cohen, another Harvard colleague now living in Seattle, the other Washington." Matt paused while the men shook each other's hands and quietly welcomed David into their group.

"We have a private table reserved at Anthony's. If everyone is ready, let's head on over and get started," Matt announced as he led the group toward the restaurant.

"Very interesting lecture today," David complimented Justin as they walked together behind Matt and the others.

"Thank you, glad you enjoyed it. We're just getting started here, and by the time you leave, you will have some very new and enlightening perspectives to take back to Seattle with you," Justin said with an air of confidence.

David was intrigued by Justin's response but decided to remain silent and simply nod his head in agreement.

The gentlemen conversed quietly while they waited for a round of cocktails to arrive. As the server placed their drinks, David couldn't help but notice that all conversation had ceased until she left the room.

Matt was the first to speak, "While at Harvard, I think every recruiter tried without any success to persuade David to join the Agency. He was the top student in our class, and he had several of the most important men at the CIA trying every trick in the book to bring him on board."

Except for David, all the men at the table seemed to find some humor in Matt's confession. David was silent; his mind began to review his days at Harvard. He was completely unaware of attempts to recruit him into any government agency. Had these efforts to steer him into government work after graduation been so covert that he was oblivious to their attempts? He began to question everyone that had befriended him at Harvard. Who were these recruiters? Why did they want him? David sat quietly, unsure of what to say as he continued to reflect on his life.

The men chatted about the Patriots and Ravens and how they managed to score tickets to both teams' games. They argued over which team was the best and which one of them might make it to the Super Bowl this year. At best, David was a weak Seahawks fan and didn't watch any NFL games on television, so he had nothing to offer to their conversation.

After their entrees were delivered, the conversation around the table took on a more serious tone. David remained quiet as Matt began to explain, "David, we need to illuminate some things for you here. Back at Harvard, your professors contacted the Central Intelligence Agency, as they often do when they recognize a stellar student such as you were. They look for students with the ability to assimilate information easily. You had, and I'm sure you still do have, all the qualities the Agency likes to see in their recruits and contract employees. By the time this conference ends, you will be much more aware of how all this works. If there's a crack in the matrix, so to speak, it's people like you and your colleagues that will prove to be helpful in patching that exposure."

"About the national security end of things," Justin added.

"National security?" David asked. "I'm a neurologist and a psychiatrist in Seattle; how in the world can I have anything to do with national security?"

Dr. Peretz spoke up, "David, we can't be omnipresent. The Agency needs psychiatrists out in the field to contact us whenever they have a patient potentially exposing national security secrets. When these problems are discovered, your responsibility would be to contact us, and we will neutralize the issue. Technically, as you may already know, we are not legally allowed to become involved in covert operations inside the United States, so we rely on people like yourself to circumvent that restriction."

"Can you explain that in a little more detail for me?" David asked, not certain he was following exactly what Dr. Peretz was referring to.

"Sure, let's say you have a patient that is trying to make sense out of an event they have seen on the news that conflicts with what they know. If this type of conflict brings someone to your office and explains that a news story is a lie, that should raise a red flag for you. For example, a patient feels that the government is targeting them with microwaves or some such conspiracy. We understand this clash between what a person believes to be true and what they have experienced through the media can be conflicting to the point of instability. It's these people that can become a threat to our national security; let's just leave it at that. I hope you understand what I am surreptitiously trying to express here."

"I believe I do understand," David acknowledged, still somewhat confused as to exactly what type of national security threat he could come upon in his practice at Harborview Medical Center.

Dr. Peretz continued, "Since what we can do legally is so limited, we create work agreements with professionals from many walks of life to assist us in keeping our country on track. For example, the JFK assassination, there's the official story which we want to remain the official story, then there are those who claim that the CIA and FBI were involved. Those people don't do our national security any good. We don't want names like de Mohrenschildt, Murchison, or Corcoran being exposed. When identities like that become mainstream, we need to get control of the situation. We must maintain the status quo, and we will discredit anyone that deviates from the official story."

"What about patients that might have legitimate information?" David asked.

"We cannot allow anything to challenge the official story; it's there for a reason. It is what it is, and it is not available to be questioned or torn apart. In other words, it's off-limits."

"Do you mean you don't want to know the truth?" David asked.

"We know the truth; this is not about the truth, David. It is about maintaining our ability to control the message, which controls the masses. We write the message, and that message cannot be mitigated," Dr. Peretz said firmly.

"Understood," David replied.

Matt felt David's hesitation and resistance; he thought it best to change the subject around the table. "What do you guys think about that trade of Brady to Tampa Bay? Will the Patriots ever get into another Super Bowl without him?"

"I don't think the Patriots have a chance of getting into a Super Bowl any time soon," Justin commented.

"If these damn NFL teams continue to kneel for our national anthem, they won't have an audience that cares if they're playing on a Sunday or in a Super Bowl," Dr. Peretz grunted.

The men continued their meaningless chatter about professional sports through the dessert course. Matt picked up the tab and thanked everyone for joining. "I've got to make a phone call and check my email; see you all bright and early in the coffee shop tomorrow."

Jim Maxey stood up at the same time, "I'm beat, see you all in the morning."

Justin finished off his Bailey's Irish Cream and announced his departure next.

Dr. Peretz smiled, "Looks like it's just the two of us. Allow me to buy us a nightcap so we can continue our conversation." He waved the server to the table before David had a chance to object.

"Two Courvoisier, please."

"Yes, sir," the server nodded.

"This will give you a great night's sleep," Dr. Peretz informed David. "Just what the good doctor ordered."

Once the server had delivered their cognacs, Dr. Peretz explained, "I'm glad you could have a nightcap with me, David. It gives us a little time for an explanation. I felt your confusion earlier, but I was uncomfortable talking in-depth with Matt's assistant at the table. Let me explain a few things to you straight up. The Agency is behind nearly everything you see on the news. We control the message, if you will. I realize that most American's have no idea that we are the agency that creates everyone's reality. We started with good intentions; unfortunately, things changed. We became the mercenary troublemakers for the global elite and the Wall Street big banks. We've perfected some things like coups and civil unrest. Occasionally, we make mistakes, and when we do, our methodically planned out event can become a threat to our national security."

"How?" David asked.

"I realize you are a busy doctor with a full patient load at a very busy hospital up there, but just because you are in the 'other Washington' as we call it, don't think that you can't be of assistance to us. I don't imagine you have much time to follow up on crazy conspiracies, as we like to call them. Let me confirm; you know that Lee Harvey Oswald was the lone shooter, right?"

David quietly nodded; he had read several books about the assassination but decided to play along with Dr. Peretz, just to see where this conversation was going.

"Good, you know we cooked up that label conspiracy theory, don't you?" Peretz inquired.

"Yes, I seem to recall that anyone questioning that magic bullet theory received a hard time and were labeled as such," David answered.

"Well, things are not always as they seem. And as Matt mentioned at dinner, sometimes there's a tear in the matrix. You see, we've created civil unrest, pulled off coups, created politicians, even presidents, and removed some as well. Everything we do is carefully planned and orchestrated. We write the script, and we set the stage, and if there's music, we manage that too. Whether we are talking about a Central American country filled with rebels murdering people or the sexual blackmail of a potential presidential candidate in our own country, we are manipulating the chess pieces behind the scenes. We are the puppet masters. Events may shock you and the public, but to us, we are only shocked when one of our carefully planned episodes is exposed for being an orchestration. There are two aspects to every situation, the actual and the perceived. The perceived is what we want you to believe, and the actual is downright horrifying. It is so evil and so upsetting that most people can't comprehend our involvement. If they do eventually manage to see through the veil and find the truth, we simply will not allow it. David, I don't know exactly how to lay this out for you. The Agency has grown so large and complex that some corners have become so opaque that light will never permeate through them. I've personally always believed that we are too compartmentalized for our own good, and that may indeed be the case. We put together an operation that someone manages to pick apart and sees right through from time to time. Over the decades, we have become like drug addicts who are above the law and with access to unlimited dope. Think about this; everything you've ever thought you knew about the world around you, both near and far, is a lie. We have gotten away with the most horrific deeds throughout my lengthy career," Dr. Peretz took a sip of his cognac, his demeanor more relaxed as he continued. "David, we have encountered a real big problem with one of our events in the recent past. You probably remember exactly where you were and what you were doing on the morning of September 11th, 2001."

"I certainly do," David confirmed.

"You probably have never questioned what you were told by every television channel, newspaper, magazine, and online article."

"As a matter of fact, I have never questioned what happened. I know what happened. Many radicalized fundamental Muslim terrorists hijacked four commercial planes and crashed them in New York, D.C., and Pennsylvania. Everyone knows what happened. What's there to question?"

"David, I hate to be the one to break this to you, but what you think you saw wasn't quite the entire story; it wasn't what happened. That was an operation of ours but let me just put it to you that way without causing too much confusion. As I mentioned, we have encountered a problem, and this is where you and your colleagues could become helpful. Not long ago, we discovered that a group of airline professionals worldwide connected on a blog a flight attendant started. By the time the agents from the FBI's counterintelligence center contacted us, it was too late. From what we read on that blog, we realized we have a big problem on our hands. Come to find out; we made some rather big mistakes that probably only airline professionals would catch. Through this flight attendant's blog, they began to pull the event apart piece by piece. We can't have this type of exposure, and we are alerting every professional we can think of to be on the lookout for any of these flight attendants or pilots that might be having psychological issues dealing with the details they have uncovered." Dr. Peretz finished off the remaining cognac, feeling a load off his chest. He thought he let David in on enough information, but not too much, to destroy his own belief and understanding of 9/11.

"I'm not sure that I understand what you are saying, Dr. Peretz. Are you telling me that what I saw on television and the photographs in the newspapers and magazines weren't what happened that day? Was it some type of Hollywood production? What the hell are you trying to tell me?" David's words were growing stronger as he felt his anger building inside. He hated being deceived. He always struggled with his anger when he discovered someone was lying to him.

"David, what I'm trying to tell you is, without going into further details, you were lied to. What we need from your profession is for you and your colleagues to contact us if and when you encounter anyone questioning the official 9/11 story."

twelve

Ruth Ann pulled the car into Vera's garage, "Jenny, that was a great idea to have dinner. Your recommendation offered the best Italian food I've ever had."

"I'm so glad you liked it; it's one of Seattle's most highly kept secrets. Not many tourists ever learn about that place. It's where the locals eat," Jenny said as they stepped out of the car. "Leave the garage door open for me; I'll run out this way. My dog is going to hate me for being out so late. Call me if you need anything, Ruth Ann."

"Will do," Ruth Ann hollered as she waited to close the garage door, then opened the door to the kitchen.

Ruth Ann was exhausted. The stress of not knowing the seriousness of Rosslyn's condition was beginning to take its toll. As she sat down on the bed, she noticed the small diary she had picked up the night before. Rosslyn's father had seen to it that she inherited all his writings. Ruth Ann's curiosity had gotten the better of her, and she began scanning through the book again.

She turned to the beginning of the small book: *Dear Rosslyn, I know one day after I am dead and gone, you'll be reading a story that you will find hard to believe. I hope you understand by now that my job required me to keep secret what I did for work. Had I and my brother, your uncle, been postal workers, things would have been much different for all of us. Having spent decades with The Company, I have seen things you will find nearly impossible to believe. I have seen first-hand how the bowels of these government agencies operate. I had direct knowledge of the involvement of the FBI spying on businessmen and politicians. When I say spying, I mean something much more sophisticated than an agent watching from a car parked outside someone's home. When the FBI wants to take down a target, they have multiple advanced technologies at their fingertips. Much of this technology is unknown to the public. From my earlier days with The Company, I understood that the FBI and The Company were collaborators for the Deep State. The Company would orchestrate missions while the FBI supplied the cleanup and cover-up crew. It was an open secret that there were directors at the FBI who were political and angry enough to set up a president for his removal from office. The FBI and The Agency work together to set up and destroy their foreign and domestic targets. Since they have control over nearly every so-called journalist in this country, it's easy for them to direct and control the message as it is delivered to the public. Those in the media that are not on our payroll have been blackmailed and risk embarrassing public exposure that will end their careers. Take the Watergate scandal in early 1972; the official story was a far cry from what happened and even further away from why it happened. Richard Nixon was forced to resign, but many people have no idea who was behind this ordeal or just how involved both the CIA and the FBI were in the break-in and the leaking of the story to the public. The FBI was constantly leaking to the press and likely never stopped. When Nixon had overlooked the guy who became known as 'Deep Throat' for the directorship, he retaliated. Some were convinced that the Watergate burglars, a group of former and current FBI and CIA agents, planned to be caught. None of us could believe that these guys, some of whom were assassins from the Kennedy event, would be so sloppy as to get caught by the night watchman.*

When the Pentagon Papers were released to the New York Times by a disgruntled Pentagon employee, they exposed the Gulf of Tonkin as a false flag and exposed falsehoods and lies that proved to be embarrassing to many in the military-industrial complex. The administrations of Kennedy, Johnson, and Nixon were exposed for their lies about the aggression and attack from the North Vietnamese. This fake claim of aggression led to an escalation of the Vietnam conflict. LBJ was caught lying to the public and congress, and the government quickly tried to cover it up. The CIA's Liddy and Hunt planned to discredit the author of the Pentagon Papers by breaking into his psychiatrist's office to find the mother lode of information on this gentleman. He had become their target for exposing the truth to the public. They were confident they would find information on his mental state in his patient files that could be used to discredit him and his reporting. Their burglary was bungled as badly as the Watergate burglary was. They found nothing that could be used against the author, and their attempt to steal his medical records was exposed. That mistake caused the espionage charges for the author to be dismissed. In a recording that was made, H.R. Haldeman described the embarrassing situation to Nixon. Rumsfeld made the point: 'To the ordinary guy, all this is a bunch of gibberish. But out of the gobbledygook comes one obvious thing. You can't trust the government; you can't believe what they say, and you can't rely on their judgment. The implicit infallibility of presidents, which has been an accepted thing in America, is badly hurt by this because it shows people do things the president wants them to do even though it's wrong, which means the president can be wrong.

A great deal of fallout came from the release of the Pentagon Papers, the break-in to the psychiatrist's office, and the ensuing attempts to discredit the messenger. It was later exposed that the Watergate prosecutor informed the author of the Pentagon Papers of an aborted plot by Liddy, along with some assassins, to "totally incapacitate" the author. It was another false flag. In Liddy's autobiography, he admitted that the plan to neutralize the author originated with E. Howard Hunt at the CIA. Their plan involved drugging the unwitting author with LSD at a fund-raising dinner in Washington to render him incoherent when it came time for him to give his speech. This was the CIA's continuing plan to discredit him. They intended to use Cuban American contract assassins at one point, but there wasn't enough time to get the Cubans into position, and the plot was aborted.

This is not unusual for The Company to use foreigners to do their dirty work. They have been doing this since I joined. It's the easiest way to be in control and yet not be held responsible. They refer to this tactic as plausible deniability.

Ruth Ann paused. Her eyes were heavy; her heart was heavy. Guilt for intruding on Rosslyn's father's life caused her to feel ashamed. She closed the book, then closed her eyes. She wondered if she should tell Rosslyn about what she had read.

thirteen

"Good afternoon, ladies and gentlemen. My name is Dr. Steven Peretz," the speaker began. "As you can see by my lack of hair and its white color, I've been around the Agency for a long time, fifty-five years, they tell me. Although those are official full-time years, of course, I started out doing contract jobs in college. I was often called upon for assistance by everyone from the Director down to the rookie agent. In all, I believe I'm pushing into my sixtieth year. If I weren't such a great guy, people wouldn't call me a 'swamp rat,'" Dr. Peretz paused to chuckle and take a slight bow. The audience applauded quietly.

Dr. Peretz continued, "So, what's this all about, you might be asking yourselves? What does this old Jewish coot have to offer me? I am, by the way, a Cuban-born Polish Russian Jew. I was raised in Europe for my early years, then spent most of my life in America. As many of you did, I attended Harvard, including our host for this conference, Matt Johnson. After I completed my medical training as a psychiatrist, I endured a short stint at MIT, where I became involved in the study of international relations. That time brought me to the State Department, where I worked with some of the country's more renowned politicians and statesmen. I've worked for the Agency under six presidential administrations, both democrat and republican. My field of expertise includes international crisis management, foreign policy, and psychological warfare," Dr. Peretz continued, "Over time, I've acquired a talent for dealing with hostage-takers. In the mid-seventies, I assisted in the hostage negotiations to release the passengers and crew of TWA Flight 356. I've always been known as a straight shooter, and that has gotten me into trouble over the years. With all of that said, I'm known around Washington as a troublemaker of sorts.

Let me explain that history to you. Many of you might think that the Central Intelligence

Agency operates solely to protect our country. By the time you walk out of this lecture, you will hopefully have a much better understanding. I have a terrible habit of going off-script, and although I have a wonderfully written speech to give you today, I probably won't use it much. I am at the end of my career, and at this point, I feel it is essential for the Republic that people know the truth. It isn't easy to swallow, so I hope you all have a bottle of water with you. To give you a short history of the Agency, we have controlled every previous president, often their parents and occasionally their grandparents. We have managed to fill every White House with our agents, control the sitting president, and leak harmful stories about him or his administration. Between us at the CIA and the Pentagon, we have managed to control every president and most of his administration for decades. We use covert methods to manipulate and control politicians that most never realize until it's too late.

Hindsight, as you know, is always twenty-twenty. What the Agency essentially is, for lack of a better word, is a shadow government. We are the military and the mercenaries for the wealthiest individuals on the planet. All of them prosper in one way or another from civil wars, rumors of wars, or disruptions of society. Everything is planned; we often work behind the scenes for a decade ahead of the well-orchestrated major event that will bring about the changes we seek. When I say we, I'm not referring to the Agency but to those we work for, which is not necessarily our government but the big money that selects our government. Politicians have referred to them as the military-industrial complex; I call it the war machine. These are the people and their bankers who profit from wars; they produce everything from the uniforms to the fighter jets and everything in between. They are the corporate fast-food outfits, the manufacturers of trucks, tires, you name it, anything, and everything that our soldiers in battle will use. They see war as a colossal money stream, a guaranteed revenue source, so they need to have us covertly interfering and interrupting countries that we can invade and control. From the early days of the Dulles brothers, the State Department and the Agency have worked hand in glove. If you pay close attention and understand our history, you will identify our patterns and techniques for everything we have done around the world. Our military research and development, known as DARPA, had a considerable role in creating social media platforms; therefore, they are under our control. We refer to this new media as our latest weapon, and I hope you will walk out of here with a new understanding and that you will also pause before you react to something online without giving thought to the many ways this weapon can be used. You will be surprised if you have been thinking all along that social media is a place to complain about political leaders or post a photo of your cat or your dinner; no harm there, right? You will be asking questions like: Why is it weaponized, and who is responsible? What's the purpose of weaponizing all media? I'll give you a hint: propaganda! Now you're probably asking, whose agenda is this. At the expense of sounding like a conspiracy nut, let me just say, there's a method to our madness, and once you learn about our methods, you might consider it madness. It's complicated, so buckle up, take a deep breath, and get ready to go deep down a rabbit hole that many never realized existed. If you are familiar with the old *hidden in plain-sight* game, I am about to shed some light on the darkness we have created for you over the decades, back to that little history lesson and my original speech. Remember, as details unfold, there are no coincidences, only the illusion of coincidences. Another word for covert is secret, and as Luke 8 says, 'For nothing is secret that will not be revealed, nor anything hidden that will not be known and brought to light.'

As most of you probably know, the Agency spawned from its earlier life known as the OSS, following the Second World War. We had our battles with the military, who all wanted to be in control of our intelligence. We won the battle and eventually became what you know as the Central Intelligence Agency. Most of us lovingly refer to the Agency as the Company with a capital 'C'; occasionally, we call it the Agency with a capital A. I bet most of you don't know that sometime around the mid-fifties, the Director of the Central Intelligence Agency oversaw the media. Not just the print media via newspapers and magazines, but all television and radio broadcasting as well. The CIA would write reports, then place them with journalists, whose messages would be repeated and cited by other reporters, printed in newspapers, and reported on television. Yes, the CIA had an agenda;

they still do. Whose agenda is it? Let me just explain; for now, the CIA has always been a friend of big banks and big business. The driving force behind us and what we do is money. Following World War Two, the International Organization of Journalists was created and controlled by the communists for propaganda purposes. Uncle Sam needed a response, and as a result, Operation Mockingbird was created to counter their communist propaganda. What started with good intentions ended up as the widespread and deliberate manipulation of the US media. In short, the CIA told you who to believe, what to believe, and where to put your allegiance. The American public was oblivious to this manipulation.

The innocent appearing box in their living room was thought to be for entertainment and honest news reporting. Eventually, Operation Mockingbird was exposed. In the early days of the Cold War, mass media was broadly used to influence public opinion by both the United States and the Soviet Union. Where the CIA once enjoyed the service of numerous journalists, they quickly learned that they would have to do so more clandestinely. The CIA publicly promised that they would drop their use of professional journalists and began using contract employees, freelancers, so-called stringers, and the like. Officially, the Agency claimed they didn't use real journalists. And so, it began," Dr. Peretz adjusted the microphone and took a sip of water.

"I bet you can't guess what happened next?" He laughed. "The CIA, as you know, is a clandestine outfit. If we get caught doing something unethical or illegal, we promise not to do it again and go right on doing what we've always done. After all, who's going to stop us? To be honest with you, nobody can. We are spies, and we spy on people all over the world, both legally and illegally. Our agents are taught to lie in training, and they are trained to lie so well that they can beat any polygraph test. When we spy, we collect data used to our advantage for many purposes, including blackmail. Everything you think you know as real and authentic is only what the Central Intelligence Agency has fed you. In our earlier years, we joined with television network program developers and Hollywood film producers to form your opinions of politicians, political parties, other countries, leaders, and even religions. Everything you have been told on the news has been manipulated for our benefit or the benefit of the United States military, better known as the Department of Defense.

How could that happen, you ask? One of my fields of expertise is Psychological Operations, commonly known as PSYOP. As you might have guessed, modern psychological warfare can also be called political warfare, MISO, or Military Information Support Operations. I am sure you remember another familiar term commonly used: *hearts and minds*. And for those of you that might be starting to scratch your heads, it's also commonly known as good old-fashioned propaganda. It's a term used to denote any action using psychological methods, intending to evoke a planned psychological reaction in a targeted group of people. These techniques are often combined with what is known as a black operation or a false flag. Did I just say false flag? You probably think that term is internet disinformation. Our government doesn't do things like that, am I right? Well, if that is what you are thinking, you are wrong, and it means we have done our jobs correctly. Black operations or false flags are covert, and a critical feature is that the entire operation is secret. So, our intelligence agencies, military, or paramilitary units are involved in a technique that is not for the public's consumption. These operations are often carried out by the CIA, FBI, and the intelligence services of many foreign countries. And, in case you're wondering, yes, we do, at times, all work together. But you didn't hear that from me," Dr. Peretz paused before continuing.

"Black operations, as opposed to secret operations, involve a degree of deception to conceal who is responsible. A false flag disguises the culprits while pinning the blame on a second party that often was not involved. The term false flag originated in naval warfare when a vessel flew the flag of a neutral or enemy country to hide its true identity. The practice began with pirates deceiving other ships and allowing them to move closer before they attacked. Sometimes people or countries will organize an attack on themselves, making the attack appear by an enemy nation or terrorist group. Israel does this all the time. False flag operations are used during peacetime and are commonly used as a pretext for war. One of the most complex false flag operations our Department of Defense proposed was known as Operation Northwoods. It was an operation to be used to initiate war with Cuba. It was denied by JFK and kept as a classified top-secret document for thirty years. The operation proposed fake hijackings of commercial flights, landing them and releasing the passengers, then claiming the Cubans shot down those planes. The plan also included terrorist bombings throughout the United States and assassinations of citizens, all blamed on Castro; what a creative way to initiate war! No wonder this type of operation and this plan were hidden from the American public. What would the American people think of our military and intelligence agencies if they discovered such a dastardly plan? As Sun Tzu wrote about, civilians like yourself don't realize that there is an art of war. And wars are planned far in advance by intelligence teams working behind the scenes before a single shot is fired. If you attended Dr. Sherwood's talk on trauma-based mind control, atrocities are created to garner the support of the public for a planned war or military conflict. Targets for psychological operations, black ops, or false flags are governments, groups, or individuals and not limited to the military. Civilians are often targeted by the mainstream media and alternative internet messaging as well. For example, we can arrange for the kidnapping of a journalist and pretend to execute him, then share a video with the public by releasing it to the media. This journalist could have been wandering around a dangerous country or war zone when we kidnap him. We write the script, and naturally, we blame it on the terrorists from the country we are targeting. We set up what appears to be a beheading, and since the terrorists are all wearing three-hole balaclavas, nobody knows who's really involved. Those, by the way, are excellent examples of the atrocity propaganda Dr. Sherwood speaks about. These were common tactics used at the beginning of the Iraq and Afghanistan invasions. By showing the American public the brutality of those we labeled terrorists, we acquired the public's support to continue the wars. After 9/11, persuasion was much easier to accomplish. Many Americans have little understanding of the Islamic religion, Arab countries, and their customs. This lack of knowledge worked in our favor with nine 9/11 and the wars that followed. Never be fooled by the media when they use a single event to trigger military involvement. Intelligence agencies use every technique available to garner support from the local civilians before they convince the American public of their plans.

Getting back to where I started, sorry I tend to go off the track giving these talks," Dr. Peretz let out a grunt as he seemed to acknowledge his reputed maverick style. "Now, where was that starting point?" He shuffled a stack of papers on the podium. "Here, yes, the weaponization of the media for propaganda purposes. Operation Mockingbird was claimed to be eliminated. I don't believe that for a split second. The CIA works closely with the Secretary of Defense, the Pentagon, and the White House to set the stage or deliver a particular message. I am reminded of the old William Shakespeare line by listening to myself speak here: All the world's a stage, and all the men and women merely players.

I think if you keep that in mind, this talk will make sense to you. It might not dawn on you until you get home, but it will eventually help you put the puzzle pieces together. Life is complicated, but it's nothing like the world of black operations and false flags. I am sharing this vital information with you professionals because you could become very helpful to us. You first must understand what has happened to your world and why. This conference provides knowledge to discover your reality. If you are familiar with the movie *The Matrix*, you will recall Neo, who feels that something is wrong with the world. Neo encounters the phrase the matrix while online, and that starts his rather bizarre journey. You might feel some connection to Neo as you continue through these precisely chosen talks for this conference. There is a purpose for everything you are hearing and learning.

As technological advances have come along and the number of television networks has increased, our challenge is to maintain control. Social media began as a research project at the Department of Defense; it was designed to monitor everything individuals say, see, or do. We call it 'data mining' of the public. Some political figures have learned how to acquire a feel for the public's opinion. It's as if we are taking the temperature of the people by reading their comments. On the downside, social media has created some narcissistic people who believe that others are interested in what they eat or how they interact with their pets. Social media taught us how many mentally ill people were not taking their medication," Dr. Peretz paused to change the image projected from his laptop.

"We discovered these social media platforms gave us a peek into a world that people didn't even share with their therapists. We realized we needed an army of keyboard warriors to control this new worldwide web and its rapidly increasing platforms. We entered a new war on truth; we had to contain and control any information that might threaten our national security. We used the same techniques we used so successfully in Operation Mockingbird. The internet became our new battlefield. Our priority and agenda had not changed, but we had to make some colossal changes. Artificial intelligence allowed us to use less human and more computer technology to maintain our control. Keywords triggered a bot to discredit a message. We placed useful politicians in front of cameras to convince the public the government was dedicated to transparency and freedom on the internet. But we were clamping down and censoring what appeared online. We learned that repetition of words, even if they are in direct opposition to reality, can convince a large portion of the population to believe even the impossible. Using the Hegelian dialectic problem, reaction, and solution, we solved the problem much as we have always done. We could not tolerate online researchers exposing our agenda; therefore, they were discredited and silenced. We will continue monopolizing this behavior," Dr. Peretz explained.

As Dr. Peretz concluded his remarks, he could not help but notice an uneasiness permeating his audience.

fourteen

When Ruth Ann woke up, the diary she had been reading was still lying open on her chest, indicating that she had not moved throughout the night. She folded a tissue and placed it in the book to mark where she had finished reading. What she had read was foggy in her memory. As she became more awake, she started to recall some of the details.

Her cell phone buzzed an incoming phone call as Randall's name appeared across the screen. "Good morning, Randall," she answered. "I was planning to give you a call later in the day. How are you managing with your kitty house guest, Mr. Dizzybear?"

"Oh, he and Blue are getting along famously. They hunt for rodents together in the evenings and sleep in windowsills during the day. They have become the best of friends," Randall explained. "I was just wondering how your trip to the Pacific Northwest is going."

"Well, Randall, that is one thing I was going to call you about. We had a nice drive to Seattle, and then we were sent to British Columbia, North Vancouver to be precise. While we were there, long story, but Rosslyn ended up with an injury, and she is in the hospital in Seattle as we speak," Ruth Ann informed him.

"Oh my, I hope she will be okay," Randall exclaimed.

"She is in a great hospital with some very experienced doctors. I hope to hear from her doctor this morning. I did want to let you know that our return to California is on an indefinite schedule. I will let you know the minute we can return."

"No problem, Ruth Ann, Dizzybear is having a grand time out here among the vineyards, and I know Blue loves the company. Please let me know any updates on Rosslyn as far as her condition goes. You can text this phone or email me any time. Her RV is fine where it is, and tell her not to worry about either her cat or her RV when you see her. I have decided to continue my research on Building 7 and might even publish my findings in a book. More on that idea later," Randall explained.

"Great idea, Randall. A book about what happened to Building 7 is needed," Ruth Ann encouraged. "Say, I have to run. I am expecting to hear from the hospital any moment."

Just as Ruth Ann was saying goodbye to Randall, an incoming call began to buzz.

"Hello," she answered.

"Ruth Ann Lowy?" The voice asked.

"Yes, this is she," Ruth Ann replied.

"This is Doctor Levine at Harborview Medical Center. I wanted to let you know I was contacted overnight that your friend is beginning to show signs of improvement. She isn't speaking yet, but every indication shows that her condition is improved. Unfortunately, I have had a family emergency and won't be able to see her this morning, but she is in good hands. I will try to get back to the hospital to do rounds early in the evening. If you visit her today, the nurses will be able to update you. I am very sorry I won't be able to examine her this morning, but I am encouraged by the report from overnight, and we should begin to see continued improvement," he explained.

"Thank you, Doctor Levine, thank you for calling. I will arrange to visit her in the late afternoon or early evening. I hope everything is okay with your emergency."

Ruth Ann sent a text to Jenny: MORNING, COFFEE READY YET?

ON MY WAY OVER. OPEN THE BACK DOOR, Jenny replied.

Ruth Ann ran downstairs and unlocked the door, holding it open as Jenny made it across the lawn, balancing a pot of coffee on a small tray with both hands.

"Any word from the hospital?" Jenny asked as she ducked inside.

"Only that her doctor is having some type of family emergency and won't be in to see her today. The nurses reported some type of improvement, but she is not speaking yet," Ruth Ann reported.

Jenny informed Ruth Ann that she would be busy tomorrow, so she would not accompany her to the hospital. She reminded Ruth Ann that Vera's property was under surveillance should she have a need, and she could probably get assistance by flashing the porch light or a loud shout-out. She informed Ruth Ann how the secret service detail first showed up when Vera married Joel. They were never obvious, but they made Jenny feel safer knowing they were present and well trained in the martial arts.

Jenny shared a cup of coffee with Ruth Ann, then excused herself to take her dog to the vet and run several errands. "Call my cell if you need anything. If I can't get it for you, I can at least direct you to where to go in the city," Jenny offered as she left.

"I think I'll stay in today and do some reading," Ruth Ann explained. "There isn't much I can do at the hospital, and the nurses have promised they will make sure I'm contacted the minute Rosslyn starts talking and making sense. I could use a day of rest and relaxation."

"You sure have earned a spa day for yourself," Jenny agreed. "I can't imagine what you two have been through."

fifteen

As the morning sun began to peek through the large hotel window, Dr. Cohen pried open his eyes to check the clock radio on the nightstand. Squinting to focus on the numbers, he felt that his head was about to split open. Another sinus headache? He pulled his feet out of the bedding and sat up; the pain grew even more intense. Staggering to his suitcase, he searched for something to stop his pain. He usually had Tylenol with him, but he must have used it all on his last trip. Nothing. He pulled the heavy drapes closed to darken the room and stumbled to the bathroom to dampen a washcloth for a warm compress.

The first conference talk of the day would start in an hour and a half. He hoped his headache would improve so he could attend. He closed his eyes and wanted to fall back asleep for another hour.

Three hours later, the headache had not improved. David was convinced that he had somehow picked up a virus, probably off the flight from Seattle. It was not uncommon for him to pick up a bug while traveling by air. He should have been more prepared with some medications, he thought to himself. He missed the first lecture of the day and hoped to attend another one later, but he would have to get pain relief if he were going to keep his attention focused on a speech.

He pulled his slacks on and grabbed a fresh shirt from the closet. He was certain the hotel had a magazine shop with travel-size necessities like aspirin and antacids. He picked up his key card and headed to the elevator.

Tylenol with a two-pack of Alka-Seltzer cold tablets, a bottle of water, and he was set.

"That will be seven dollars and sixteen cents," the woman working the register announced in a soft voice that seemed at least two decibels too loud. He handed her his debit card and began to tear open the Tylenol as she passed a paper receipt toward him for his signature.

"Thanks," he grunted as he exited the small shop looking for a chair. He intended to sit down, take the Tylenol, and drink the entire bottle of water. Maybe he was dehydrated.

"Dr. Cohen?" A man's voice asked.

David looked up, "Yes, do I know you?"

"No, sir, you do not know me, but I have seen you at this conference, and I have a question for you if you don't mind." The young man explained.

David quickly swallowed the Tylenol and drank half the bottle of water as he waited for the man's question.

"I'm curious if you are buying into any of this intelligence operation here?" He asked.

"What exactly are you referring to?" David questioned. "And who are you anyway?"

"My name is Josh Miller; I'm an investigative reporter for the Wall Street Journal," he explained briefly.

"Exactly what are you referring to with your question?" David asked.

"I suppose I should start from the beginning if you have a few minutes to allow me to explain," he stated.

"Sure, go ahead; you've captured my attention now," David replied as he settled back into one of the leather chairs lining the lobby. "Please, have a seat," he invited the young man to join him.

"Have they been trying to recruit you?" Josh asked David.

David chuckled, "I understand they tried back when I was at Harvard, but I was too involved in my studies to figure it out. Looking back now, I recall missing a meeting with one of my professors, and someone he said was from the government. At the time, I was not interested in anything the government had to offer me."

"I mean here, at the conference, have they tried to convince you that you will be patriotic or that you owe service to your country by working for them?" Josh asked.

David thought quietly to himself. Was he being recruited into some government intelligence agency? Is this what the entire conference was for? Why would they want him? For what purpose?

"Let me explain why I am asking. I have a good friend from college who was approached by the CIA while studying international business at Stanford. He went straight to Langley after graduating. He attended training at Camp Peary, a place those inside refer to as the Farm. A couple of weeks into his rather intensive training, he caught wind from one of the instructors that the Agency had pulled off some horrific events. One day, he confided in me that he had overheard a cryptic comment from an instructor. This instructor was about to retire. He revealed how the CIA, along with other intelligence agencies, often masqueraded as something they weren't. For example, they would pretend to be a local shopkeeper or a postal worker in foreign countries. Near the end of his training, he was involved in a conversation about the terror attacks of 9/11. That discussion changed his mind about staying on as a spy or having any involvement with the Agency. It encouraged him to investigate their history of previous operations. His first alarming discovery involved protocols following 9/11. Agents were convinced in training that all Arabs were potential terrorists and not to be trusted. It was reinforced throughout their training that all men in the middle east were out to kill Americans. After years of therapy, he was able to deprogram from what he considered professional brainwashing. Later, he was approached by a senate staffer assigned to research enhanced interrogation practices that the CIA was involved in at Abu Ghraib prison in Iraq. The staffer discovered that the CIA hired two quack psychologists that created the most horrific human torture techniques one can imagine. These charlatans knew full well that torture is never effective in getting to the truth; it will only produce the desired response. In other words, the tortured person may know nothing about what he is accused of but will admit to whatever he is being forced to say. The agency hired these two to formulate and administer torture sessions, which gave the agency plausible deniability. They were paid roughly eighty million dollars to instruct agents to torture men that had nothing to do with the terror attacks. Immediately after 9/11, the Bush administration classified captured Middle Eastern men as detainees, which placed them outside the protections of the Geneva Convention. They incarcerated them in rendition sites. President Bush signed a directive giving the CIA the power to interrogate all detainees. They were beaten, exposed to extreme cold, suspended from the ceiling by their arms, shocked and waterboarded."

"Are you saying the CIA was allowed to detain anyone they felt threatened by and torture them, even without any proof that they were involved in the terror attacks?" David asked.

"Precisely! The CIA knew they didn't have support from the Justice Department, so what they were doing was illegal. Within a couple of months, the CIA's general counsel began considering the legality of this torture. He justified it by, and I quote, '*The Israeli example of using physical force against hundreds of detainees could serve as a possible basis for arguing that torture was necessary to prevent imminent, significant physical harm to persons where there are no other available means to prevent the harm,'* end of quote."

"Well, the Israelis have a very different system than we do in the United States," David said.

"Yes, sir, they do. The CIA hired these two whacked-out psychologists to reverse engineer the military survival technique known as SERE, to break an individual and coerce him to confess to a crime he didn't commit," Josh explained. "Documents showed after lengthy discussions inside the Bush White House; the National Security Advisor told the director of the CIA that Vice President Cheney approved these techniques. The CIA later learned that these two psychologists misrepresented their claims of the effectiveness of torture techniques which often resulted in death," Josh stopped for a moment to allow his words to penetrate Doctor Cohen's psyche.

David felt his sinus headache begin to fade away, but he found it replaced by nausea upon hearing the failures and poor judgment of the CIA. "Go on," he sighed.

"You are probably wondering how the CIA got away with torturing people. Let me answer that for you. The Bush administration's Department of Justice claimed that the interrogators did not *intend* to inflict severe pain or suffering. But, according to the U.S. Justice Department's own memos, if an interrogator could proclaim that they did not *believe* what they were doing caused pain or suffering, they were immune from prosecution."

"Was no one at the CIA concerned that this torture might breed real terrorists once these detainees were released? I can't imagine the degree of anger and hatred a human would have after experiencing such brutality," David said.

"Good point, Doctor," Josh agreed. "But it gets much worse. The CIA's reign of terror throughout the Middle East included hundreds of innocent detainees. All the classic brainwashing techniques were used on them. I hope you don't think of me as an internet conspiracy theorist because that is not where my information has come from. While in training, my friend was privy to a conversation between a group of top CIA officials. They were laughing amongst themselves as they discussed the use of foreign intelligence assets to create memorable identities and faces for the accused nineteen hijackers. There were three sets of decoys, art students, a drug ring, and fake hijackers, working together and sharing one mission. That mission was to pull off the scenario or government story presented to the public on 9/11. To do that, these groups of decoys flew around the country using similar identities to make lasting impressions that the public would refer to after the horrific event. They rented apartments, cars, hotel rooms and opened bank accounts, using the identity and names of the hijackers. They frequented restaurants and acted in a way that drew memorable attention to themselves, such as being rude, boisterous, and obnoxious. The CIA officials laughed about how their decoys escaped on a 747 out of JFK the afternoon of September 11th. The CIA officials reconfirmed that there were no real hijackers on those four planes. There were no security cameras to film the passengers, hijackers, or crew members boarding those planes. The CIA made certain that all airport cameras had been disabled. These officials had been involved in the planning and orchestration of the 9/11 deception. My friend was disenchanted, learning that he accepted a job with the people who were responsible for 9/11. When the reality sunk in, he became frightened and felt his life was in danger. He became so paranoid and fearful that his overall health began to suffer. His declining health provided a perfect cover story for his resignation from the CIA. He was able to reveal this information to me secretly. He told me these details, and I was stunned. What the CIA is doing at this conference is getting a feel for any doctors they might recruit. If you ask me, they are afraid that someone will find details they thought were hidden, which could expose the truth about 9/11. Most likely, it will be someone from inside the aviation industry, someone whose training could pick out the flaws in their story. Right now, the CIA is laughing all the way to the bank over what they believe was a huge success. The attack gave them an unlimited budget. They operate above the law and what they have done is far beyond evil," Josh said as he leaned back into his chair.

David was shocked by the young man's presentation. His mind reviewed the lectures he had attended as well as the conversations about Harvard. Why would they want him? He again questioned silently. "Let me get this straight. You are telling me that your friend was hired and trained by the CIA, then he discovered them admitting to controlling the hijackers who were never onboard those planes? That entire event was some type of intelligence…"

"And military operation," Josh completed David's sentence. "I have been following this conference, and I can tell you that Dr. Sherwood and Dr. Peretz were not originally scheduled to be keynote speakers. They were a last-minute change; exactly when they were added, I don't know, it could have been last night. I know they seemed to be prepared; I sat in on both their talks. But the question I have is, why these two?"

David felt a rush of mixed emotions as he analyzed his situation. Was this young man's story about the CIA true? Did they have that much power and control that they could stage a fraud on the public, then run roughshod through the Middle East making accusations of terrorism? He knew from his travels that most middle eastern people had little understanding of the English language, let alone the events of 9/11. He felt his blood pressure begin to rise and his face become flush. He pulled out his wallet and found a business card, "Please, Josh, here's my card; I would like to continue our conversation sometime."

"Dr. Cohen, I understand one reason none of these accused terrorists in Guantanamo have ever gone to trial is that in the discovery phase, the government would not be able to prove they had anything to do with 9/11. The government cannot afford for that truth to surface. Imagine their reaction if the world learned the truth after nearly two decades of wars in Iraq, Afghanistan, Syria, and other countries. There would be nothing left of the media, our government would be damaged beyond repair, and the intelligence community would cease to exist. The degree of outrage over this fakery would be devastating in many ways. My friend believes that many politicians in D.C., from both sides of the aisle, are invested in the war machine and will do anything to prevent the truth from coming out. I can understand their position, but it is not right. Someone must expose the truth and set our nation free from these globalist warmongers. There are only a few safe ways for us to make contact; I suggest you consider a private encrypted email account for our future contacts," Josh said as he handed David his business card.

Dr. Cohen's knees felt weak as he stood up. He nervously checked his watch. He couldn't recall ever being as rattled as he felt at this moment. He needed time to think. What was the reason he had been contacted about this conference? Was Matt Johnson aware of everything this young reporter told him? What about Dr. Peretz, did he know? Was Justin Sherwood enmeshed in this outrageous plot?

"I really have to be moving along; I need to contact my colleague and check on a new patient," David said.

Just then, David's cell phone rang. He hurriedly walked toward the bank of elevators to take the call.

"David, your new patient is starting to talk. She is in good physical health and has no underlying conditions. The strangest thing, however, is what she is saying. She makes perfect sense and seems to be coherent in every aspect. But she is claiming she saw one of the airline captains from 9/11 still alive in North Vancouver. Everyone knows there were no survivors on those four planes. This makes no sense. I was doing an extra round just now and was standing at her bedside when she started to speak. She clearly described having dinner and seeing a captain that she thought was dead," Dr. Levine explained.

David was shocked by this report, considering what he just learned from the young reporter. He struggled to find words, "I'm leaving this conference early; I'll call you when I get to the airport. I want to interview her and will be there as fast as I can get packed and get a cab to the airport."

David pushed the elevator call button and waited. Then, as he was about to call Alaska Airlines to inquire about the next available flight to Seattle, Matt walked up, "David, I understand you missed the morning lecture."

"Matt, I'm glad I ran into you. I have an emergency at the hospital and will be leaving shortly. The craziest thing happened, I admitted a new patient who was catatonic the day I flew down here. I just learned that she has begun to speak, and she is claiming that she saw a pilot from 9/11 who is still alive."

Matt raised his eyebrows, "Really? How nice."

"No, it is not 'nice,' Matt. Do you understand? She is claiming that she saw and spoke with one of the pilots from the planes on 9/11. She must be experiencing some strange parallel universe type of thing. We all know there were no survivors on those planes. This is the kind of patient a psychiatrist dreams about. This could end up being the patient case of my lifetime. I'm on my way to Seattle as soon as I pack my suitcase," David explained. The elevator chimed its arrival to the lobby level, and David jumped in. "Are you going up?" He asked.

Matt Johnson smiled calmly. "No, no, thank you, I'm looking for Dr. Peretz," Matt's voice carried a strange tone that David had not heard before.

The elevator doors closed. David felt his heart skip a beat, maybe two. His stomach felt like he was on a roller coaster ride. When the elevator doors opened, he realized what Josh Miller told him about the CIA and the terror attacks was true. Had he just made the mistake of his lifetime?

sixteen

Even though Ruth Ann spent the day relaxing and reading, she still felt exhausted. She was worried about Rosslyn. Her reading in Rosslyn's father's diary had also been very troubling, as it filled her mind with more angst than she could bear. As sunset approached, she felt a walk on the beach would clear her head and return some solace to her soul.

She marveled at the radiance of the sun as it reflected off the buildings across the Puget Sound in downtown Seattle. She hurried out the back door and down the terraced steps to the beach. She took her shoes off and left them on the bottom step. She walked along the beach, wandering into the water to let the contrast between beach and water register in her brain. Finally, she felt both her mind and body begin to relax. She walked until she came to a jetty and decided to turn around and return. She rolled up her pants to the knees and waded in the water, splashing like a child.

It was almost dark when she arrived at Vera's house. She turned and started to jog up toward the steps. Unfortunately, her right foot stepped into a hole and caused her to stumble and fall headfirst into the sand. In addition, there was a sharp pain in her right ankle which caused her to scream. She questioned if she could manage her way up the steps and into the house. Almost immediately, a gentleman was standing behind her, offering his assistance. "May I help you?" He asked.

"Why, thank you, sir, I appreciate it. I'm staying at a house just up the stairs. My name is Ruth Ann."

"My name is Charles. I'm one of the four Secret Service agents assigned to protect the First Lady's home. We are also charged with protecting anyone staying at her residence, so we have been aware of your visit. You're going to need to put some ice on that. Let me help you into the house," he added.

"Jenny told me you guys were lurking around and usually out of sight," Ruth Ann said.

Charles helped her up, took the weight off her right leg, and guided her up the stairs and into the house.

"I think I will be fine from here. I'll soak my ankle in ice water tonight and see how it feels in the morning," Ruth Ann said.

"I am off duty tomorrow, so I can come by and check on you if you'd like," Charles replied.

"Thank you. That would be lovely," Ruth Ann said.

In the morning, Ruth Ann's ankle felt better; the swelling had gone down but putting her weight on that leg caused discomfort. She wasn't sure if she would be able to navigate the trip to the hospital to see Rosslyn. Just then, Charles knocked at the back door. Ruth Ann motioned for him to come inside.

"Good morning," she said. "Would you like a cup of coffee?"

"I would love some," replied Charles.

Ruth Ann handed him a cup of hot coffee and joined him at the kitchen table.

"So, how is the ankle this morning?" Asked Charles.

"Oh, it is much better, but I am hesitant to drive to Harborview Medical Center to see my friend Rosslyn," Ruth Ann demurred.

"Why is she there?" Charles asked.

"She has a head injury and is in a catatonic state," Ruth Ann explained.

"I'd be pleased to drive you if you would like a ride. I've always wanted to see Capitol Hill, but I haven't had an opportunity yet. What time do you want to go?" He inquired.

"I am waiting to hear from the doctors monitoring her, and I can go any time after that call," Ruth Ann said.

"I'm ready whenever you are. Text me when you want to head out. I'm driving a big black government-issued SUV," he said with a laugh.

"Let's hope I'm able to climb into that beast by myself," Ruth Ann said.

Later that afternoon, Dr. Cohen called and informed Ruth Ann that he had just landed at SeaTac. He said that Rosslyn was beginning to speak, and he was headed directly to the hospital as soon as he retrieved his luggage and his car.

If Rosslyn was awake and lucid, she wanted to get to the hospital as soon as possible. So, she sent a text to Charles saying she would be ready to go in five minutes.

"Thank you for driving me. I really appreciate it. If Rosslyn is awake, I'm sure she will enjoy meeting you," Ruth Ann explained.

"It's really no problem. This assignment can be boring, and I'm grateful for a little excitement even if it does mean going to a hospital."

They both laughed.

When they arrived at the hospital, Ruth Ann led the way to Rosslyn's room.

As they passed the nurses' station, Ruth Ann asked if it would be okay to visit Rosslyn.

"Sure," replied the nurse, "she has been awake and has begun to talk. A doctor is in with her now, but that shouldn't be a problem. Although I must admit, I didn't recognize that doctor."

That comment confused Ruth Ann. She was expecting to see Dr. Levine or Dr. Cohen.

Ruth Ann held the door to Rosslyn's room for Charles to enter. Before she could squeeze in behind him, she heard him shout, "Doug! What are you doing? You're not a doctor!"

Charles pulled his service weapon from his shoulder holster and pointed it at Doug, "Move away from her and stand next to the wall."

Ruth Ann stood behind Charles but wanted to see what the excitement was all about.

Doug held a syringe in his hand, and instead of backing against the wall, he lunged toward Rosslyn and attempted to insert the syringe into her IV portal.

"Move away from her, or I will blow you to hell," shouted Charles.

Doug ignored Charles' command.

Without hesitation, Charles fired his weapon and hit Doug square in the chest. The impact pushed him into the wall, but it did not kill him. Staggering to his feet, Doug lunged toward Rosslyn, hoping to empty the syringe. Instead, Charles fired again, blowing Doug through the window. If he was not dead from the second bullet, he certainly was when he hit the ground seven floors below.

Dr. Cohen rushed into Rosslyn's room. "What the hell is going on in here?" He shouted, relieved to see Rosslyn sitting up in her bed and still very much alive.

"I just took out a CIA assassin who was trying to kill Rosslyn. I am sure the fluid in that syringe is a lethal toxin," claimed Charles.

"And who exactly are you?" Questioned Dr. Cohen.

"Charles Lee Smith, United States Secret Service assigned to protect the First Lady's home and anyone staying there. And that is exactly what I did. Let me explain something before the authorities show up. Doug Ross, the man on the pavement below, and I have known each other for years. We were in the academy together. We were both expert marksmen and were recruited by the CIA. Clandestine operations appealed to Doug, so he took the job. I was more interested in police work and chose the secret service. We kept track of each other in the ensuing years until it became obvious that Doug had become an assassin. I had not thought about him until I entered this room and saw him hovering over Rosslyn's IV. I knew immediately he was assigned to kill her. I gave him every chance to back down, but he persisted, and I had no choice but to shoot him."

Dr. Cohen looked at Ruth Ann, who nodded in agreement. He began to reflect on what he had learned while in Las Vegas. It was not difficult to believe what Charles told him, and it made him angry. Did Matt Johnson tell Dr. Peretz about Rosslyn? Did the CIA send this assassin to kill her? Why would she be such a threat? Could it be something she has been saying about an airline captain she saw in Vancouver? He wanted to question her, but under the present circumstances, he thought the better of it. He walked to the broken window and looked down. Police cars were beginning to arrive.

Ruth Ann felt a compelling urge to phone Max. She excused herself and stepped into the hallway. "Max, something terrible has happened. I'm at the hospital with Charles Smith, one of the agents assigned to protect Vera's house. He recognized and shot an assassin who was trying to kill Rosslyn. I can't imagine why anyone wants to kill her. I don't feel we are safe anymore, even at Vera's house. We need to get out of here as soon as we can before this becomes more complicated," Ruth Ann explained.

"Have the police arrived yet?" Asked Max.

"Not yet, but I think they're on their way up."

"Give me a few minutes to commandeer an aircraft for you. Deal with the police, and if they give you any trouble, call me back, and I'll get this mess cleared up from here."

"Okay, Max, will do," Ruth Ann replied.

Just then, four Seattle policemen exited the elevator. Ruth Ann could see the receptionist point them down the hallway toward Rosslyn's room.

Charles held his service weapon by the barrel and handed it to one of the officers along with his Secret Service credentials. "I shot the man who is down on the pavement with this weapon, and I'm prepared to answer all your questions," offered agent Smith.

"Who else was in the room when this happened?" Asked the officer holding Charles' gun.

"I was," answered Ruth Ann.

"Very well, follow my partner, ma'am, and he will question you," he ordered Ruth Ann.

The police lieutenant escorted Ruth Ann to a vacant patient room down the hall and started questioning her. He was surprised to learn that Ruth Ann and Rosslyn were friends of the First Lady. Upon learning that detail, his demeanor became much more polite.

The detective questioned Charles at length while Dr. Cohen did his best to comfort and calm Rosslyn.

As the police officers finished their questioning, it became clear that Charles was telling the truth. Doug Ross was using an alias which only made him more suspicious and corroborated what Charles told them. Charles' and Ruth Ann's accounts precisely matched, adding credence to their story. After a few hours, they decided to release Charles without pressing charges but insisted he is available for any further questioning. He reassured them his assignment to protect the First Lady's beach house would have him in Seattle for another eighteen months.

Ruth Ann persuaded Dr. Cohen to release Rosslyn. He would have preferred to keep her in the hospital for several more days, but considering someone tried to kill her, he concluded it would be best to let her leave with Ruth Ann and agent Smith.

After Ruth Ann and Charles helped Rosslyn into the back of the SUV, Ruth Ann called Max, "We are on our way to Vera's house now to gather our belongings."

"Great, you guys have that agent stay outside and keep watch. Get your things out of there as quickly as you can. Do you know where Moses Lake is?"

"Not really," replied Ruth Ann.

"I will send the information to your phone. Can that agent drive you?"

"It's his day off, but I would think he can," Ruth Ann answered.

"Okay, here's the situation, the Secretary of Transportation is in Portland today. I have commandeered his jet and am having it sent to Moses Lake to fly you back to D.C. I'll make other arrangements for the secretary, or he can fly back commercial, which might be good for both him and the public. The jet should be waiting for you in the general aviation area by the time you arrive at Moses Lake," Max said.

"Thanks, Max; I guess we will see you tomorrow then," Ruth Ann said. "If agent Smith can't drive us or we have any other problems, I will call you back."

Ruth Ann quickly loaded their belongings into the back of the SUV.

"Charles, is it possible for you to drive us to Moses Lake right now?" Ruth Ann asked.

"No problem, what's going on at Moses Lake?" Asked Charles.

"There is a government jet waiting to take us to the other Washington," Ruth Ann answered. "And I have a huge favor to ask of you. Can you return my rental car for me tomorrow?"

"I can do that; just don't forget to give me the key. You certainly have some high-level connections," Charles responded.

"The First Lady and I shared a life-changing experience a while back; as a result, we are pretty close. We are both cautious of anyone in intelligence," Ruth Ann explained. "Now that Rosslyn can speak, I'm hoping she can explain why someone tried to kill her. If you hear anything that surprises you, you will need to keep it to yourself. As far as you are concerned, we are just two crazy middle-aged women with a drinking problem. Got it?"

"Whatever you say, ma'am, Secret is my first name, and Service is my last."

seventeen

"Max made arrangements for a private jet to pick us up at Moses Lake and fly us to Washington. We will stay in a hotel there," Ruth Ann explained to Rosslyn as they sat together in the back seat of Charles' SUV.

Rosslyn nodded but did not say anything.

Ruth Ann continued, "Charles will drive us to Moses Lake."

"Who's Charles?" Rosslyn asked quietly.

"Charles is one of the Secret Service agents assigned to Vera's house.

Rosslyn nodded again and softly replied, "Thank you, Charles. I feel like I've been in the twilight zone; everything seems unreal."

"You are very welcome, Rosslyn," Charles said. "I'd like to say all in a day's work, but I have to admit watching an empty house doesn't usually offer this kind of excitement."

Ruth Ann chuckled, "You will be happy to be back to guarding an empty house after today."

"I flew into the Moses Lake airport a few years back. So, I know where it is and how to get there, but I could not tell you a thing about the city; we drove to a remote area in Canada after we landed," Charles explained.

Traffic was exceptionally light eastbound on I-90, and they arrived at Moses Lake in under three hours. Charles drove the SUV onto the tarmac right up to the jet, waiting with its stairs extended. The two women bid Charles goodbye and thanked him for all he had done. Ruth Ann tossed him the keys to their rental car, then quickly climbed the stairs into the private jet for their trip back to D.C. Within moments, the plane was in the air, and in no time, both women were sound asleep.

Ruth Ann began to stir and opened her eyes to see that Rosslyn was already awake and was staring out the window.

"That was quite the experience in the hospital. Do you remember what happened?" Asked Ruth Ann.

"I know Charles shot and killed some guy in my room, but I don't know who he was or why he was there," Rosslyn replied.

"Charles recognized that man as an assassin," Ruth Ann confirmed.

"But why would he want to kill me?" Rosslyn asked, confused.

"That's something we need to get to the bottom of," Ruth Ann said.

Rosslyn nodded in agreement.

"I have a feeling it has something to do with what happened in Vancouver. By the way, when you woke up, did you mention anything about that event to anyone?"

"I don't recall exactly, but I might have said something to the nurses. I probably yammered a lot. I was happy to feel alive again," stated Rosslyn.

"It might be a good idea to call Dr. Cohen and find out if he knows anything that will help us solve this puzzle," Ruth Ann said. She reached for her cell phone and dialed the hospital. "It's nice that you can use your phone in the air on these government planes," Ruth Ann said.

"Dr. Cohen, this is Ruth Ann," she said when he answered.

"Where are you two?" He asked.

"We are on a flight back to D.C.," she replied.

"How were you able to get on a flight out of SeaTac that quickly? That's amazing!" He exclaimed.

Ruth Ann chose not to respond to that comment. She did not feel he needed to know more about their business than the little he already knew. She followed by saying, "Dr. Cohen, when were you informed that Rosslyn regained consciousness? When she began to talk, do you know what kind of things she was saying? We're trying to tie up some of the loose ends surrounding today's events."

"Right before I left Las Vegas, Dr. Levine called me with the news. He mentioned Rosslyn started talking about being a flight attendant and something about a pilot who was supposed to be dead that she saw in Vancouver. Other than that, I don't know what she said," Dr. Cohen replied.

"Did you happen to mention what you just told me to anyone before you left Las Vegas?" Ruth Ann asked.

"I did say something to my good friend Matt Johnson about a patient that saw a pilot involved in 9/11. I don't recall exactly what I said, however," the doctor replied.

At that moment, it became clear to Dr. Cohen that Matt must have said something to Sherwood or Peretz, and they could have ordered the hit on Rosslyn. His heart sank, thinking he was in any way responsible. But, based on what he learned at the conference, he knew the CIA was both capable and vindictive enough to kill someone they deemed a threat to their version of history."

"That certainly answers some of my questions. I appreciate all you were able to do for Rosslyn and your candid responses. I do not hold you in any way responsible for today's events," Ruth Ann said.

Ruth Ann turned to Rosslyn and said, "I have a confession to make to you. When I brought your things into Vera's house, one of your father's diaries fell out of your tote bag. I opened it and began reading. It was one of the most fascinating things I have ever read. I knew it was wrong of me to read something meant for you, but I could not stop myself. I stayed up most of the night reading."

"Oh, Ruth Ann, it's no problem; I intended to share them with you anyway," Rosslyn said.

Ruth Ann dialed Max's number and was surprised when it rang more than three times before he answered.

"Okay, where are you two?" Max inquired when he answered the phone.

"I would guess we are over North Dakota about now. We had a very uneventful ride to Moses Lake, and the plane was waiting for us, ready to go. I want to thank you for taking such good care of us even if it was at the Secretary of Transportation's expense," Ruth Ann remarked.

"Oh, he is fine; I made other arrangements for him," replied Max.

"We should arrive at Andrews in about two and a half hours. Will you be the one to come pick us up?" Ruth Ann asked.

"I've made a reservation at the Willard Hotel for you two. I will meet you at Andrews and take you to the hotel," Max explained.

"I look forward to seeing you again, Max. See you in a few," Ruth Ann said.

eighteen

On the drive to the hotel from the airport, Ruth Ann asked, "Rosslyn, do you remember any more details about North Vancouver?"

"I'm beginning to recall our time at Vera's house and the traffic as we left Seattle. I remember seeing a view of the Space Needle and Elliot Bay as we drove north. But after that, everything still feels like a dream to me," Rosslyn explained.

"When we get to the hotel, I think we should share a room; let's ask for a suite with two queen beds, and that way, if you feel dizzy or not well, I will be right there with you," Ruth Ann suggested.

"Oh, that is a great idea, Ruth Ann. I do have a slight sense of pressure in the back of my head like a headache might be sneaking up on me. It's a very strange sensation. I know I should be getting used to strange happenings, but I am feeling a little unsure of being alone."

When they arrived at the Willard Hotel, Ruth Ann insisted that Rosslyn sit on a nearby sofa with their luggage while she registered.

"We are all set; the bellman will bring our things," Ruth Ann helped Rosslyn to her feet. The bellman was directly behind Ruth Ann and quickly loaded their belongings onto a luggage dolly.

At check-in, Ruth Ann ordered a bottle of red wine with cheese and fruit to be delivered to their room. It arrived right after the women changed into their sleeping attire.

"Ruth Ann, this is just what the doctor ordered," Rosslyn said.

"If only the doctor knew where you were," Ruth Ann laughed.

"To a successful adventure!" Rosslyn held out her wine goblet to toast.

"From what read in that diary of your father's, I think you might have enough material to write a spy novel one day," Ruth Ann suggested.

Rosslyn picked up the diary that Ruth Ann referred to. "Maybe since you're here, I am brave enough to take a peek into his world." She opened the book and flipped past the few pages

she had read earlier. Her eyes caught some printed numbers on a page, so she backed up and began to read:

Dear Rosslyn, I have transcribed some of the details of a top-secret document. This will explain a great deal about how several government agencies work and work together. The degree of corruption is beyond most American's imagination. This is how the CIA set up the most extensive drug and money laundering system in the world. It involved Operation Eagle II, Operation Studebaker, Operation Clean Room, and Operation Supermarket. Their main aim was to create money for the CIA's covert black operations. There is a copy of the actual FBI document for you among the papers Uncle Greg gave you. I wanted to write as much of it as I could in a diary in case our history ends up shredded.

Rosslyn quietly read several pages, then exclaimed, "Ruth Ann, you have got to hear this!"

"What is it?" Ruth Ann asked.

Rosslyn read:

"FEDERAL BUREAU OF INVESTIGATION

Date: July 7, 1989

To: Senator Edward Kennedy (FOR HIS EYES ONLY)

Classification: TOP SECRET

Dear Senator:

Per your oral request of June 5, 1989, requesting a full report on the 'Japanese/ Singapore/New Zealand/Kentucky' connection, what follows is a complete investigation of all available files of the Bureau, the Department of Defense, the Central Intelligence Agency, the Departments of the Navy, Army, and Marine Corps, as well as records of the

World War II Office of Strategic Services (OSS). We have included a full report into the present assignment of a man called the Colonel and his total work history from 1942 to the present. That investigation is as complete as possible, considering the difficulty we have met whenever we have mentioned his name.

"Wow! Whoever this guy is, he sounds like he could give James Bond a run for his money," Ruth Ann interjected.

"No kidding! You have to wonder why all the secrecy," Rosslyn agreed, then continued reading aloud:

"During the tenure of Richard Helms as Director of the Central Intelligence Agency, decisions were made with the approval of the Oval Office to draft a plan by which the CIA could have as much money as needed, without knowledge or control of the Congress. This would accomplish the dual purpose of carrying out clandestine and covert operations and avoid the necessity of having to request funds from Congress.

The FBI intercepted Director Helms' memo to the Oval Office in which he said, in part, 'If Congress or any other uninformed do-gooders ever become aware of this operation, this agency will invoke the CIA Act of 1949, which exempts the CIA from requiring the disclosure of functions, names, official titles, salaries, and numbers of personnel employed by the agency.' Using this as the cloak of legality, Director Helms put together a team of five top people."

"The FBI intercepted Helms' communications with the Oval Office? That's interesting," Ruth Ann said as she opened her iPad. "To put this into a period, Helms was the Director of the CIA from June 30, 1966, until February 2, 1973. I would say that was the height of the Viet Nam War. The Oval Office was occupied by Lyndon Johnson until January 1969, then Richard Nixon until August of 1974. So, the Oval Office was in on this conspiracy."

"Looks like the CIA was setting up off the books ways to fund themselves so they wouldn't have to ever deal with Congress," Rosslyn said, then continued reading:

"The five experts chosen were, General Edward Lansdale, who ran CIA activities in Vietnam; William Colby, who was put in total command of the operation; George H.W.

Bush, who asked and received approval to have his top aid, Richard Armitage be brought aboard, and the man we refer to as the Colonel, a top CIA asset."

"I'm beginning to get the feeling that we are about to discover why JFK was no fan of the Central Intelligence Agency," Rosslyn added then continued:

"Four of the five were hand-picked for their exceptional abilities: Bush was chosen for his knowledge of China and his war-time flying experience, as well as being on the way up within the CIA. General Lansdale brought his expertise as a top CIA asset. William Colby was picked for his knowledge of Southeast Asia. The Colonel was included because of his experience as a pilot, his command of over a dozen languages, and his position as founder of the Special Forces. These names were submitted to the Godfather of the CIA, Allen Dulles, who gave the plan his total blessing."

"That's interesting! JFK ousted Allen Dulles from the CIA in 1961. This sounds like he was still running the show until he died eight years later. General Lansdale was one of the plotters of Operation Northwoods. He was the General who proposed using false-flag provocations to incite war with Cuba. Remember Operation Northwoods?" Ruth Ann asked.

"Sounds vaguely familiar to me," Rosslyn said as she reached for a slice of brie cheese. Then she held her wine glass up towards Ruth Ann, who was refilling her glass. "If this account is real, then this arrangement was set up and approved sometime before January 1969," Rosslyn added, then continued reading:

"The plan called for a second airline to be set up by the CIA (the first was Flying Tigers). This was done, and the airline was named Overseas National Airline (ONA). Suddenly, this airline received contracts as a civilian carrier and à military cargo into the Pacific Rim and Southeast Asia without owning any aircraft.

The CIA was to enter the drug smuggling business. Each of the five planners would have his field to handle. As the secret head of ONA, Bush would handle the shipping of the drugs under forged waybills. Armitage would be the gopher for the group and the intermediary with any undesirables. General Lansdale would manage all the distribution network and collection services within the military in Viet Nam. William Colby was to handle all the manpower from runners, peddlers, pushers, and collectors. Colby would also direct the elimination of any who might prove to be uncontrollable, be they American or Vietnamese. The Colonel was to use his contacts to obtain aid from various governments. The operation was given the code name of Eagle II, although there is some evidence that a different name may have referred to it. Colby started his phase of elimination of dissidents under the code name: Phoenix Program. Colby soon became insane with power, and before he was finished with Phoenix, over 20,000 suspects were executed.

Helms later tried to have Colby eliminated but discovered that Colby's copies of all plans and secret recordings of their meetings were being held as an insurance policy. Finally, Helms agreed with Colby in exchange for his resignation, that he (Colby) would eventually become the Director of the CIA."

"So much for earning the directorship," Ruth Ann commented. "Rosslyn, this is mind-blowing information. He earned that top position by keeping his mouth shut about the CIA running drugs."

"It's rather telling, isn't it?" Rosslyn agreed. "Should I continue?"

"Yes, you should. This is information that the government has denied for decades. But, my God, George H.W. Bush not only became the Director of the CIA but a Vice President and President of the United States. What were these men up to?"

Rosslyn continued reading from the diary:

"Bush, for his cooperation and silence, would become Director of the CIA, where he managed to increase the CIA's drug operation ten-fold. The plan was in full force when the United States government met opposition from the Japanese ruling party. To put CIA-controlled people in power, Bush chose a bankrupt obscure party to back in the takeover of the Japanese government. The Liberal Democratic Party needed a vast amount of money to buy memberships and votes. Before they finally achieved power, a sum of over 300 billion Japanese Yen had been funneled to them by the CIA.

That appeared to be about the time of the beginning of the CIA's drug-running operation, which evolved into what you refer to as the 'Japanese/Singapore/New Zealand/Kentucky' connection. The Kentucky connection came about strangely, and were it not for unforeseen circumstances, there would not now be any such connection. We believe another code name was used in this operation, and that was Studebaker, again, which could be a misdirection.

All the players fit neatly into the puzzle, except concerning anything about the Colonel. It's impossible to get the Agency, the Pentagon, or any branch of the military to so much as admitting to any such person ever existing. Our strong suspicion is that the Colonel is now the top worldwide CIA free agent, in charge of all covert operations and, if needed, assassinations. He reports and is responsible only to the real and secret director of the CIA, Mr. Helms. We have taped conversations between the Colonel and Helms. The Colonel is so deeply buried in secrecy that not even those within the upper levels of the CIA confess to any knowledge of him.

He has dozens of aliases, and our most trusted agents within all agencies cannot unearth an iota of information on his actual job, purpose, or present mission. All we have been able to gather of his current work is that he is helping an individual named Marion Horn. He has withdrawn from any assignments with either the military or the CIA until Mr. Horn collects all the money that is due him. The amount in question to be given to Mr. Horn totals 318 billion Japanese Yen, resulting from the sale of drugs by the CIA.

In 1973, Helms decided that he could better control international operations from outside the CIA. Colby assumed the post of Director, and the next hand-picked Director was George H.W. Bush. The seventies were not a peaceful time for the Agency; Helm's puppet, Prime Minister Kakuei Tanaka, was caught in a bribery scandal involving the Lockheed Aircraft Company,"

Ruth Ann typed a query into her iPad, "Kakuei Tanaka was the Prime Minister and head of the Liberal Democratic Party until December 1974. He was indicted for scandalous activities on August 16, 1976. George H.W. Bush was the Director of the CIA at the time."

"This story does seem to follow a truthful timeline," Rosslyn noted as she continued to read:

"Helms formed a strong relationship with a representative of the Rothschild banking empire, and together they decided to start different clandestine operations. This gave Helms and the Rothschild empire control over any new drug operation in the world. When Prime Minister Tanaka was forced to resign, a decision was reached to have George Bush wash away any evidence of their operation."

"Absolutely, this reads like a spy novel, but it's real, and it is about people that have had a great deal of power during our lifetimes. Jimmy Carter was sworn in as President January 20th 1977, to keep things in perspective," Ruth Ann interjected. "And George Bush's term as the Director of the CIA ended on the day Carter was inaugurated. So please, if you are not too tired, continue; this is fascinating."

Rosslyn continued reading the FBI report:

"Armitage continued the operation by changing locations, with the knowledge of Bush. Bush's hands were tied because of the information secreted by Armitage. It appears that certain steps were taken to eliminate Armitage by natural causes, and his secret partner, Sununu, of whom we have given you the proof of his bisexuality."

"John Sununu was bisexual? Does anything get past the FBI? This sounds like the FBI spied on politicians, insiders, and even Directors of the CIA," Ruth Ann said.

"The FBI was even spying on the President of the United States!" Rosslyn added.

Ruth Ann scrolled through her iPad, "Oh, here is an article that says Reagan signed a top-secret document called the National Security Decision Directive 17, which gave the CIA the power to recruit and support a 500-man force of Nicaraguan rebels to conduct covert actions against the leftist Sandinista regime, that established a $19 million-dollar budget. It looks like this was signed November 23rd, 1981."

"Back to the spy novel," Rosslyn said, then continued, "*At this point, Senator, how much is fact and how much is fiction is hard to tell but, we believe that the records prove that this is as close to fact as possible in a complicated covert operation like this. Helms realized he needed funds to aid the Contras in Nicaragua. His solution was to continue the operation under the control of Armitage, with the full knowledge of Bush, but not of President Reagan.*

The Colonel had to be kept in the dark because of his total aversion to the drug trade. So, instead, Lt. Colonel Oliver North was brought in to run this operation.

Helms has made mistakes, but nothing as significant as allowing Armitage to oversee the continuation of this operation. Armitage became the consummate double-dealer and the perfect triple-crosser. We have documentation showing that Helms and the CIA are in possession of all the proof needed of the actions by Armitage. It is estimated that Armitage has amassed a sum of more than one hundred billion dollars. Our agents within the Oval Office suspect that Armitage has invested it all in gold and that gold is deposited in banks around the world."

Ruth Ann refilled their wine glasses, "The FBI has agents within the Oval Office? And Senator Kennedy is aware of this? Yet, the FBI is fine with Armitage amassing this money and then investing it in gold. That doesn't seem legal."

"It's starting to look that way, isn't it?" Rosslyn took a sip of wine. "This is quite a story, not what you expect from the FBI, the CIA, a Senator, or the President of the United States. I keep waiting for an honest man to rise in this story. So far, it seems that the FBI is aware of the CIA running drugs and amassing billions of dollars then hiding that money offshore. I mean, this report reads as a matter of fact, yet there is no mention of holding these men to the legal standards the rest of us would be held to."

"Please, read on." Ruth Ann encouraged.

Rosslyn continued, "*The Colonel discovered the names of our agents within the CIA, as well as our agents in several U.S. Embassies abroad. He started to feed that information to Casey. Per the orders of the former director, we set out to destroy any credibility that the Colonel might have. We used paid informants and runners to destroy him. The Bureau has tried to investigate this; however, orders have come down from Justice and State that both men are considered untouchable. As a result, all inquiries about the Colonel and Horn were stopped, and all documentation in our files to be shredded. We orchestrated two attempts on the Colonel within the past two years, failing in both. Now, he is under the protection of the White House.*"

"That would be the George H. W. Bush White House," Ruth Ann interjected. This report says that the FBI made two *attempts*. That sounds like they are admitting to the Senator that they tried to kill the Colonel. I would interpret that as attempted assassinations."

"It sure does sound like that," Rosslyn agreed. "Do you want to hear more?"

"Read on, please."

"*We had as many as two dozen agents assigned to monitor all movements of the Colonel, but when he started to approach our agents and reprimand them for their terribly sloppy methods of tailing, we decided to abort. Future inquiries about these operations must be obtained from the non-existing files of the CIA. If the Colonel does not exist, then there are no files to be found.*

The Colonel sent a report detailing drug dealing by Noriega and other Panamanian military officers to the White House, where it quickly disappeared. Noriega had been dropped from the Agency's payroll when Admiral Turner became the Director. Still, the Panamanian was restored to the Agency's good graces when the Reagan administration came into office. The Colonel continued to complain to the CIA about Noriega until Noriega found out about it from Casey in 1985. Noriega revealed all about the CIA's drug operation to Castro.

The agency had to have funds for Oliver North. Our files show that Casey set about establishing his own kingdom without consulting Helms, with him as the emperor. Casey put Barry Seal in charge of the drug routes to obtain the funds for Oliver North's operation with the Contras."

"My God, Rosslyn, this is bringing all the truth to the surface. Your father said there is a copy of this actual document with the other diaries and papers your uncle gave you? I wonder if it has been declassified by now. This account brings everything together, and the FBI and Senator Kennedy were aware of these activities. Yet, I don't recall ever hearing that any of these men were brought to justice over any of this," Ruth Ann's head was reeling. "Oh, please don't stop; if there is more, let's hear it all."

Rosslyn continued:

"Noriega controlled a network of remote landing strips in Panama that he agreed to provide to Seal. In return, Noriega received a $500,000,000 cash bribe plus a one percent cut of the value of every shipment of drugs that came through Panama. The CIA would use Panama's banking laws to launder the Medellin Cartel drug profits. Casey agreed to arm Noriega and clandestinely see to it that Noriega's enemies were eliminated.

As Casey saw the problem, the Soviet Union was about to set up a Central American beachhead via the Sandinista government of Nicaragua. The solution was to eliminate the Sandinista regime. An American military invasion was out of the question, and the only CIA man with contacts to Noriega was the Colonel who would not agree to drug smuggling into the U.S., so Casey created a covert paramilitary operation."

"The Boland Amendment prohibited that action. I think it was in 1982," Ruth Ann added. "That really messed up the CIA's covert war machine."

"From what I can figure, this Gang of Five had been funding their covert operations since somewhere around 1968; I recall Noriega was a good guy then a bad guy. He must have served his purpose, so they took him down," Rosslyn said and continued reading:

"The CIA established a connection with the drug lords of Columbia. Barry Seal was ordered to contact the Medellin Cartel. The Cartel's bosses wanted to smuggle tons of cocaine in single shipments instead of hundreds of kilos by individual runners. Along came Seal with his airline, which in truth was Casey's airline, and they set up the perfect system for smuggling tons of cocaine into the United States. Barry Seal was the most important organizer, facilitator, and impresario of the partnership between the CIA and organized crime. Seal earned over thirty million dollars as his share of the drug smuggling operation. Casey ordered the subordination of drug enforcement and allowed two southern states to be used as major distribution points for Latin American narcotics. Seal first met the Colonel in early 1972, when he was helping the organization trying to overthrow Fidel Castro. Seal agreed to smuggle seven tons of C-4 explosives to the Mexican base, from which the CIA was preparing to dispatch teams of saboteurs into Cuba. The Colonel knew

of Seal and did not like him, so he had Seal arrested for violating the Neutrality Act, and yet, the case against Seal was thrown out by the Court.

Seal was a favorite of Casey's and was given the funds to set up his smuggling businesses with the full knowledge of the CIA. He ran guns to the Contras for Casey, drugs back into the US, and was always found innocent of any court accusations. This was all run through the Mena, Arkansas airport under the knowledge and cooperation of Governor Bill Clinton and his administration.

The Colonel got wind that Seal was involved in running drugs into the United States and did not know or care that Seal was working for Director Casey. By asking Casey that Seal be eliminated, he was risking the toppling of the drug money machine for Col. Oliver North.

Our tapes of phone conversations between Director Casey and the Colonel show that the Colonel informed him that he had proof of who the real leader of the drug cartel in the U.S. was. The Colonel asked if he would step on anyone's toes if he stopped Seal, that 'fat son-of-a-bitch'. Director Casey claimed that Seal was not working for the Agency. Casey tried to contact Seal but was not successful. In the meantime, the Colonel's men were successful. On the evening of February 19, 1986, at precisely 6 P.M., Barry Seal got out of his Cadillac in a parking lot and was dead instantly. The Bureau has copies of all tapes of these conversations with Casey and copies of all the police reports.

Casey continued secret operations to keep the Contras armed and supplied. He changed the name of the operation again, possibly to Black-Eagle. The operation went ahead through a Casey confidant, Michael Harari. Harari was the former Head of Operations in Central America for the Israeli intelligence, Mossad. Harari was a man steeped in the darker arts of modern espionage and was a key operative for Mossad murder squads that rampaged throughout Europe. While serving in the Mossad, Harari went into the import-export business in Panama City. His link with the Mossad allowed him to arrange twenty million dollars' worth of Israeli arms for the Panamanian military, plus Mossad training and Israeli-made Uzi submachine guns for Noriega's intelligence operatives.

The Colonel had his mole in the government of Panama. Dr. Hugo Spadafora, Panama's vice-minister of Health, under dictator Omar Torrijos. Following the unexplained death of Torrijos in a plane crash, Spadafora learned that Noriega was involved in drug smuggling. Spadafora found out that Noriega was being paid $250,000 per year by Casey from the CIA, while at the same time Noriega was supplying information to Fidel Castro. Noriega also offered the Israeli's the use of Panama as a conduit for embargoed arms to Israel.

Casey had the idea of using Vice President Bush's office as a cover for their operation, arranging it via Bush's Chief of Staff, Donald Gregg, a former CIA officer. The CIA concluded that it was time to put distance between Noriega and their drug operation. A revised operation code-named the 'Supermarket' was then set up by Casey. Noriega only had a small role in this new operation. Michael Harari was to take full command, and his contact was Lt. Col. Oliver North."

"If this story is indicative, Ruth Ann, of what my dad was involved in, I am not sure I want to read all of those other diaries and papers. How awful can our government be? We have just read about plans to fake hijackings, a multi-billion-dollar drug-running operation, assassinations, and control of foreign governments. I don't know whether my stomach or my heart can handle any more of this. And I sure don't want to know how deeply involved with this type of activity my father was."

"Let's hope everyone in the Agency is not a sociopath or a psychopath. But, from what you just read, it's not looking good now. However, but they must have people who hired on not knowing what they were getting into. It's like membership in a gang or organized crime; it's nearly impossible to retire or get out alive," Ruth Ann said.

nineteen

Jim knocked on Max's office door as he pushed it open, "Max, I've got everything copied, and I think I have enough for everyone on the team."

"Great, I have made copies for everyone too; here's one for you," Max said. Tom sent over a huge file of information from Chip. It's everything he was working on before his unexpected death. Some of it concerns details you already know, but I am sure there is new information here. Unfortunately, Tom suspects that Chip may have uncovered information that caused him to be silenced. We will know more when the autopsy report is available. There are a few documents that I read last night that I found intriguing. I clipped them together, and they are on the top of the stack I just gave you. So that you know, Ruth Ann and her friend Rosslyn flew into town last night and are at the Willard Hotel. Rosslyn had a horrific encounter in North Vancouver, about which I am still waiting for details. I sent them to visit an American Airline's pilot that contacted the webpage and was not willing to share details over the phone. Along with everything you are bringing to the table and what Ruth Ann and Rosslyn have discovered in their travels, I think it's a good idea to arrange a meeting with President Sherman, Vera, and the group. What does your schedule look like for the next few days?"

"I can make myself available any time," Jim replied.

"Great, I will make arrangements with the White House and get Tom here. Hopefully, we can get started tomorrow," Max explained.

"How many people do you expect will be at this meeting?" Jim asked.

"It looks like we will have eight people there. Why don't you make certain we have ten sets of everything while I get on the horn and lock in an early morning meeting," Max said.

"Do you have any idea what Ruth Ann and Rosslyn are bringing to this meeting?" Jim inquired.

"I'm not certain what all they have, but I understand Rosslyn spent some time in the hospital after something happened on their trip to North Vancouver. Then, a few days later, an assassin was caught in her room. I am sure we will get an update. I will call Ruth Ann once I get the White House committed to a start time tomorrow, and I will have those two write a report."

"Great, I am looking forward to hearing all about their trip and how she ended up in the hospital with an assassin," Jim replied. "Text me the moment you have the meeting arranged and let me know if there are any other documents we might want to add. I will work on a presentation of everything you and I have so far, and I will look over Chip's file this afternoon. If you can get Tom here, see if he can present what he feels is the most pertinent information to share with the group. I couldn't get the original copies of those manifests, but I did manage to get some photos taken on my cell phone. I will get those printed up for everyone. Max, I understand why these airline people were so afraid to come forward; the FBI was crawling all over the minute those towers exploded. Many of the ticket agents and flight crews were harassed and threatened by FBI agents, and it really rattled them. The manifests alone are no doubt posing a huge threat to those behind this deception."

"Make sure that information is emphasized in the meeting. I will call everyone in the group the minute I lock in the time."

twenty

President Sherman stood as the room became quiet. "Thank you all for your presence here. I know that all of you have done a great deal of research. Vera and I and our country appreciate all your hard work. I have cleared my schedule for the next few days, so if we need more time to go over everything, I can arrange for that. I want each of you to feel free to take as much time as you need to present your material. Without further delay, I'd like to ask Jim Bowman to lead this meeting. If you will, Jim, please begin."

"Thank you, President Sherman. Welcome to everyone and a quick introduction; if you have not met our newest team member yet, I would like to introduce Rosslyn Langley. She's a retired flight attendant, and I understand she has some very interesting information to contribute. She was an International Purser with American Airlines and had some thirty-plus years of seniority."

Rosslyn lifted her right hand slightly and waved as the others in the room tipped their heads, nodding a silent welcome, "Thirty-six years to be exact."

"Now, before I go any further, I have a great deal of information to share, so I'll not be standing to present it all to you. Unfortunately, I'm not as young as I once was, and my back will be giving me heck if I stand up for as long as this will probably take," Jim explained as he made himself comfortable in the winged-back chair next to the sofas in the Oval Office. "And thank you, Mr. President, for freeing up time in your schedule and you too, First Lady. Although there's a great deal of information for us to review, I'm hopeful we can get through it all in two or three days," Jim said as he handed everyone in the room a thick manila envelope filled with documents.

"As some of you already know, I was invited to view the original passenger manifests from a couple of the flights on 9/11. The customer service agent I met with did indeed have the original manifests. Those of us from the airline industry will recognize the type of paper they were printed on. When she heard her company was involved, the first thing she did was to print a copy of the manifests for the flights in question. She was curious to see if any non-revenue passengers or employees were onboard or riding the jump seat. She informed me that she noticed federal agents in the departure area as soon as she had run a printout from a gate computer. She said they wore curly wire earpieces and dark suits, making them stand out as government agents. She quickly tucked the manifests under her blouse, and while walking to the employee break room, she was stopped by another customer service agent. This other agent informed her that the FBI was on the property, asking questions lots of questions. They were looking for anyone that had access to viewing the passenger manifests. Strange question indeed, since every employee with knowledge of the flight numbers could have printed out the manifests."

Vera shook her head in agreement, "Every single employee anywhere near a company computer at any airport throughout the entire system could have printed copies of the manifests."

"Right, Vera," Jim agreed, then continued. "So, back to the manifests, I saw. Just exactly like the customer service agent reported, there were no Arab names listed… none in first class, business class, or coach. Not one of the Arab names the FBI later claimed were listed on the manifests were there, which indicates they were lying."

"If there were no Arab hijackers, then they weren't being hijacked," Vera spoke aloud as her mind began to ponder the possibilities. "If it wasn't an actual hijacking and the FBI knew it, that would explain why they were questioning what those gate agents knew and if they had printed the passenger manifests. They needed to conceal the truth."

"Right off the bat, I have to say the FBI was doing their usual clean-up job. They were hiding the truth about the manifests, those stinking rascals. Lots of us knew this was an inside job; we just couldn't figure it out. We kept thinking those darn Arabs were actually flying those planes. We should have known the FBI was up to no good." Max said.

Jim agreed, "Max, I am afraid what we are about to unravel is a more horrific story than that fantasy tale the media and government have been touting."

Ruth Ann noticed the color change in Rosslyn's face, "Rosslyn, honey, are you feeling alright?" She placed an opened bottle of water in her hand, "have some cold water; you'll be okay."

Joel stood up, "Let's all take a few minutes to stretch.

Vera added, "I'll have coffee service brought in for us along with something for us to nibble on. The White House chef has the most delightful pastries and snacks. Please, let's take a ten-minute break, then get right back into this meeting."

Rosslyn sensed the room return to full focus. She felt Ruth Ann's hand on her right shoulder and heard Vera ask, "Is she feeling alright, Ruth Ann? Is there anything we can get her?"

Rosslyn answered, "I'm okay; I was a little faint there for a moment; I'm fine now, thank you." She took a sip of water. The men were returning one by one as a server announced his presence.

"The coffee service is here. Rosslyn, how do you take your coffee?" Vera asked while the server stood at attention, waiting to be released.

"Cream, no sugar, thank you," Rosslyn answered, feeling a need to pinch herself, being in the White House and having the First Lady serving her coffee.

Vera thanked the servers and poured a cup of coffee for Rosslyn.

The ten-minute break passed quickly; Jim stood up to speak, "The real passenger manifests, tells us first and foremost that the FBI was lying to the world. But during that first week, they claimed a half a dozen names were listed on the manifests that were either still alive or have never been to the United States. The media aided them by never questioning their false accusations. As a result, most people were never aware of their gross mistakes."

Max interrupted, "The Federal Boys of Incompetency, lied? Imagine that."

"And they blamed the Arabs," Vera commented.

President Sherman added, "And this country has been involved in wars ever since."

"Those seams on britches," Max growled.

Jim loudly cleared his throat, "Let's bring this meeting back into focus by looking at the rest of our findings. To keep this as simple as possible, let me start with the first flight to push back from the gate at Boston's Logan International, American Flight 11. Those of us in the airline industry know that the only way a passenger's name can end up on the final manifest is to be onboard. At the time, most airlines were pulling the stubs of the boarding passes, and those stubs would also show everyone who was on the plane. Those stubs have never been released to the public. All we have are claims from the FBI, and you'll soon see for yourselves why those claims cannot be trusted. Initially, the FBI alleged that there were four different Arab names on the manifest, three of those people were very much alive, and one had died in a small plane crash exactly one year earlier. On Flight 11, Mohammad Atta was the only original name the FBI retained."

Ruth Ann piped up with a question, "Jim, are you saying that the FBI initially asserted that the accused hijackers were Mohammad Atta and four others whose names were later changed?

Jim replied, "good question. Why *was* the FBI lying, and *where* did those names come from?" The FBI claimed that in Atta's luggage that missed the flight was a list of the other eighteen hijackers. But of those listed, I have figured out that at least ten of them are still alive. Two had fake IDs, and the others are quite possibly intelligence agents. In fact, upon further investigation, the actual manifest showed a very different story than what the FBI was telling. I found out that none of the accused hijackers from Flight 11 were dead. Atta's parents were both shocked to be tracked by the media and asked about their son, especially since they were told he died in the plane that crashed into the North Tower. Shocking because they both received phone calls from him after 9/11."

Max interrupted, "Uh-hum, so let me get this straight. So, the guy that the FBI claimed was the pilot and the ringleader, Atta, was alive and spoke with his parents?"

"That's correct, Max," Jim said as he positioned a new illustration on the easel. "The

FBI made false accusations about others they claimed were listed on the manifests that had nothing to do with the events of that day. It might be easiest for me to show you this chart. The dishonesty problem for the FBI continues; the official story alleges that Atta rented a car and drove to Portland, Maine. Then the following morning, he flew back to Boston with barely enough time to make Flight 11. A few days later, his rental car was found, not in Portland, Maine, where it should have been, but in a parking lot at Boston's Logan airport. The FBI has never explained this, nor has the media ever questioned how Atta's rental car found its way back to Boston. I guess the FBI thought an improbable explanation would have drawn attention to their fake story."

"Seriously? Didn't the FBI say that the airlines provided them with the manifests?" Ruth Ann asked. "How could the airline give the FBI the manifests only to have the FBI add fake passengers who were not on board?" Why would the airlines remain silent?"

"That is a very big mystery. I can't be certain that the airlines gave manifests to the FBI, but you would think the airlines might have said something about such a discrepancy. Yet, a full year later, Atta's parents both claimed he was still alive and was on the run from what they referred to as American security forces," Jim added. "Reading through thousands of FBI interview form 302's, I can testify that there were many anomalies that were never addressed."

"What about that Saudi passport they found on the street in New York City? Was that Mohammad Atta's?" Joel asked.

"It was found on Murray Street if I remember correctly," Vera said. "I was always suspicious of that because it was found a couple of blocks north of the north tower, and come on; a paper passport is all that survived from that huge aircraft. I remember hearing that it wasn't even singed."

"I always questioned why the mayor of New York never went into his command center in Building 7 that day too," Ruth Ann added.

"Later on, in a television interview, he said that he did go into the emergency command center, but he evacuated the office the moment the first tower was hit," Vera said.

"If that was true, why would he have gone into the command center that morning before the North Tower being struck?" Ruth Ann asked.

"That was a lie," Max added. "That passport found on Murray Street was eventually given to the New York Police Commissioner. Interesting tidbit… he just returned from Israel the last week of August. He was attending a conference on terrorism. He no sooner arrives home than the biggest act of terrorism happens right in his city. Like I always say, there are no coincidences. That's why I call them 'coinky-dinks.' A similar situation occurred in Shanksville. The only things to survive there were two hijackers' passports. There were no titanium engine parts, no landing gear, no tail section, no bodies, nor luggage, just two Middle Eastern passports. And finding the passport on Murray Street was an impossibility. It would have had to have flown out the window before impact to land where it did. But since we know that the four planes landed at Westover, this passport had to have been planted there by someone. Now, who would have done that?"

"The passport found on Murray Street had the wrong photo in it. It had the photo of one of the accused hijackers from American Flight 77. The media originally said it was Atta's passport, but later they said it belonged to Satam Suqami, but the photograph was not of him. This passport photo mix-up clearly shows that at least two of these accused hijackers were using fake identities. Once I discovered the FBI made false claims about the manifests, I started looking at the other flights more closely. Why were the feds lying, and who was involved? If we are to believe Atta's parents, and we have no reason not to, then Atta was not only alive but was employed by Israeli intelligence," Jim said.

Jerry Reitz questioned, "Atta's parents said he was working for the Israeli Mossad?"

"That's correct, Jerry," Jim answered. "I was going to cover this later, but since we are on the subject, let me just say Atta is not the only one that had connections to either our military, FBI, CIA, and or to the Israeli Mossad."

"If I recall," Vera chimed in, "a flight attendant on Flight 11 referred to only one passenger giving them trouble. When she was on the phone with a reservation agent, she referred to the troublemaker as a 'he,' which to me indicated there was only one hijacker. She said, 'he stood upstairs, he sprayed pepper spray or mace, he's coming back from business class.' Do you remember she also said, 'I don't know, we might be being hijacked?' There isn't a flight attendant in the world that would not know if there was a hijacker on board. That's our job to know when our passengers are in any danger. One hijacker would be noticed, but five hijackers, I think I could manage to get that out of my mouth in at least three different languages! But we have learned that there weren't any hijackers on board. So, what does this say about this flight attendant?"

"You are correct, Vera. I was able to find several different FBI 302 interview notes from her four-minute recorded call into a reservations line. She appeared not to know what was going on, she repeated information that was not helpful, and she repeated several times that she was sitting in her jump seat. She didn't even say how any hijacker breached the cockpit if they had," Jim said. "Her main complaint was that the pilots were not answering her calls to the flight deck. Other than an unscheduled descent minutes after take-off, I could never figure out why a coach-class flight attendant would be calling the cockpit so early in the flight."

"Jim, that's probably the reason she was trying to call the pilots. They were descending, not climbing to their cruise altitude," Vera added. "No matter who was doing what, if they landed at Westover, barely twenty minutes into the flight, someone had to be checking seat belts and stowing carry-on luggage."

"How could a flight attendant not know if her aircraft was being hijacked? And why wouldn't she speak specifically about the most important detail?" Rosslyn asked, looking toward Vera, then said, "And she would have been far away from the cockpit doing her inflight duties in coach. It makes no sense that she would call into a reservations line that early in the flight. It sounded like she didn't walk up the aisle to see what was going on, but someone must have come back to tell her. Why didn't she call crew scheduling which would have been able to scramble the military? By calling into reservations, she delayed help from arriving in time to stop the hijacking."

"That never made any sense to me," Vera said, "but if there were no hijackers on the plane and she kept referring to just one guy, then definitely something else was going on. None of the FAA hijack protocols were followed by any of the crew members. There must be a logical explanation. Every year in recurrent training, those protocols are hammered into us."

"What about the other flight attendant that initially alleged the sole hijacker was seated in 9B? That passenger was an Israeli special forces operative. I have family in Israel that tell me there's at least one monument honoring him, and he has gone down in history as a hero. His fellow soldiers in the IDF said he could kill any human with a pen and a credit card. He surely was traveling with both of those items. And to make matters even more unbelievable, he was fluent in English, Hebrew, and Arabic. So, if anyone seated behind him were planning to take over the airplane, he surely would have heard and understood every word," Ruth Ann added.

Jim continued, "according to our own government's story, most of the accused hijackers did not have command of the English language; they would have been speaking Arabic."

"We only have two phone callers from that flight, both working crew members and both referring to a single hijacker. Those two flight attendants gave conflicting details about their situation. If there were no hijackers, Jim, could it have been the passenger in 9B that was coming back from business class who sprayed the mace or pepper spray?" Ruth Ann asked.

"If a passenger sprayed mace in a pressurized cabin, everyone, and I mean everyone, would suffer the consequences. All of the passengers, the flight attendants, the pilots, and the hijackers would have been affected," Rosslyn added. "I remember a Hawaiian Airlines flight from California to Hawaii that someone accidentally discharged pepper spray, and several of the crew and passengers were transported to the hospital."

"Yes, that's true, Rosslyn, and neither flight attendant complained of the effects on them or the passengers. I believe only one flight attendant mentioned mace, and she was sitting in the jump seat at the back of the plane. Oh, my, it just hit me," Vera said, staring straight at Rosslyn, "What was the hijack protocol if you were not the flight attendant directly dealing with the hijacker?"

"We were to sit down in a passenger seat, remove our name tag and wings, cover our uniform with a coat or blanket and not draw attention to ourselves," Rosslyn answered.

"Why then was this flight attendant sitting in her jump seat in uniform talking on a phone for nearly half an hour?" Vera asked. "Jim, do you have those typed transcripts of her taped call into reservations?"

"You all should have a copy of those; there are three or four different versions," Jim said.

Max interrupted, "How can that be, Jim? Form 302's are the original interview notes, and if it is a recorded call, how can there be different renditions of a recording?"

Jim nodded, "If this were a legitimate FBI investigation, there would only be one 302. I have highlighted in yellow the omissions and changes. These multiple unexplained missteps by what is purported to be the premier investigative law enforcement agency in the world are blatant."

"Jim and I deduced that the planes were on the ground when the calls were made. That explains why the mace or pepper spray didn't affect anyone in coach. The plane was no longer pressurized," Vera said.

"Some of the hijackers were not even real people, according to the Department of Justice and the Attorney General. Yet, years later, the Department of Justice used their photos on a poster warning of identity theft," Jim continued. "Trust me, once I made these connections, the airline pilot in me became an investigator. The most difficult step for me was to expunge the official story, which became easier after I saw the actual passenger manifests."

"If the DOJ says the hijackers used stolen identity, we have two photos switched on passports, and the FBI making false allegations about names on manifests, who were those people taking flight lessons in Florida and around the country?" Max asked.

"Max, that is the sixty-four-thousand-dollar question," Ruth Ann said.

Jim looked down at his watch and directed his question to President Sherman, "What do you say we take a break for lunch?"

"That sounds like a good idea. Let's make it a two-hour break. Vera and I must stay inside the White House, but if any of you would like, you may join me in the dining room of the residence."

The men jumped at the chance to sit with the President for a private luncheon and followed him out the door.

Vera suggested the women meet in the formal dining room downstairs. She wanted to chat with Rosslyn about her airline career. She also wanted to hear all the details about the assassination attempt at the hospital.

twenty-one

Vera sat at the head of the large mahogany dining table and invited Ruth Ann and Rosslyn to sit on either side of her. "I have ordered lunch for us, and the staff will be bringing it shortly. When they deliver the food, we should stop talking. The White House walls might not have ears, but we are certain that some staff do and have connections to the media. We don't want the press to know we are discussing 9/11."

"Understood," Ruth Ann acknowledged.

Rosslyn nodded in agreement.

"I am dying to hear all the details of your journey to North Vancouver and how you ended up in the hospital. And who would have sent an assassin to kill you? Is that connected to what happened in Vancouver?" Vera asked.

Rosslyn tried to relive her experience in North Vancouver. She closed her eyes and took a deep breath as more details slowly returned to her memory. His face became crystal clear in her mind. Silently, she recalled their first trip together to Bogota, Columbia. It was a two-day layover. The crew met both evenings for dinner, and she remembered he picked up the entire bill both nights. Each evening after dinner, he took the crew to a karaoke bar, and he was by far the most entertaining person to hit the stage. That made both him and the trip memorable. She remembered he liked to drink scotch. So, when she saw him in Canada, she asked him if she could buy him a drink. And that's when it happened.

"I hope you don't think I am crazy, but I… I saw one of our captains who is supposed to be dead! That's who Patrick was referring to; he recognized him too. He was right; I knew exactly who he was the minute I laid eyes on him. His plane crashed on 9/11, and he is supposed to be dead. But he is alive! Oh my God, that's who I saw! That's who hit me!" Rosslyn exclaimed.

"Oh, Rosslyn! This is the game-changer we discussed on our way to Canada! My God!" Ruth Ann exclaimed.

"That reconfirms what Jim and I discovered; the pilots were involved!" Vera affirmed.

"The next thing I remember, I was in a hospital bed in Seattle with a man yelling at someone in my room. Then, there were gunshots fired." Rosslyn said.

Ruth Ann finished telling Rosslyn's story, "One of the agents assigned to guard your house accompanied me to the hospital. Thankfully, he recognized the man as a CIA assassin and shot him before he could kill Rosslyn."

"That means the captain likely had some association with the CIA. Could he have notified the CIA, and they sent someone to kill you?" Vera asked, completely occupied with the possibilities.

"It's starting to appear that way, isn't it?" Rosslyn agreed.

Vera heard the staff approaching with their food and hushed the women.

A server wheeled in the food beautifully presented on a silver serving cart. He tossed a large Caesar salad then offered them a choice of salmon or chicken to top it off. He poured each of them a glass of water and quietly backed out of the room.

"Wait until the guys hear about this! We can share your story with them, can't we, Rosslyn?" Vera asked.

"Of course, we can! I am still having a hard time believing it myself. Ruth Ann, you are correct; this is a definite game-changer. I bet he never dreamed that someone he knew would walk into that Yacht Club one day and recognize him. I must have shocked him to get that reaction. He was always so friendly to everyone on the crew. That reaction wasn't what anyone that knew him would expect." Rosslyn added.

"I wonder how many people on board were involved. And how many have been what, allowed to live under a new identity?" Ruth Ann asked.

"That's a good question, Ruth Ann. The identity protection program is facilitated by the FBI, which would indicate that they were complicit, at least in the cover-up," Vera said.

"What kind of questions did the airline employees ask on your blog?" Vera asked.

"Everyone began to open their eyes and question the official story about five or six years after 9/11. For a while, it was a taboo subject to discuss on company property. And I mean any company property and any airline. They would not allow questioning of the government narrative. Many of them commented that it was great to have a forum where the official story could be questioned or discussed without fear of retaliation," Rosslyn said.

"I want to know what was going on inside those cabins. Were the flight attendants in on the charade? You've already answered the question about the pilots' involvement," Vera remarked.

"Some crew members wondered if a government agency boarded with the crew and convinced them that they would be part of a hijacking drill. I can't imagine any flight attendant or pilot going along with such a scheme. We board the plane and barely have enough time to stow our luggage and check our emergency equipment before the agent sends passengers down the jetway. How would anyone manage to explain the details of a drill to the crew with so little time? Imagine how upset every crew member would be if something like that happened; we all have plans for the minute we arrive at the layover hotel. No, this would never happen, not unless everyone was under duress. A federal agent would have needed to show a gun to pull off something that insane. It is much more likely that the crew rehearsed what to do. Several people thought the four aircraft were taken over remotely, using the flight termination system. However, one captain claimed the pilots were involved because they were needed to steer the aircraft into the hangars. That's why none of them squawked the hijack code on the radio," Rosslyn explained.

"That makes perfect sense," Ruth Ann commented.

"If the crew members were involved, this was planned well in advance, and everyone played their assigned role," Vera said.

"Vera, remember when the kid at Mojave reported that a US Airways 757 was flying out of the boneyard on weekends? He fueled that plane and said that a busload of what appeared to be flight attendants boarded it every Saturday night for weeks before 9/11?" Ruth Ann asked.

"Yes, I remember. That also explains why some of the flight attendants told their parents they were enrolled in special terrorist training," Vera said.

"No airline has ever had terrorist training. We only do our yearly recurrent training, except when new equipment is added to our fleet. And all our training takes place on company property," Rosslyn confirmed.

"The public tried to put a square peg into a round hole trying to make the official story work in their minds. The fact that so few people outside of the airline industry know how flight crews train allowed conspiracy theories to be concocted by people who don't know anything about your jobs," Vera said.

"If the flight attendants were involved, how do you explain their calls on Flight 11?" Ruth Ann asked

"If you think about it, their involvement actually explains a lot of the problems with the official story. On that first flight, neither of the flight attendants followed their training, and some of the things they said were just outlandish," Rosslyn said. "They gave conflicting and false information and basically did everything wrong. In a hijacking, the crew's goal is to prevent the passengers and fellow crew members from being harmed or killed. Every crew member failed to do that, yet the media elevated them all to hero status before the sunset that day."

"They sure did, Rosslyn. That always seemed so odd to me. A different outcome would be needed for them to become heroes. Maybe the media promoted that idea so we would not suspect any of the crew members. Jim managed to find copies of the real passenger manifests; I am sure other agents printed copies and are afraid to expose the truth. Imagine knowing that and watching the nonsense the media promoted. Anyone with that type of knowledge would be scared to death to share it. That was the first brick to fall. Rosslyn running into one of the pilots was brick number two," Vera said.

Ruth Ann asked, "what would cause professional airline employees to get involved in something this horrendous?"

Vera smiled and said, "Everyone has their price, and there are plenty of examples. On Flight 11, a B-scale flight attendant rented and furnished an expensive apartment in Boston's Beacon Hill area. There is no way a two-year flight attendant on that low salary could dream of affording a place in such an expensive neighborhood. She would be lucky to be able to pay the monthly utilities."

Rosslyn added, "I flew with pilots who were some of the biggest tightwads in the world. If someone offered to pay off their ex-wives and buy them a nice big boat, they would break both legs jumping at the chance."

Vera started to laugh, and as she did, Rosslyn joined in until they were both laughing hysterically.

"On Flight 11 out of Boston, both flight attendants may have been removed from the aircraft and taken to different offices inside a hangar. That would explain their conflicting statements. Betty said she was in her jump seat multiple times, yet Amy reported they were both seated in the last row in coach. According to the manifest, a passenger was seated across from Betty's jump seat; that passenger would have heard every word she said. At the same time, Amy was telling her supervisor the coach passengers had no idea anything abnormal was happening," Rosslyn explained.

"That passenger seated across from Betty's jump seat was a Raytheon employee," Vera added. "I remember thinking it strange that he would be seated in coach on such a long flight. I remember there were five employees of Raytheon on those flights that day."

"I always thought it strange that Betty told the reservations agent that someone was coming back from business class, yet she didn't offer any explanation. It was also weird that Betty didn't know if they were hijacked," Rosslyn said.

Vera interrupted, "If there were a hijacker on board, every crew member would know it. The hijacker would be in the aisle, making demands and being unruly. Hijackers don't just sit in their seats. They usually act out, are loud, and make a scene to instill fear in front of the passengers. So, it was inexplainable that Betty didn't know if the flight was being hijacked."

"Betty's comment that *he stood upstairs* was puzzling," Rosslyn added.

Ruth Ann had been quietly typing, then suddenly picked up her iPad and said, "ladies, I give you a C-5-Galaxy-sized hangar at Westover. Check in the corner behind that airplane; there are bright yellow stairs!"

"Oh my, I just had a flashback from a final scene in the movie *Wag the Dog*. They were in a large military hangar and were in an office with phones overlooking the hangar bay," Vera exclaimed.

"Another oddball detail I remember reading was Betty telling the reservation agent 'we're up in the air.' Why would a flight attendant say that when a hijacking only takes place in the air?" Rosslyn asked.

"Sounds like she was trying to convince someone she was in a hijacking," Vera said.

"What about the fact that Amy referred to a hijacker seated in 9B, but neither of them mentioned a group of five?" Rosslyn asked.

"Both men sitting in 9A and B were Jewish, I know because I recognize the last names. Two Jewish men were also seated in row 2 of first-class. I see an interesting Jewish pattern here," Ruth Ann let out a sigh. "Sometimes, being Jewish can be an asset. There were no Arabs, but I spot at least half a dozen Jewish men in business and first-class. I can mention this detail without the fear of being labeled as an anti-Semite."

"I have always wondered about Amy. She was a last-minute addition to the crew, and she was missing her child's first day of kindergarten. I cannot think of a flight attendant senior enough to hold a schedule that would choose to miss such an important day," Vera said.

"The lead flight attendant and the Israeli assassin in 9B were supposedly killed. What a perfect cover; it's an old trick. Nobody would suspect dead people of being involved. Maybe that's why the media referred to them as heroes when they did nothing to protect the passengers," Ruth Ann commented.

"I've always suspected the media was involved in the cover-up," Vera admitted.

"If these two flight attendants were able to make phone calls for half an hour, what were the other crew members doing? Eyewitnesses saw Flight 11 land at Westover twenty minutes after departure. The phone calls started at about that same time. In normal situations, twenty minutes into the flight, passengers would have reclined their seats, pulled out laptops or books, and prepared for a six-hour flight. The flight attendants would be in the aisles serving. That plane would have been at twenty thousand feet when it began descending into Westover. The flight attendants would have immediately begun to prepare the passengers and cabin for landing," Rosslyn explained.

Ruth Ann said, "It just occurred to me, they would have had to prevent everyone from making phone calls. Someone must have had a signal jammer to prevent anyone from making a cell call. The airphones could have been deactivated by the pilots pulling a circuit breaker in the cockpit. In that case, Betty had to have been off the plane when she called."

"In the FBI transcripts, Betty said, 'we're the first.' That leads me to believe she knew the entire scenario for the day," Vera added.

"Maybe on the 757 flying out of Mojave, the participants were told of the scenario for the entire day. That might explain why Betty made that comment. Hijackings had not happened in the U.S. for decades; why would she think there would be more than one happening on that day? Unless someone briefed her on the events of the day," Ruth Ann said.

"When I started investigating 9/11 with Jim, I wanted to believe the remote-control system took over the flights. That explained why Betty could not call the cockpit since the onboard interphone system would not work once the flight termination system controlled the plane. In a hijacking, it is of the utmost importance for the cabin crew to give the flight deck exact information about the hijacker, his demands, and his whereabouts in the cabin. But that system would have only been activated by the pilots…" Vera stopped.

"Now that Jim has seen proof of the big lie, we must look at the situation with open eyes and let go of the idea that no airline employees were involved. We know that one junior flight attendant took a job with the CIA; how many other crew members did? That would explain a lot of things, wouldn't it? I'm sure Jim will have more to share with us, but right now, my gut is telling me this was a faked hijacking. As much as this disturbs me, I am mentally prepared to look deeper than I have in the past," Vera sadly admitted.

"Oh my, I'm getting a headache trying to keep all this straight," Rosslyn moaned. "I am sad to think that airline employees could have been involved, but there has to be an explanation to what really happened. Jim's discovery forces us to explore possibilities we don't want to contemplate."

Vera noticed the time, "We had better be getting back to the Oval Office. This has been a very enlightening luncheon, and I am so glad we had this conversation. Rosslyn, I am looking forward to comparing more notes with you. I feel like we will leave these meetings with a complete understanding of what happened that day. We have already uncovered so much, and I am sure Jim has a lot more in store for us."

"I am sure he does," Rosslyn agreed.

"Vera, this was absolutely beautiful; thank you so much for suggesting that we meet and dine together," Ruth Ann complimented.

twenty-two

Before Jim started the afternoon meeting, Vera revealed what Rosslyn shared with them at lunch to the men.

The men were stunned at the revelation as chatter filled the room.

Eventually, Jim calmed the room and continued, "As the truth about the dishonest FBI continued to sink in, I began to question everyone who was on board, especially the last-minute passengers and crew. There must have been a last-minute decision made to place certain people onboard. A review of the crew convinced me that the decision to unleash the scheme was made the afternoon of September 10th. I felt as though I was reverse engineering a crime. Whoever was the mastermind of 9/11 knew the outcome they wanted, but they needed to construct the details of their crime. In this case, they created hijackings, but they made huge mistakes. They didn't know how flight crew members would act or react in a hijack emergency. I also questioned the load factors. All four flights had at least a hundred empty seats. It is possible someone in reservations manipulated the bookings or state-sponsored cyber hackers were involved."

"People in the NSA could have lent a blind eye or hit the delete key. However, government employees are not above breaking the law, and some are more dedicated to what they feel is their other home country. Dual citizens," Jerry admitted.

Vera glanced toward Rosslyn, raised her eyebrows, and asked, "Do you remember loads ever being that light on any day in 2001?"

"No way!" Rosslyn exclaimed. "We were operating every day of the week at near capacity. I was shocked to hear how light the passenger loads were that morning."

"American Airlines Flight 11 had the heaviest passenger load with seventy-six passengers.

At least a dozen of them were last minute. I recreated a seating chart," Jim explained as he handed each person a copy. "The passengers that were last-minute additions are marked in red. A short biography of each passenger is on the backside, all open-source information from obituaries, commentaries, or newspaper articles."

"Wow, Jim, this is how we used to take beverage and entrée orders in the old days. Did someone teach you how to do this?" Vera laughed as she began to study the names.

"Among the last-minute passengers were two Raytheon electronic warfare specialists and one Hollywood producer with his wife, a college Rugby star, and of course the Israeli special forces guy. Not an easy crowd to take control of, that's for certain," Jim said.

"For an early morning departure, that is an unlikely number of last-minute passengers," Rosslyn added.

Jim continued, "Having read as many books as I could get my hands on about intelligence agencies and how they train and recruit, anyone of these last-minute passengers could have been a contract operative for an intelligence agency, not necessarily ours. Israel or the United Kingdom are commonly used to provide plausible deniability. Examining the crew on Flight 11, both pilots were assigned to the flight the afternoon of the tenth. Seven of the nine flight attendants were added to the crew the afternoon of the tenth or the morning of the eleventh," Jim commented.

"I wonder who the original crew members were and why they have never come forward. It is highly unusual, especially for a Tuesday morning transcontinental flight, to have so many of the original crew replaced," Rosslyn added.

Vera chimed in, "Jim, we looked into the episode with the purser from Miami who had been assigned to Flight 11. After she commuted to Boston, someone claiming to be crew scheduling called and removed her, that is not just strange; it's downright impossible."

"Yes, and you remember when she got home, she found a strange message on her phone recorder. A woman with a heavy accent talking with a couple of men, saying: 'if this had anything to do with Israel, there will be hell to pay.' It's still a mystery to me. Who left that message? Was it someone that was given the crew orders before she was replaced?

How would anyone obtain her home phone number?" Jim questioned. "Unfortunately, she is not the only mystery surrounding the crew of Flight 11. Most of them were single, and two of them attended Boston University."

"Boston University?" Max asked, "what does that have to do with anything?"

"Since the mid-seventies, Boston University employed a retired paramilitary CIA spy to run their athletic department. He had been shot down over China during the Korean War and held captive for twenty-one years. Shortly after his release, he joined the faculty of Boston University," Jim said.

"A CIA campus recruiter?" Vera asked.

"That is very likely," Jim continued, "he retired from the university in 1989, so any student before that time, especially if they were college athletes, could have been recruited. One of the pilots and one of the flight attendants on that flight were both college athletes, and both graduated from Boston University before 1989. The university does not hide its association with the CIA; they have a spy school on campus. And might I add, many professors are recruiters. Many universities have active recruiters on their faculties. The connection between academia and the intelligence communities is eye-opening. For example, the University of Denver has the Joseph Korbel School of International Studies, which is a well-known CIA hotspot."

Ruth Ann asked, "Isn't Joseph Korbel Madeline Albright's father?"

Max piped up, "Right you are. Maybe that is why she became the Secretary of State and a well-known globalist."

"One of the Boston University alumni and first-class passengers on Flight 11 was a close friend of Hillary Clinton. It is common knowledge that the Clintons have been involved with the CIA since the 1960s. You can't find much information about her or her husband, which is often an obvious indicator of intelligence involvement. Her family was close friends with Senators Edward Kennedy and John Kerry. Finding rock-solid evidence of CIA connections when you are taking apart a crime of this magnitude is difficult. Therefore, we must look with an open eye for all links to everyone on board," Jim explained.

"Good point, Jim. If irrefutable evidence of government involvement were easily uncovered, it would indicate they did a darn sloppy job. When I was a kid, I loved to watch Perry Mason and Columbo, and sometimes circumstantial evidence is all that can be gathered, but it usually exposes the culprits," Max said.

"If you look at the seating chart, you can see that the official story of Mohammad Atta getting up on climb-out and taking over the cockpit would be no easy task. The highly trained Israeli assassin was seated on the aisle diagonally and behind him. The Israeli anti-hijack specialist should have prevented Atta from entering the cockpit," Jim continued.

"But that is irrelevant since we now know Atta was not onboard. The government's entire official story becomes highly questionable," President Sherman mumbled under his breath.

"There are several intriguing anomalies concerning the captain of this flight. For decades, his father was an executive at Standard Oil, and we all know where that might lead. The captain scheduled an important event on his farm to which he invited several officials from the U.S. Department of Agriculture and special guests from Asia. He built his flight schedule to be home on September 11th for this event. Later, his wife, a flight attendant, explained that he received a phone call late in the afternoon of the 10th and was forced to pilot Flight 11. She knew that was impossible. He had plenty of seniority not to be forced to fly on his scheduled days off. Years later, a newspaper article reported that his daughter took a job with USAID, which is a well-known CIA front organization," Jim explained.

Airline employees are pretty possessive of their days off. That's when they make plans as this captain did. His wife never claimed crew scheduling called, only that he received a phone call and had to fly the following day," Vera added.

Jim replied, "Several years later, the son of the first officer on that flight became a pilot for American Airlines. But, of course, that's the last thing I would expect a child of either a passenger or crew member from one of those flights to do."

"I cannot imagine that!" Ruth Ann exclaimed, "If one of my parents had been killed in a hijacking, getting on an airplane would be difficult, but doing it for a living would be impossible."

"I feel the same way," Rosslyn agreed.

"I am beginning to wonder if every major event in my life has been a deception," Max grumbled.

Jim continued, "United 175 only had seven passengers in First Class that morning and eleven in Business class. There was a professional hockey player seated in business class and another younger hockey player near the front of coach, who coincidentally also attended Boston University. Those two would have cross-checked anyone trying to get into the cockpit. Both passengers that made phone calls from that flight were also alumni from Boston University. They both worked for military-industrial complex corporations involved with DARPA, Homeland Security, and the intelligence world. One of the flight attendants attended the University of Denver, and another one admitted to being offered a job with the CIA. This second flight attendant was a black belt in martial arts, had worked alongside several federal agencies, and seemed to have foreknowledge of what was about to play out. Three of the flight attendants on board learned to parachute, and one of the three reported to her parents that she was attending special terrorist training in the weeks before 9/11."

"Flight attendants, that learned how to parachute?" Vera questioned, "I never met one flight attendant that would jump out of a perfectly good airplane. That is a very unusual finding, Jim."

"Yes, it is a coincidence the CIA rehired a retired officer to teach recruits jump training shortly before 9/11. I discovered at least four other flight attendants were also parachutists, and three told their parents they were involved in some special terrorist training. On Flight 175, one of the flight attendants called everyone in his large family the night before, which could show he had foreknowledge. And of the seven flight attendants on United 175, five of them were last-minute additions to the crew orders. One of the strangest stories I discovered was the reporting in a New York newspaper of a male flight attendant on United

175 was pass-riding, but he was actually a working crew member on that flight," Jim said.

"How would the media obtain that information? If he were working crew, which the official story tells us he was, his name would have been on the crew orders. If he were pass-riding, his name would have been on the passenger manifest. So that is an improbable story at best," Rosslyn said.

"We know the media is a branch of the intelligence community's operation mockingbird, and he was the CIA's guy onboard. The Agency made an obvious mistake releasing his name as a passenger," Max said.

"The fact that he was trained in martial arts and could kill anyone with his bare hands was conveniently left out of the official story," Jim said.

"His work position on that flight was in first class. He would have been either in his jump seat or busy in the galley that early in the flight. There is no way he would have allowed a hijacking to occur," Rosslyn added.

"So, if there were a hijacker on board, he would have had to get past two professional hockey players and a martial arts expert working right outside the cockpit door?" Vera asked.

"Exactly, Vera. Hard to believe, isn't it?" Jim asked.

"Extremely," Vera agreed.

Jim continued, "On this particular flight, we have only two passengers that made phone calls, and both made more than one cell phone call. I don't need to remind you that cell phones did not make successful calls above eighteen hundred feet and still don't as of today. That's less than a minute after take-off. The bizarre details these two callers gave are worth reviewing."

"Both passengers who made calls worked for government contractors, and they were both graduates from…"

Max finished Jim's sentence, "from Boston University."

"Exactly, Max," Jim nodded as he continued. "From what I have been able to dig up, both were seated in row 31, Brian on aircraft left and Peter on aircraft right. At the time they called, the plane was supposed to be over the Hudson River. Brian would have been overlooking Newark's Liberty International Airport and Newark Bay. Most adults would easily recognize what was out his window, yet he told his mother that he thought the aircraft was over Ohio. Newark Airport is very distinct, and this guy was a military pilot. How he could make a mistake like that is beyond belief. He was trained at the Top Gun School at Miramar, California, and from what I could gather, he was the guy you'd want around if you were in a bar fight. He flew Tomcats in the Gulf War and was a radar intercept officer. If he were on that plane and it was where the official story claims, there is no way he didn't recognize Newark airport or the Manhattan skyline."

Rosslyn shook her head, "Even a junior flight attendant would recognize those landmarks!"

"According to the FBI interviews, he led his mother to believe that he was about to be killed, but then he made one very large mistake. He told his mother that he and some other passengers were going to rush the cockpit and take it back from the hijackers. But that was the 'Let's Roll' scenario from United Flight 93. How did he know those details from the other United flight when that hadn't happened yet? That information wasn't made public until later the following day. Had he been briefed on the entire scenario?" Jim explained.

Max commented, "Jimbo that makes sense. If he were on the phone in an office in a hangar and were asked where he was, he would have no idea where that plane was supposed to be."

Jim confirmed. "A pilot would know that the flight time from Boston to Ohio is roughly an hour and thirty minutes, but he called his mother forty-five minutes after take-off. There is no way he could think he was near Ohio. This is unexplainable, but it falls in line with the anomalies from the other passenger. The passenger on the aircraft right phoned his father twice and told him mace was sprayed in the cabin. However, he was not coughing or experiencing any difficulties breathing yet; he said people seated around him were getting sick. Somehow from clear back at row 31, he knew a flight attendant had been stabbed in the front of the plane. He told his father that the hijackers told him they were going to fly to Chicago and *into* a building!"

"What?" Rosslyn asked. "That's crazy! Who would have cooked up that scenario before 9/11? According to the official story, even if you believe hijackers were on the plane, they didn't speak English. So how would he have come up with that story unless he too had been briefed on the entire operation?"

Jim continued. "After he called his father, his dad called the local police, and they called the FBI. According to his father's interview with the FBI, he immediately called the Kennedy Space Center in Florida. He told a woman working security that his son called from a hijacked plane. He has information that the hijackers told his son that eight aircraft were going to be hijacked. The problem is, he said his son was on United Flight 11, but Flight 11 was American Airlines, and his son was on United Flight 175. How would his son have known the flight number for American Airlines that supposedly crashed into the north tower minutes earlier?"

Max interjected, "it does sound like his son knew the entire scenario and got the flight numbers mixed up."

"Jim, that story is unbelievable. How does the Kennedy Space Center fit in? Was the woman he called a relative? Did the father have some connection to NASA?" Vera asked.

"I have not been able to find a connection. I found the FBI report of her receiving the call, but it did not explain why the father called from Connecticut to Florida with this information."

"How do you explain this passenger was not struggling with the effects of the pepper spray or mace that the other passengers were reportedly vomiting from?" Ruth Ann asked.

"Ruth Ann, it's just one of many broken links in this story. It goes along with the flight crew failing to follow FAA hijack protocols," Jim answered. "It doesn't make any sense according to the official story, but as you will see when we use logic, we will conclude something much more believable.

Vera nodded in agreement and said, "Her supervisor asked one flight attendant on Flight 11 for her location, and she answered, 'I see water, I see buildings.' How could she not have recognized New York City? However, of the four people who called on these two flights, one said they were over Ohio, one said they were flying to Chicago, and the two flight attendants did not recognize New York City. The big picture is coming into focus now. We were all lied to."

Rosslyn agreed, "If the passengers were not given a good reason for landing prematurely, they would have needed someone trained in martial arts to control them."

"So true, Rosslyn," Jim continued. "Both of the pilots were not originally scheduled to be on United 175. They also did something highly unusual. They phoned their wives from the cockpit, having left home only hours earlier. The first officer's wife was a teacher. I found it odd that he would call her as she was either driving to work or already in her classroom. By the time he would have completed his walk around to check the fuselage and kick the tires, it would have been close to their scheduled departure. Pilots don't usually make phone calls from the flight deck. Once we file the flight plan, get into the cockpit, and check the equipment, it's time to start the departure checklist. The most peculiar detail is what the captain said to his wife. He reminded her to winterize their swimming pool. She found that request so strange that she repeated the story to several reporters," Jim said.

Vera added, "They were on a two-day trip, and it was the first week of September. So why would he remind her to winterize their swimming pool? Do you think he knew he was not coming home?"

Ruth Ann piped up, "September is nice weather in that neck of the woods; even an early freeze would not cause any damage. He could have winterized it when he got home."

Jim chuckled, "Both pilots were military trained. The first officer was a Marine, and the captain was a Naval aviator. I have never understood why if there was an intrusion into the cockpit, why neither pilot fought back using the crash axe."

Vera spoke, "I have always wondered about that, Jim. The idea that anyone could commandeer a cockpit from two military-trained pilots is incomprehensible. I am still thinking about the black belt martial arts flight attendant working right outside the cockpit door."

Rosslyn chimed in, "I have been thinking while you've been explaining these details. The most important positions for flight attendants would have been those in first-class closest to the cockpit door. The purser would have played a vitally important role in preventing hijackers from entering the cockpit. With a martial arts expert in her galley, that would have been even easier."

Jim picked up again, "The parents of the purser mentioned to the media that she was attending special terrorist training. They would not have known no such training existed. She used that as an excuse to her parents to explain why she was on the flights out of Mojave. If that were the case, it explains why her actions onboard were never mentioned by the media."

Rosslyn agreed, "I never heard the word 'terrorist' used in our yearly recurrent training. It was always hijackers, except when we discussed the Achille Lauro. You remember the Italian cruise ship that was hijacked; it was sailing from Alexandria to Ashdod, Israel."

Ruth Ann commented, "There was also an Israeli citizen on United 175 from Ashdod, Israel. My cousin told me about her. She served in the Israeli Defense Forces, and like the Israeli commando on Flight 11, she too has been immortalized in her hometown as a hero."

"I didn't find her listed as a last-minute passenger, but I did take note of her Israeli military background. Our friend Max here would call this a coinky-dink. Intelligence agencies have historically recruited agents who are athletic, competitive, and show an interest in international business and travel," said Jim.

"That description fits several flight attendants that I flew with over the years," Rosslyn said as she thought about her past airline career.

Jim added, "The martial arts expert arranged for his wife to meet him in New England to sign life insurance papers the weekend before 9/11."

"That's odd. We signed all insurance and beneficiary forms on graduation day from initial training. That is another indication he had foreknowledge," Vera commented.

Jim interjected, "Anything is possible, except for the official story. Another incongruent detail I came across was that his son later became a flight attendant for United Airlines. So again, like the first officer on Flight 11, we have a family member entering a profession you would never expect."

Max shook his head in disbelief. "The masterminds behind this were certainly in control of the media, and they would ridicule anyone questioning the details. I'm sure they never thought anybody would ever look close enough to find all their errors. With the inside knowledge we have in this room, I feel like we are peeling this stinky onion, layer by layer."

President Sherman sat quietly, taking notes on a yellow legal pad. He hadn't said much, but he had taken plenty of notes. Vera knew a long conversation between them was coming.

"I think this is a good time for us to call it a day," Vera suggested. "Can we continue this tomorrow morning?"

Everyone agreed on a 9 am start time.

twenty-three

Ruth Ann slid her keycard into the slot opening the door to their hotel room. "What sounds good to you? Another bottle of wine and some snacks like we had last night?"

Rosslyn was slipping off her heels, "Ruth Ann, I could use a small salad with blue cheese dressing, that cheese tray we had last night, and if you are up for sharing anything chocolate for dessert, I'm game for that too. And that same wine would be perfect."

Ruth Ann ordered room service, then announced she was taking a quick shower, "If room service arrives before I'm out, sign my name to the bill and add a twenty percent tip."

"Will do. In the meantime, I think I'm ready for more diary reading tonight, are you?" Rosslyn asked.

"Definitely!" Ruth Ann shouted from the bathroom.

Rosslyn removed the journal from her tote bag, noticed a bright green cover of another diary near the bottom of the bag, and placed it on the nightstand.

Ruth Ann finished her shower just as their order was delivered. The room service attendant opened the wine then positioned the table between their beds.

Rosslyn slipped into her favorite lounging sweats and grabbed two extra pillows from the closet. She propped them against the headboard and nestled in. She held her wine glass toward Ruth Ann and said, "to another reading adventure."

"Indeed!" Ruth Ann's glass tapped the edge of Rosslyn's.

"I found another diary in my tote bag. You can read through this one and share anything you find interesting." Rosslyn tossed the small green book onto Ruth Ann's bed.

"Oh, my, this could be a very interesting evening!" Ruth Ann exclaimed. "But first, we should enjoy some of this food."

The women dined on their salads and left the chocolate cheesecake and cheese tray to nibble on as they read.

It wasn't long before Rosslyn broke the silence, "Ruth Ann, listen to this! It sounds like my dad belonged to a team that nobody would be proud to admit. This is unbelievable! If the American public knew what the CIA did around the world, they would be very upset. But learning this makes it much easier to believe they were responsible for the entire 9/11 event."

Rosslyn read, "*One of our assignments was to assassinate General Alvarez, the CIA co-operating Army Chief of Staff in Honduras. We carried out this task in 1989. At the same time, my partner was involved in the assassination of former Israeli Mossad agent Amiram Nir. Nir was scheduled to testify in front of a Senate sub-committee, and it was feared he would reveal the truth. Instead, he perished when his helicopter was shot down from a missile fired from one of our helicopters. My partner was the pilot of that chopper.*

Some of the methods we used to neutralize our targets were unorthodox. For the sake of your security, I will refer to the following targeted individual as Mr. Jones. He was a leader of one of the largest CIA-backed Contra groups who had recently testified before the US Senate Intelligence Committee. During his Senate testimony, he denied any knowledge of CIA involvement in the narcotics trade. Mr. Jones had been recruited into the CIA by Director William Casey with the help of Oliver North.

When Nicaraguan leader Daniel Ortega announced free elections, Mr. Jones asked President H.W. Bush to ensure he be given a prominent position in the new Nicaraguan government in return for his years of service to the CIA. Mr. Jones didn't politely or respectfully request Bush's help; he threatened to publicly expose Bush's role in the drug trade. Threatening Bush was not a smart move, and one of our special activity teams was assigned to neutralize him. We chose to use Scopolamine, a tasteless, odorless drug, often called the Voodoo drug. It had been determined that Mr. Jones could be a useful future asset if he were to be effectively compromised.

Mr. Jones was invited to spend a relaxing weekend at a luxury hotel as the guest of his friend George H. W. Bush. The evening started with cocktails and was followed by an exquisite meal. Nothing but the best were the orders. Following the meal, he was ushered into the suite of a blonde honeypot supplied by the CIA. A dose of Scopolamine had been slipped into his pre-dinner cocktail. Mr. Jones was a gentleman with the blonde as they moved into the bedroom where video cameras were already set up in one corner. In short order, she had Jones standing naked in front of her, slipping his manhood into her mouth. Slipping off her clothes, the blonde instructed Mr. Jones to reciprocate the act. Naked, the blonde boasted a large erect penis; Mr. Jones obliged. Their sexual activities were all recorded on video.

Two weeks later, Mr. Jones was visited in his office. He was presented with a copy of the video footage along with instructions. Not only did it reveal his homosexuality, but it also revealed his bestiality and satanic worship rituals. As frame after frame flicked by, Mr. Jones was forced to watch himself kill and gut his honeypot and then eat the still-warm heart. He had been neutralized, precisely the way Bush had ordered. Mr. Jones became a leading member of the Nicaraguan government and would never threaten the Bush-Clinton Enterprise again. He was now under our complete control."

"That's horrific!" Ruth Ann exclaimed, "So last night we read a much milder story about how Bush senior and the CIA gained control of the Japanese government, now this. It makes you wonder what Mr. Jones was providing to the CIA that they needed to keep him under their control. I have a feeling he wasn't providing soda pop at a discount."

"I think I need another glass of wine after reading that story," Rosslyn said as she reached for the wine bottle.

The women quietly returned to reading the diaries with an occasional break to nibble on a slice of cheese or fruit.

Rosslyn broke the silence again, "take a listen to this; it looks like that newspaper guy Gary Webb who wrote about the CIA running crack cocaine was more correct than people knew."

She read aloud: "*Our team worked with Special Forces all over the world. Around this time, most of our agents trained Contras in violation of the Boland Amendment. Special Forces camps were built on the border between Nicaragua and Honduras during the early 1980s. Several of the soldiers were involved in the cocaine shipments brought into the United States through Panama. They understood the deal. There were no Contras to train without drug profits, and there would be no equipment to train them with since Congress had cut off the funding. Soldiers out in the middle of nowhere depend on their teammates to survive, whether they are in the jungles of Southeast Asia, Central America, or the desert of Afghanistan.*"

"So, the CIA uses Special Forces soldiers as their private military? No wonder they killed Gary Webb for revealing his information. Our government was saying 'just say no' while shipping tons of drugs into the country. Now, that gives a whole new slant to what our military has been up to for decades." Ruth Ann commented, then read from her diary aloud:

"*George H. W. Bush was CIA prior to the assassination of John F. Kennedy in 1963. Later, the Governor of Arkansas, Bill Clinton, aided the CIA at the Mena airport, which was the CIA's cocaine shipping station. Bill Clinton was CIA since the late '60s. CIA agent Cord Meyer was named as Bill Clinton's handler. Other names associated with the CIA are not as well known, for example, Ruth Paine. On orders from CIA officer William Casey, she was assigned to find and recruit an individual with communist ties and some type of anti-American background. Once Ruth Paine found such an individual, she notified her CIA contact, identified as George de Mohrenschildt, who contacted his CIA supervisor, George H. W. Bush. The individual found by Ruth Paine was identified as Lee Harvey Oswald. FBI records after the assassination of President Kennedy reflect that George H. W. Bush met with FBI Director J. Edgar Hoover. Bush was concerned that the FBI might have stumbled onto the Ruth Paine-Lee Harvey Oswald connection, which would have confirmed the CIA's involvement in the assassination.*"

Rosslyn quietly typed into an internet search 'Ruth Paine' the moment Ruth Ann mentioned the name. "Ruth Ann, check this out; much *has been rumored about Ruth and*

Michael Paine's ties to the CIA. According to declassified CIA documents, Ruth's sister Sylvia Hyde Hoke was listed as an employee of the Agency in 1961. Ruth visited and stayed with Sylvia in September of 1963."

"Just a couple months before Kennedy's assassination," Ruth Ann interjected.

"*Ruth's father, William Avery Hyde, was an insurance executive who worked for USAID, the US Agency for International Development, a well-known cover for CIA personnel. Mr. Hyde had contacts with the CIA, which considered him for use in an operation in Viet Nam. Michael Paine's mother, also named Ruth, was a friend of Allen Dulles' mistress and fellow spy, Mary Bancroft. Michael's mother would invite Dulles and Bancroft to the Forbes private island near Martha's Vineyard. Michael and Ruth Paine were frequent visitors to the island as well,*" Rosslyn read.

"That could explain how Ruth Paine was recruited into the CIA," Ruth Ann suggested.

"Oh my, listen to this," Rosslyn continued, "*two CIA employment applications for Ruth Paine's brother-in-law John Hoke, her sister Sylvia's husband, confirm her employment with the CIA, and USAID hired him.*"

"Wait, so Ruth Paine's father, sister, and brother-in-law were employed by the CIA, and Michael Paine's mother was from the famous Forbes-Cabot families and was friends with Allen Dulles and his mistress who she entertained on the Forbes family private island? Ruth and Michael moved to Dallas, where they met Lee Harvey Oswald and his Russian wife. Both Ruth and Michael Paine were from the upper class. Why would they ever associate with a defector and his wife, neither of whom had wealth or prestige? They all became acquainted with George de Mohrenschildt, a Russian Jewish immigrant who became friends with the wealthy Bouvier family. Their daughter Jacqueline would later marry John F. Kennedy, who this defector Oswald would be accused of assassinating. That's a lot of connection to the intelligence world like what we have uncovered so far with those involved in 9/11," Ruth Ann explained.

"It seems to be more than a coincidence, doesn't it?" Rosslyn agreed, then continued reading aloud from the diary: "*The Colonel, I referenced elsewhere, was a paymaster for both US military intelligence personnel and the CIA. He was a 'made man' in the New York Mafia and the liaison between the New York Police and the Mafia. He was the middleman between CIA factions and multiple Mafia families that ran illegal enterprises in New York City.*

The Colonel was also a representative of the Bank of Credit and Commerce International, commonly called the BCCI, founded by the CIA to launder money and finance black operations worldwide.

In 1976, a CIA operation brought over 100 military-style cargo planeloads of cocaine out of Colombia into the Albrook Air Station in Panama. Jackson Stephens was a financial backer of both George H.W. Bush and Bill Clinton's presidential campaigns. Stephens also bought Alltel, whose subsidiary, Systematics, used a version of the PROMIS software. Jackson Stephens paid off politicians from Arkansas to look the other way and ignore the CIA's cocaine operation in Mena. Stephens and the CIA own a lot of people. They have a lot of money. They get things done. We all answer to Stephens indirectly. We answer to his money, and so does everyone else at the CIA where Stephens has influence."

"So, Stephens financed both political parties and was connected to the CIA as well as their money laundering, arms deals, and cocaine smuggling?" Ruth Ann asked.

"Exactly!" Rosslyn replied, then continued reading: "*My partner attended a meeting of government drug smugglers held in a bunker at Camp Robinson, an Army facility outside Little Rock, Arkansas. In addition to Governor Bill Clinton and his aide Bob Nash, the guest list included Max Gomez aka Felix Rodriguez, John Cathey aka Oliver North, resident CIA agent Akihide Sawahata, and Agency contractor Terry Reed. The man in charge of this meeting went by the name of Robert Johnson, but he was actually CIA agent William Barr. He was the representative for CIA Director William Casey. Later, Barr was appointed US Attorney General by George H. W. Bush. A large amount of money was missing from the Enterprise. Robert Johnson admonished Clinton for double-dipping and becoming greedy. Clinton made a deal to help launder money for the CIA. Robert Johnson, William Barr, pulled the drug smuggling operation out of Arkansas and sternly threatened Clinton into compliance. He informed Clinton that the CIA didn't need 'live' liabilities.*

Later, the prosecutor, Lawrence Walsh, covered up the high crimes and misdemeanors of George H. W. Bush in the Iran-Contra scandal. Kenneth Starr covered up CIA drug trafficking by using the Bill Clinton-Monica Lewinsky sex-capades during the Clinton impeachment. This corruption led to permanent networks involving both oil and drugs, or more specifically, petrodollars and narcodollars. These networks, particularly in the Middle East, have become so important that they affect U.S. foreign policy and the behavior of the U.S. government, U.S. banks, and U.S. corporations.

We later discovered when George Bush, CIA Director Bill Casey, and Oliver North started their own plan of government-sanctioned drug smuggling. They envisioned using 500 men; they ended up using about 5,000 operatives and making well over $35 billion. In addition, the operation became a government within a government, eventually involving thirty to forty thousand people."

"I recall George H.W. Bush was either in Washington DC or New York City the morning of 9/11. So let me do a quick internet search. Oh, dear!" Ruth Ann exclaimed, then read the words on her screen: *"George Herbert Walker Bush was meeting with none other than Shafiq bin Laden, the brother of Osama bin Laden!"*

"No!" Rosslyn exclaimed in disbelief. "Are you kidding me?"

Ruth Ann continued reading: "*It was a routine business meeting on September 10th through the 11th. There is no conflict of interest, no relationship to the 9/11 attacks, and no FBI investigation into the links between the Bush and bin Laden families. What is presented below is a factual account confirmed by the Washington Post. Investors of the Carlyle Group, including Osama's brother Shafiq bin Laden and former President George H. W. Bush, met in the plush surroundings of the Ritz-Carlton Hotel on September 10th and 11th. Their business encounter was unfortunately interrupted by the 9/11 attacks.*"

Rosslyn said, "I have read several conflicting reports about where George Bush Sr. and Barbara were and what they did that morning."

"Well, will you take a look at this Newsweek article from November 6, 2014? George H. W. Bush himself writes it. This story says: *on September 12th, 2001, George H. W. wrote to the journalist Hugh Sidey telling of the advice he had given to his son the day before. He had concerns that American Muslims might be demonized as the Japanese had been after a similar surprise attack on America at Pearl Harbor in 1941,*" Ruth Ann read.

"How could he have said that to his son on September 11th?" Rosslyn asked, "Nobody knew who was responsible for the hijackings. It sounds like Bush Sr. knew about the plot, and all of it would be blamed on Muslims. It is noteworthy that he mentioned the attack on Pearl Harbor since 9/11 was referred to as a 'New Pearl Harbor' by some rather suspicious characters."

Ruth Ann continued reading the Newsweek article, "*Barbara and I were flying to St. Paul, Minnesota after spending the night at the White House when we got diverted to Milwaukee. We were whisked off to a motel outside the city limits.*"

"So, all those stories about Bush attending the Carlyle Group conference are what? Bogus? Where did that story come from?" Rosslyn asked. "This Newsweek article stinks to high heaven. Is it just fake news? Why all the confusion?"

"It sure does stink, and it probably is fake news. Several articles put Bush Sr. at that Carlyle Group conference with the bin Laden brother. Wikipedia says bin Laden was the guest of honor and the main speaker at the Washington Ritz-Carlton on September 11th. It looks like old man Bush was rewriting history with his Newsweek story," Ruth Ann agreed.

Ruth Ann was about to close the Newsweek article when she noticed a telling exposure, "Rosslyn, in Bush's September 12th letter, he admits: *Abroad, the Arab leaders now have condemned the attack. The Taliban claimed, 'We didn't do it. Nor did Osama Bin Laden.' Their words rang hollow. They must be a little apprehensive, our president having declared properly and forcefully that those who knowingly harbor terrorists will also pay a price.*"

"It seems like old George is doing a little CYA if you get my drift," Rosslyn said and shook her head.

"It sure does," Ruth Ann agreed.

Rosslyn continued reading the pages in the diary. "Ruth Ann listen: *The corporate media cartel covers up CIA's criminal activities, despite documented evidence from many whistleblowers. Director Casey's program made a mockery of the free press in the US and spread propaganda denying it. When discovered in the seventies, journalists and media executives became more careful and covert about hiding their association with the CIA. Everything on television, in Hollywood movies, and the news is crafted to control the public's viewpoint toward worldwide events. It is presented to brainwash the masses into thinking and reacting like the CIA's psychiatrists desire. The MK-Ultra program of mind control is highly effective and delivered so covertly that unless you are aware of what is happening, you would never know that your mind is being manipulated to train you to love or hate a person, a country, a religion, or a skin color.*"

Ruth Ann interrupted, "I've heard the media refer to the MK-Ultra program as a conspiracy theory, but apparently, your father knew differently."

"Unfortunately, he did," Rosslyn continued reading. "*Everything is a rich man's trick. If you organize the information within these diaries, it will connect many events of your lifetime. This cabal has been working behind the scenes for a very long time. Their motivation is power and control. They finance their missions through the billions of dollars they generate from running narcotics, trafficking children, and illegal arms sales. If you have ever wondered how African tribes or the Taliban of Afghanistan lack shoes but manage to carry a rocket-propelled grenade launcher. Look to the Agency; you'll find your answer. Foreign leaders are paid off with weapons in exchange for what they can provide to the US war machine. This madness has gone on for decades. It is the driving force behind the evil deep state cabal that orchestrates events, conflicts, and wars. This war machine forms the basis of our economy. Following World War II, we brought thousands of Nazi scientists to America; most were placed in government agencies, such as the Central Intelligence Agency and the State Department. Their progeny has remained in these government agencies, and they're the ones who write the script for the corporate-controlled media to deliver to the masses in order to stir conflict. Once conflict begins, they take control of all valuable natural resources, oil, gas, minerals, or drugs.*

Every CIA operative involved in the assassination of JFK became embroiled in drug-running, arms dealings, and money laundering. Their names find their way into our living rooms via the nightly news and will be involved in future false flag operations, including events on US soil. There is nothing this group of elitists will not do to promote their agenda of world domination. It has been methodically planned and will be carried out under the auspices of a new age or a new world order. President Bush Sr. spoke of the new world order, as did presidents that followed him. Unfortunately, only the elite understand what that term means for the public. First, they will take away our freedoms through a power grab following an orchestrated event that they claim to be terrorism or a pandemic. Then they will install a government that will resemble a third-world dictatorship. Unfortunately, most Americans will not know what has happened until it is too late.

It is an open secret in government that the elite players are blackmailed or compromised by the Agency or the FBI. They become controlled assets to be used whenever necessary, such as voting or appearing on a Sunday news show to deliver a message. We own and control everyone. We claim plausible deniability by working closely with all the other intelligence agencies around the world. The Agency does the bidding for the elites, the international bankers, and the military-industrial complex corporations. They say all wars are banker's wars because that is who we work for. Everyone in Washington DC knows how to follow instructions and execute our game plan. When there is a terrorist attack, we blame it on a target country. As you go through life, Rosslyn, remember one of my favorite sayings, 'things are not always as they seem.' I have lived a life of illusion and deception as a highly trained liar and assassin, trapped in a world of darkness beyond your imagination. Darkness, along with greed, is the power that controls the world. This agenda is unstoppable, although I wish I could leave you with a solution to do just that. What is planned for our nation is the same communism Americans fought against for decades. The fight is a charade. We invited the communists and fascists into our own government. I will close now and ponder a way to help you expose and stop this evil. If

I figure out a suggestion for you, I will write it in one of the diaries... so keep reading."

Ruth Ann said, "I realize this information from your father's diaries may be personal, but it needs to be shared with the group. Our futures and our freedoms depend on us exposing what you just read."

"I agree with you, and I believe my father would want this information to be shared. How else can these agendas be stopped?" Rosslyn concurred.

twenty-four

The following morning, Jim brought the meeting to order, "I want to continue with the next two flights starting with Flight 77. We are taking apart a covert operation that changed not only American's lives but the lives of everyone around the world. We have several pieces of evidence, but we don't have enough to convince a skeptic that they were lied to. However, we have more than enough evidence to build a far more believable case than the official government story.

Flight 77 had at least half a dozen last-minute passengers that were mentioned in the media. The most famous last-minute passenger was the television commentator, Barbara Olson. It's difficult to find a starting point because there are so many inconsistencies in her stories. Her husband, the Solicitor General, claimed she called his office two, three, or four times. He never kept his story straight. At first, he claimed she phoned his office collect from a cell phone, then changed the story, claiming she called collect from an air-phone. Let me stop right there. I have been sent documentation from American Airlines that shows they deactivated the air-phones on their 757 fleet by January 2001. So, we know she couldn't have called using an air-phone. We also know that you cannot and never could call collect using a cellular phone. So, again, that is not true, besides the fact that cell phones did not work at altitude."

Max piped up, "So her husband was lying. Is it possible that he made the entire story up? Any idea why he lied?"

"A few interesting details about him, Max, he was instrumental in seeing to it that George W. Bush won the disputed presidential election in 2000. Another interesting connection is that he was the attorney for the Israeli spy Jonathan Pollard who passed classified information to South Africa and tried to sell secrets to several hostile countries. Pollard worked directly under the Israeli Mossad's top spy, Rafi Eitan, who stole the PROMIS software from the DOJ. Barbara was also Jewish. She spent a decade in Hollywood, but I have been unable to find one piece of information about her time there other than working for Stacy Keach. Following her stint in Hollywood, she attended the Yeshiva University's Ben Cardozo School of Law, an Orthodox Jewish school in New York City. The Solicitor General was her second husband but, everything has been scrubbed from the internet about her life. On the phone calls to her husband, she claimed that all the passengers had been moved to the back of the plane and indicated that the hijackers were armed with knives and boxcutters. Only through her husband's statements to the press did we learn the hijackers used knives and boxcutters. Neither Barbara's cell phone records nor any telephone company records of her calls have been made public. In the Zacharia Moussaoui trial, the FBI claimed that Barbara only called her husband one time and that call failed to connect."

"So, if her husband cannot be trusted to tell the truth about her phone calls, how can his story about boxcutters or any of his details be trusted?" Ruth Ann asked.

"Great point, Ruth Ann," Jim agreed. "There are so many conflicting statements by the Solicitor General that it is impossible to know for certain if she even called him at all. I have never found anywhere that she described the hijackers. His story changed every time he told it for the next year or so."

"Any experienced attorney knows that whenever a person changes his story, he is most likely lying. Her husband was certainly experienced," Jerry Reitz commented.

"I'll say, he had experience both with the law and the Israeli Mossad," Max chuckled.

"The entire passenger list was filled with employees from Boeing, Raytheon, BAE Systems, Lockheed Martin, and the Department of Defense. Let me touch on the last-minute passengers that I was able to confirm. Other than Barbara, there was a senior scientist with the U.S. Navy. He was a third-generation physicist whose work was so classified that his family knew nothing about it. They didn't even know he was flying to Los Angeles. The passenger load was light with only fifty-three passengers, most of whom were somehow connected to the government," Jim concluded.

"It looks like anyone on that flight might have been useful in creating a faked hijacking scenario," Max said.

"Very true, Max," Jim agreed. "I am not suggesting we implicate anyone, but we must examine who could potentially have been involved. I can't imagine anyone willingly cooperating with a hoax. But, on the other hand, I can understand a military person or anyone connected to the intelligence world being involved."

"Military personnel would do anything they were asked," Joel Sherman explained.

"Exactly, Mr. President," Jim confirmed. "I discovered another interesting element from a last-minute passenger who was a scientist for a biotech company. Since no plane parts from a 757 were found at the Pentagon, this story should rattle your cage. This account appeared six years after 9/11. This passenger wrote a note to her husband on a sheet of hotel stationery. For some unexplained reason, she dated and timestamped the note at the bottom: *9/11/01 7:15 am PST (I think)*. The message simply read: *I love you, please, take care of our two children for me.* The article did not include when or where the note was found amongst the rubble of the Pentagon. The stationary was found intact with only a slight water stain. The FBI claimed they found this note and returned it to her husband. What struck me as utterly impossible was how a piece of paper survived the crash, the fire, the water from multiple fire engines, and the collapse of the Pentagon. Even odder was that she noted the time as *7:15 am Pacific Standard Time*. That made me question the validity of the letter."

"Why would an educated scientist not know the time when she was traveling with meetings to attend and flights to catch? How did the FBI figure out who her husband was since no name was written in the note? Why did it take so long for this story to appear?" Asked Jerry Reitz.

"Sounds to me like a plant," Max bellowed.

Jerry agreed, "That certainly is how the FBI operates."

"Didn't Flight 77 crash at 9:37 am? Her timestamp of 7:15 am Pacific indicated it was

10:15 am on the east coast," Vera questioned.

"It's an easy mistake to make to write PST for Pacific Standard Time, but the country was still on Daylight Savings Time until late October. If you are going to note the time zone, how could you not know it was still Daylight Savings Time?" Rosslyn asked. "And why would she feel compelled to indicate the time in a note? If her flight was hijacked and she felt her life was endangered, why would she write a note to her husband in California? I agree; it seems like a phony story to me."

"Why didn't she just call her husband like Barbara Olson did?" Vera asked. She did not know what time it was when she wrote this note because she put 'I think' in parenthesis after her timestamp."

Max explained, "If the FBI wrote this phony note, maybe it was written months or years later, and it was after the fall time change back to standard time. That would be a detail they missed."

"You could be on to something there, Max. That would also explain why she didn't mention hijackers in her note. If she was alive at 10:15 am Eastern, that also indicates Flight 77 did not crash at 9:37 am. If she were still alive but convinced that she was not going to live through whatever she was observing at Westover, then she would have written a note," Jim explained. "So Max, I think you may be right."

"Jim, since we know Flight 77 landed at Westover, and they were on the ground when Barbara and the flight attendant Rene made phone calls, someone must have collected wallets, watches, and cell phones, that would explain why she didn't know the time," Vera interjected.

"I have always wondered what prevented every passenger and crew member from making phone calls," Ruth Ann commented.

"It makes sense that someone would have confiscated everyone's cell phones. But who would willingly give up their phone?" Rosslyn questioned.

"You would be amazed what people will do with a gun pointed at their head," Max responded.

"If they also removed wallets, watches, and jewelry, that could explain these unbelievable stories about rings and credit cards being found years later at ground zero, Shanksville and the Pentagon," President Sherman added.

"This story made public years later is typical of the deep state; it's how they kept their deception alive," Max added.

"I believe that is true, Max; as I said earlier, I have read every article concerning 9/11. Some stories don't make sense, and it is worth further investigation when far-fetched accounts coincide with a last-minute passenger or crew member. The 9/11 charade is chock-full of evolving narratives that the media and others claim to be miracles," Jim explained.

"Believe it or not, I had co-workers that were convinced those impossible cell phone calls from cruise altitude were made possible by a miracle of God," Rosslyn chuckled.

"Speaking of paper that survived the crash at the Pentagon, in the captain's wallet was a prayer card which survived, but his wallet didn't," Jim said.

Jerry Reitz asked, "Wasn't there another phone call made from Flight 77?"

"Yes, Jerry, the lead flight attendant, phoned her parents in Nevada. They reported to the FBI that Rene phoned, and they could hear a male voice in the background reciting American Airlines phone numbers to her," Jim explained.

"Why would someone have to give her specific phone numbers to call when she had been a flight attendant for at least a dozen years? Any flight attendant would have memorized the toll-free number for crew scheduling. So, who would have been giving those directives?" Vera asked.

"All good questions, Vera," Jim agreed. "There was only one male flight attendant on that plane, and he too was a last-minute addition to the crew orders. His aunt was an employee of the FBI, and his wife, who was also on board as a flight attendant, had an uncle who worked in the Pentagon."

"To convince a senior flight attendant to call her parents during a hijacking, instead of directly to a company number, would be a fete in itself," Rosslyn explained.

"She also had the number of hijackers wrong and never said anything about anyone breaching the cockpit. Her account, much like the calls from the other flights, gave conflicting information," Jim added.

Vera had been quietly typing, "Oh, my, listen to this! The captain's prayer card read *I did not die, do not stand at my grave and weep. I am not there…*"

The room fell silent.

twenty-five

Jim continued after the lunch break, "all four of the flight attendants on Flight 77 were not the originally scheduled crew. This information was not easily unearthed. I searched and read every article I could find. After reading everything, including obituaries, I put two and two together. It appears all four flight attendants were added on the afternoon of the tenth."

"The entire cabin crew were last-minute replacements?" Rosslyn questioned.

"That's right, Rosslyn, Jim resumed, "as I was investigating the First Officer; I found an obituary for his father, Roland J. Charlebois, in the Washington Post. The obituary mentioned his son was a pilot on Flight 77 that crashed into the Pentagon on 9/11."

"Charlebois, as in the First Officer David Charlebois from American Flight 77?" Rosslyn asked.

"Right again," Jim said, "the obituary boasted that his father was a retired CIA officer and linguist. He learned to speak Chinese during World War II and taught high school French and Latin before joining the CIA in 1954. He was an instructor overseas for international security officers. He was a lieutenant colonel in the Air Force Reserves and lived in Arlington, Virginia. He was survived at the time by his wife Vivienne, who later died in 2014. Coincidently, she was born in Chicopee, Massachusetts."

"Chicopee, you mean right there where Westover Air Force base is?" Vera laughed.

"Indeed, a coincidence," Jim replied, then continued, "she joined the Marine Corps after her brother was killed in World War II. Her obituary mentioned that her favorite posting was Paris, where she could take cooking classes with Julia Childs. That detail took me down the rabbit hole to clarify whether Julia Childs was CIA or not. In addition, the discovery that the first officer's father was an international recruiter and trainer for the CIA sheds a very new light on the 9/11 operation. The First Officer's family connection to the CIA was eye-opening."

"Charlebois would have been easy for the CIA to recruit with those relatives. But you know what they say, nobody ever retires from the Mafia or the CIA until they are dead," Max inserted.

"Jim said. "In researching the CIA, I found it is common for the children of intelligence operatives to follow their parents into the world of espionage and black operations."

"You mentioned Julia Childs. My mother loved to watch her cooking shows. I remember hearing once that she was involved with the Central Intelligence Agency," Ruth Ann added.

"Everyone knows Julia Childs was associated with the OSS, the precursor to the CIA. She had quite an interesting life story. Julia was the daughter of a wealthy heiress. She stood six feet two inches tall and grew up in a family wealthy enough to have their own cook. However, she didn't learn to cook until she met her husband-to-be. He was also an OSS officer for many years. Julia tried to enlist in the Women's Army Corps and the Navy WAVES, but she was too tall, so she joined the Office of Strategic Services and began her career as a typist. Soon, she was given more responsibilities that required a top-secret clearance. She worked directly under the head of the OSS, General William J. Donovan," Jim explained.

Max slowly shook his head, "Old Wild Bill Donovan, she worked directly with 'Wild Bill'? He was the only person to have received all four of the United States highest awards, the Medal of Honor, the Distinguished Service Cross, the Distinguished Service Medal, and the National Security Medal. He was also the recipient of the Purple Heart, the Silver Star, and many other medals from foreign countries. By the time World War II came along, old Bill had years under his belt setting himself up as a mover and shaker in international business affairs. He honed his skills as an intelligence gatherer and met with many foreign leaders, including Mussolini. He had many Jewish clients throughout

Europe and was no friend of the Nazis. During his many trips to Europe leading up to the war, he met with Winston Churchill, British diplomats, and the U.S. ambassador to Britain, Joseph Kennedy."

"It's a very tight circle," Jerry said.

"Exactly!" Max exclaimed. "Roosevelt signed an order naming Donovan the Coordinator of Information known as the COI. There was no formal spy agency at that time, but Donovan laid the groundwork for a future centralized intelligence agency. He organized the COI's New York headquarters in the Rockefeller Center and asked Allen Dulles to head it. Dulles's office was on the floor directly above the New York branch of Britain's MI6. Donovan set up espionage and sabotage schools, set up front companies, and arranged clandestine collaborations with many international corporations, including the Vatican. In 1942, the COI ceased being a White House operation and was placed under the Joint Chiefs of Staff, at which time the name was changed to the OSS. However, it wasn't all peaches and cream for old Wild Bill. He was jockeying for power between J. Edgar Hoover at the FBI and General Douglas MacArthur. Donovan was active in every theatre during the war and even had a group of Catholic priests across Europe engaging in espionage without the Pope's knowledge. By 1946, he resumed his law practice and began writing a history of American Intelligence, which he never finished. He badly wanted to be chosen to head the CIA, but since that wasn't in the cards for him, he worked behind the scenes to promote Allen Dulles to fill that position. He went on to become the Ambassador to Thailand, and it is rumored that he worked clandestinely for the CIA to set up their operations in Southeast Asia and Vietnam. Yep, he was quite the man."

"Max, how do you know so much about him?" Vera asked.

"I recently read a couple of books on the man," Max admitted. "Sorry to sidetrack your presentation there, Jimbo."

"Not a problem at all, Max. Now, where was I?" Jim asked. "Oh, yes, Julia Childs. She and her husband moved back to Paris after their marriage, where he continued to work for the State Department. Her files were declassified in 2008. I discovered that from the early days of the OSS, Donovan and future directors of the CIA produced some of the most hare-brained schemes you can imagine. During World War II, while stationed in Thailand and Burma, Donovan and Julia, her future husband Paul, and a few other agents used nefarious schemes to demoralize Japanese troops. They would leave satchels of food that appeared to be abandoned along a roadway. The Japanese troops were hungry, so they would grab up the satchels but discovered the food had been booby-trapped or poisoned. They broadcasted propaganda about losses on the front lines and political disarray in Japan. They broadcasted offensive political material to the Thai and Burmese people and blamed it on the Japanese. One of the OSS trainers became a target of the McCarthy probes because she had been a member of the Communist Party. Behind the scenes, McCarthy was diligently trying to embarrass Donovan and expose the left-wing people he hired into the OSS."

Jerry Reitz interrupted, "so that was when the communist infiltration of our State Department and intelligence community started."

"The FBI's director J. Edgar Hoover wanted all the power to himself and his organization. Because of their closeness to some of these communists in the OSS, the Childs's were also pulled into the McCarthy probes. Paul Childs was put under a full loyalty inquiry because he was still a government employee working in propaganda. At one point, he was even accused of being a homosexual despite his marriage to Julia. Interestingly, the FBI and their investigations ignored Julia. They either didn't have any dirt on her, or her wealthy family connections provided her protection," Jim clarified. "Before I understood their history, I had no idea the CIA was meddling around the world. They were busy creating unrest, military coups, running drugs or arms, and seating dictators around the world."

Ruth Ann piped up, "Julia Childs' husband was a propagandist for the United States? Who would have guessed? I have always heard about Tokyo Rose's broadcasts, but you're saying our own intelligence agencies were sending propaganda. You know what the Nazis said, always accuse the other side of that which you are guilty."

"How is that any different from what is going on today? Every channel is creating fake news and making up stories for political gain," Max said.

"What other connections to the intelligence world did you find, Jim?" Vera asked.

Jim cleared his throat and continued, "there were other associations to the military or intelligence agencies on Flight 77. For example, the captain was known for his *take-charge* attitude. He served in the Pentagon while in the reserves, and rumor has it that he designed military war games, including one in which a 757 struck the Pentagon."

Max's jaw dropped, "Now, Jimbo, you say that is a rumor, but if there is any truth to that, it is a mega-coinky-dink!"

"No kidding, Max," Jim laughed. "I have never found proof he designed that war game, but nothing would shock me. I uncovered that the pentagon drilled for more than one scenario, including a plane strike. I also discovered that another 757 qualified Captain was pass-riding that day with his wife. They were not listed as last-minute passengers, but employees fly standby and do not make reservations weeks in advance. They watch the passenger loads on all flights leaving the day they plan to travel and list themselves as a non-revenue passenger within twenty-four hours of departure. This recently retired captain didn't book into first-class; he and his wife flew coach. That is not something an airline employee would typically do on a six-and-a-half-hour flight. There were plenty of seats available in first class. He, his wife, and a friend of theirs sat squeezed into seats at row 22."

Rosslyn spoke up, "I would imagine if he were a retired captain out of the Washington base, he would have been known to most of the flight attendants, and they would have offered him first-class seats. That's what every flight attendant I know would have done."

"Very true, maybe there was a reason he needed to be in coach," Vera added.

"In addition to being a retired American Airlines captain, he was also a retired Rear Admiral in the Navy. In a crew base the size of Americans in D.C., he had to have known the captain on Flight 77, who had spent twenty years in the Naval Reserves in the Pentagon. Both men retired from the Navy within a year of each other and were involved in military exercise planning. This retired captain seated in the rear of the plane would have been familiar with the FAA hijack protocols. If you have ever known any naval aviators, you know they would not sit still and allow anyone to take command of an aircraft. Since there were no Arabs on the plane, this pass-riding captain could have played an entirely different role than that of a helpless victim. Pass-riding flight attendants were denied boarding on all the flights. They could have thrown a monkey wrench into a staged scenario. That same circumstance should have held true for the pilots," Jim said.

"Unless… could he have been involved?" Ruth Ann questioned.

"That brings up the question if Barbara Olson and the lead flight attendant had no problem calling, why didn't this retired pilot make a call?" Joel Sherman asked.

"Nothing but troubling questions surround this man. I am sorry to say, but not having been on board, I can only guess what his role could have been. That's a good que stion, Mr. President. We know he did not make any phone calls," Jim responded.

Max agreed. "Once you get the official story of the hijackers out of your head, you can think much clearer, and you can see a whole new world of probabilities."

Vera added. "On Flight 77, they claim the lead flight attendant was ushered to the back of the aircraft with all the passengers. Right there, I have to say; no way would any lead flight attendant leave their first-class passengers alone with a hijacker. Likewise, no flight attendant worth a Diet Coke and a taco would leave the cockpit door unattended."

"Both callers did not give any pertinent details about the hijackers, their demands, or their weapons. The lead flight attendant even reported the number of hijackers wrong, saying there were six, not five, deviating from the official story," Rosslyn added.

"I would like to move on to discuss United Flight 93, but first, I want to mention that all of the accused hijackers on Flight 77 were discovered alive after this event. The passport found on the street in Manhattan bore the photograph of one of the accused hijackers from Flight 77 under the name of an accused terrorist on Flight 11, proving that they did a poor job faking identities," Jim said.

Max laughed, "And a piss-poor job at that."

"I've got an incoming call from Qatar that was scheduled weeks ago. I don't want to reschedule it, and I certainly don't want to miss one minute of these meetings, so can we close for the day and pick this up in the morning?" President Sherman asked.

twenty-six

Dr. Cohen slept late, something he rarely did. He was stuck in the early morning traffic that he despised. His cell phone rang.

"Dr. Cohen, are you coming in today? Is everything okay?" Judy asked.

"Everything is fine Judy, if it were not for this ridiculous traffic, I would probably be there by now. I slept late, but if this traffic starts moving, I should be there in about ten minutes," Dr. Cohen replied.

"There were just two men in suits here demanding information on your patient Rosslyn Langley. They were not about to take no for an answer. They were quite threatening," Judy admitted.

"Did you give them any information about her? What were they looking for? Obviously, they were not insurance agents," Dr. Cohen fired his questions to his receptionist.

"I had no choice, Dr. Cohen; they were making strange threats to my kids and even mentioned my dog by name and how it would be a shame if Jasper were killed or hit by a car or something. I am so rattled just thinking about it; I can't remember exactly what they said. I am sorry, I gave them her personal information like name and address, which satisfied them. They were not asking for a diagnosis or anything like that. I got the feeling they wanted to find her," Judy replied.

"Judy, if the security camera was running when they came in, would you pull that clip and save it for me?" Dr. Cohen asked.

"I think it was turned off by then, doctor, but I will check right now and save any images that might have been captured," Judy replied.

"Thank you, Judy; after you check, take a few deep breaths and write down every detail you can recall about those two men. No need to make it a court document or anything, I know you have a great memory, and you will recall every detail when you write it down. I will be there as soon as this darn Seattle traffic allows."

"What in the hell is going on?" Dr. Cohen thought to himself as he merged into the far-left lane and was finally able to hit the gas.

twenty-seven

The meeting reconvened the following morning in the Oval Office.

Jim adjusted a new chart on the easel, making it visible to everyone in the room. "I have mentioned the light passenger loads on the first three flights. United 93 is no exception, but it is extraordinary that at least sixteen were last-minute additions of the thirty-three passengers. That means that the original load was under twenty, which was highly unusual for any transcontinental flight. So, of course, I had to look at everyone that was a last-minute addition, including the flight crew. Only one out of the seven crew members was originally scheduled to be on this flight. The reasons given for being last-minute additions by both passengers and crew were unconvincing. I found it curious that the media felt it necessary to explain why each crew member had been added to the flight at the last minute. How the media found out about a crew member's schedule change and why they found it necessary to tell the public caught my attention. In a typical incident involving an airline, the media would not be inclined to report such a detail," Jim explained.

"When I was junior, I bid a horrific six-stops per day trip for five days, just to be home for Christmas," Rosslyn admitted. "I have to agree with you, Jim. Why would the media feel they needed to explain a crew member's schedule change?"

"I smell Operation Mockingbird," Max grumbled. "Flight crews fly; nobody would have questioned why they were flying. Jimbo, now I think *you're* on to something."

Vera was quietly nodding in agreement. She, too, had questioned the media's motive for elaborating on the reasons everyone was onboard.

"Had it not been for the media pointing out specific reasons for each crew member being on board, I would not have given it a second thought. It was like a criminal that says he's not guilty when nobody accused him of a crime. I also discovered that every last-minute passenger and crew member that day has a scholarship program, a foundation, or a fund in their name. Many of these foundations and funds are still actively collecting money. In addition, several passengers' wives were given significant book deals."

"Their wives were offered book deals?" Rosslyn asked. "What would be the purpose of writing a book if you were not on board and didn't have sufficient knowledge to share?"

"Exactly! And the publishing houses even supplied ghostwriters for them. These book deals could be part of the government propaganda to legitimize the fake story," Jim added.

Max spoke up, "I always think of some hidden pay-off whenever I see book deals offered to people like that. It reminds me of the money Look magazine gave for the JFK assassination film."

Joel Sherman slowly nodded his head as he listened, "that is interesting about the financial payouts since the federal government's victim fund paid the families millions of dollars. I have always wondered why our federal government felt it was their responsibility to pay for what they claimed were acts of terror from foreign agents. Why weren't their countries of origin held financially responsible?"

"The victims' families were not only paid by the government, but they also received substantial insurance payouts from the airlines. Getting back to the last-minute passengers, of the sixteen, more than a third of them made phone calls," Jim explained.

"One of those calls came from a lavatory. You can guarantee *that* call was not from an air-phone, there were no air-phones in the lavatories. Didn't the FBI attempt to rewrite history by claiming that all calls were from air-phones?" Rosslyn asked.

Jim answered, "That's a good point, Rosslyn. Yes, the FBI did realize their mistake and attempted to change the narrative about cell phones working at thirty-thousand feet."

Max laughed, "I guess those FBI goons were accustomed to having telephone access from thirty-thousand feet. They forgot how the rest of us travel. They made several mistakes putting this ruse together, and their bull-shittery about cell phones stinks to high heaven."

"That wasn't their only mistake. Everyone seated in first-class made phone calls, except Mark Rothenberg, who they claimed was stabbed," Jim added.

"I see a pattern here. This is the exact same story as on Flight 11. A Jewish man is stabbed to death, so we are not supposed to suspect him. Several Jewish men were on these flights, and we were told that two of them were killed. But what if they weren't …" Ruth Ann questioned.

"Dead men tell no tales, and in this case, they wouldn't be suspected of involvement in the charade," Max blurted out.

"That's an interesting point. If a man was stabbed to death in first-class, why didn't any callers mention a murder? It would have been very bloody if the only weapon used was a boxcutter. I think one caller mentioned a stabbing but not a murder. You would think a murder would be the first detail mentioned. One couple called family members and gave the strangest comments. The woman conveyed the combination to her safe to her sister and said she hoped to see her again in person. Her partner called his father and told him there were 'terrorists' on the plane and that he loved him. His father said that his son sounded sad, which is not the reaction you would expect from someone with terrorists on their flight. Their stories were incongruent. The woman never mentioned hijackers, yet her partner used the term terrorist," Jim said.

"That is very strange, Jim," Vera said.

"Let me refresh your memories about this flight. It took off after a traffic delay, departing Newark. It was late getting off the ground by forty minutes. Wheels up time was 8:42 am, taking off to the north then turning to the west only a moment before the first explosion at the North Tower. The first phone call began one minute before the official story claims the hijacking even started. According to his wife's testimony, he used a cell phone to call," Jim continued.

"Wasn't his wife also a flight attendant for Delta? I wonder why he didn't fly on Delta?" Rosslyn interrupted.

"Yes, she was, and why he didn't fly on Delta is a question that has always bothered me.

When his wife noticed the caller ID was from her husband's cell phone, she was shocked when he told her he was on a plane that was hijacked. She knew what we all know; cell phones didn't work at cruise altitude. They didn't work then, and they don't work now. He ended up placing four cell phone calls to her, each one connected with no problem. With each call, he gave her more information, and like on the other flights, those details conflicted with the other callers' accounts. And the details of those calls did not match the FAA's claim of a rapid descent. Several callers sounded certain they were about to be killed, although they didn't mention how that might occur. One woman showed clear signs of the Stockholm Syndrome as she left a message on her home recorder telling her husband there had been a slight problem on the plane, and *they* were very kind to the passengers." Jim added.

"*They* were being kind? Who was she referring to? The flight attendants or someone else? Why wouldn't she mention hijackers if they were onboard? Oh, wait, that's right, there were no hijackers on her plane," Vera commented.

Jim continued, "Exactly, Vera, so who was she referring to? You'd think, at the very least, she would use the term hijack. And why didn't any of these callers describe the hijackers?"

"It's difficult to accurately describe hijackers that don't exist," Max joked.

"Getting back to the phone calls," Jim continued, "The passenger that called from the lavatory is the only person who reported white smoke in the cabin, meant to indicate that the plane had been shot down. He also reported that the plane was full of passengers. He did manage to declare there was a hijacking. However, his phone call was made while the FAA claimed the plane was upside down. For some reason, the FBI kept his identity a secret for six months. I can't explain that since every detail about everyone else on board was made public immediately."

"If the plane was upside down, there's no way he was in a lavatory; he would have been on the ceiling with a big blue water problem," Max laughed.

"Why would he claim the flight was full?" Ruth Ann asked.

"Only thirty-three passengers on a 757 is a very empty aircraft; if he was on this flight, he knew it wasn't anywhere close to capacity," Rosslyn added.

"The FAA alleged the aircraft was upside down yet traveling at more than five hundred miles per hour. This was when both flight attendants made their phone calls to their spouses. Neither of them mentioned the plane was descending or upside down, but they did say there was a hijacking. One of them explained to her husband they planned to break through the cockpit door with the help of passengers. They had a meal cart with pots of hot water on top and intended to crash through the cockpit door to take back the flight deck," Jim said.

"That's ridiculous! There's no way they had a cart in the aisle if the plane was upside down. And flight attendants would never allow passengers to be in the aisle during a hijacking. Taking water like that into the cockpit would short circuit the onboard flight computer and an immediate loss of control. A dozen phone calls were made from this flight, yet none of them said the pilots were dead or not in the cockpit," Vera exclaimed.

"The flight deck is way too small for two dead pilots and two hijackers. If the pilots had been killed, their bodies would have been drug into the cabin. It would have been extremely difficult to roll a cart with hot water over a couple of dead bodies," Rosslyn added.

"That's right, none of the callers mentioned the pilots were not flying the aircraft. If they were, why would you throw hot water on them? Only the flight attendant's unbelievable claim that passengers were involved with carts and hot water led us to think that the pilots were not in control. Why wouldn't the first passenger that called report dead pilots in the cabin and hijackers inside the cockpit? The scenario the flight attendant painted was insane. Who did they think had the flying skills to upright that aircraft and land it safely?" Jim asked.

"That detail has never been explained, and I think we all can see why," Vera said.

"The entire government version of this flight and what occurred is outrageous. The flight attendants broke FAA protocols by calling their spouses and failing to follow instructions to keep the passengers safe. Yet, they were immediately labeled as heroes by the media," Rosslyn said.

"Heroes do something heroic, but in this case, nobody did anything, not passenger or crew," Vera said.

Jim continued, "One caller phoned his mother and used both his first and last names when she answered. He explained that his plane was hijacked and then asked her if she believed him. Another caller who was a college judo champion called his family and talked for twenty minutes. He described the hijackers as Iranian-looking and said they had a bomb. Why he didn't use his Judo skills to prevent the hijacking is inconceivable."

"I remember him; he was Jewish also. He was six foot four two twenty-five, and he certainly could have controlled those small Arab hijackers if they had been on board," Ruth Ann commented.

Jim began again, "the most noteworthy caller attempted to phone his wife using an airphone unsuccessfully. He then called the operator, who offered to connect him with his wife, but he refused. Instead, he stayed on the phone with the operator praying and giving information about the passengers and crew. Even more damning is that his cell phone continued accepting calls and taking messages for nearly eight hours after the designated crash time. That indicates his cell phone was not destroyed."

"Maybe his wife could tell if he was lying," Max suggested.

Jim chuckled, "that's one explanation, Max, wives are like that. This last caller I mentioned worked for Oracle, and his CEO broke the 'Let's Roll' story a full day before the FBI released that information. The official hero scenario of that day has one huge flaw; all the men were on phone calls for the last twenty minutes of the flight, they were all seated several rows away from each other. They had no time to plan an assault with the flight attendants. I have seen my fair share of airplane crash aftermaths, and the site at Shanksville lacked any sign of a 757 accident. Even the local coroner said there were no bodies, no airplane parts, and nothing that resembled a large commercial plane. Days later, someone planted a flight attendant's uniform purse and a paper passport supposedly from a hijacker who the FBI claimed was piloting the aircraft."

Vera spoke, "Considering everything we have discussed; it looks like this last flight was designed to humanize the innocent victims, tug at the heartstrings of the American public and cause us to believe the unbelievable. Most of the men on this flight were athletic, strong, competitive, and alpha male types. I can honestly say that such male passengers would not sit on their hands and do nothing to prevent abnormal onboard behavior from other passengers. If one of these men tried to prevent someone from entering the cockpit, other men would have joined in and helped. The fact that none of them got up gives us reason to question why they didn't."

Jim added, "the men you are referring to were all last-minute passengers."

"Everything about this flight was disjointed. It was as if they were making it up for a made for television movie," Max stated.

"So true, Max," Vera agreed.

twenty-eight

"Thank you for sticking with me. I realize this is a lot of information to keep straight. At one time, I had a great deal of respect for the FBI. Eventually, I dropped the belief that the FBI was investigating 9/11. They were not. In retrospect, they were throwing everything against the wall to see what might stick," Jim said.

"You mean to see what the public would swallow," Max interjected.

"The government and the media want us to believe the Arabs were the bad guys, and maybe they were; they just were not hijackers on board those four planes. To keep it simple, I will try to use only the first names of the hijackers. According to the Central Intelligence Agency, the first accused terrorists to hit our shores were Khalid and Nawaf. The CIA claimed they were two important Al Qaeda members. In news articles written a few weeks after 9/11, Nawaf was portrayed as Osama bin Laden's right-hand man. These two were monitored by intelligence while attending an Al Qaeda summit in Kuala Lumpur," Jim explained.

Max chuckled, "We know the CIA was arming and funding rebel groups in Afghanistan since before the eighties. When Osama bin Laden was a CIA asset known as Tim Osman, he bought arms for the Mujahideen to fight the Soviets. So maybe the CIA wasn't watching the Al Qaeda summit as much as they were shopping for recruits."

Jim resumed, "Max, that explains what happens next. These two young Saudi nationals arrived at LAX, and according to the official government story, they met another Saudi national who was suspected of being an intelligence agent. However, the Saudi's claimed he was not one of theirs; the CIA asserted they had no association with this guy, and the Israeli Mossad was never mentioned. The account claimed this Saudi gentleman was having dinner in the arrivals area at LAX and invited these two young Arabs to join him."

Rosslyn looked confused, "Jim, did the government really claim this man was eating dinner in the arrivals area at LAX? I was based at LAX and flew my fair share of international flights. There are no restaurants in the arrivals area. There is no place for anyone to eat anywhere near the international arrivals area."

"I believe you are correct," Vera agreed.

"I had not thought of that, but Rosslyn, you might have identified another flaw in the official account. After their meeting, this mysterious Saudi national helped these two set up banking accounts, apartments and place ads on internet dating sites. He gave them money and later introduced them to a well-known FBI informant whom they would eventually live with. It was from this informant's home that one of these young men placed several calls to Yemen," Jim said.

Jerry Reitz interrupted, "That would have been impossible. At that time, the NSA monitored every international phone call placed from the United States. We hired an Israeli company to monitor all domestic long-distance calls for billing purposes, but the NSA collected all international long-distance call data."

"Unless the NSA didn't want to know what was going on," Max declared.

Jim asked, "What do you mean by that, Jerry?"

Jerry responded, "At that time, the NSA monitored all international calls made from the United States, especially to a country like Yemen. There is no way we would have missed his calls unless it was masked. Their calls would have been tracked unless they were working for one of our own agencies. That could explain why the CIA stopped following these two the minute they landed. Those two had to be protected from being discovered."

"Interesting, Jerry, these two young Saudis arrived at LAX only weeks after the Millennium bomber was arrested. You would think that security was on high alert," Jim explained.

"If I remember his story correctly, the Millennium bomber, Ahmed Ressam, had more than one passport and three different IDs, along with credit cards in his fake names. Those are all hallmarks of an intelligence agent. Ressam's arrest caused the entire country to be on high alert. Suppose two Al Qaeda members, who were associates of Osama bin Laden arrived in this country shortly after his arrest. In that case, there could only be one explanation for why our intelligence did not surveil these Saudis," Jerry Reitz added.

"There was never an explanation given for military-grade explosives found in his car," Max added.

"I remember the New Year Eve celebration at the Space Needle was canceled out of fear that there was an attack planned," Vera recalled. "But Jerry, didn't the FBI fail to connect Ressam to any specific location for an attack?"

"Yes, he never did confess to any specific target. It's possible that the FBI used Ressam in a sting operation. He might have been paid to drive the explosives into the United States to set a tone for future staged terror attacks which would be blamed on Middle Eastern men. The FBI was running around the country trying to connect every Middle Eastern man to Ressam. There was an increased vigilance from the west coast to New York and every major city in between," Jerry recalled.

"We look at Al Qaeda as an enemy because of how the media has conditioned us. The CIA may see them as assets. The CIA armed and funded the Mujahideen, which became Al Qaeda until they morphed into ISIS. Considering the heightened security the Millennium bomber stirred up; there is no way the CIA or FBI would have stopped their surveillance on Khalid and Nawaf, if they were real terrorists," Jim said.

"The FBI has a reputation for corruption, and they lied more than once about the passenger manifests. So, we are safe to assume that these first two were more than likely involved in the staging than the event itself," Max concluded.

"Five months later, Marwan or someone claiming to be him arrived at Newark's Liberty Airport. The following week Atta or someone claiming to be him arrived at the same airport. A few months later, these same two traveled to Norman, Oklahoma, to check out a flight school. Eventually, they ended up in Venice, Florida, where they enrolled at Huffman Aviation, a flight school recently purchased by a Dutch intelligence operative. They rented a room there from a known CIA pilot that was involved in the Iran-Contra scandal," Jim explained.

"So, these two manage to find a CIA pilot and a Dutch intelligence source? Now, that's what I call a real coinky-dink," Max shook his head in disbelief.

"Coinky-dink, Max? This is just the beginning; wait until you see how this all plays out," Jim said. "Keep in mind; Atta was under surveillance in Germany by several intelligence agencies for months before he flew to the United States."

"More Kabuki theater," Max commented.

"In Germany, Atta went to the U.S. Embassy and was given a five-year visa in one day," Jim added.

"Wait a minute; most people would have to wait weeks to obtain a visa. Only an ally intelligence operative could be granted a visa in one day," Jerry said.

"There was considerable confusion as to when Atta and Marwan arrived in New Jersey. One intelligence operation known as Able Danger claimed they were monitoring these two in January and February of 2000, nearly six months before they arrived in the United States," Jim said.

"They would have filled out an I-94 Immigration form on their flight into the United States. That form was stamped with the date and flight number. There should be no confusion as to when they arrived," Vera added.

"That's a good point, Vera. Atta and Marwan visited several cities and attended a few different flight schools in 2000. The following year, Marwan flew to Morocco, and Atta flew to Spain. They returned to the United States and visited a flight school in Georgia. They rented a post office box in Virginia Beach, VA, then returned to Georgia. They later rented an apartment in Coral Springs, Florida. After that, Atta flew to Boston, San Francisco, and Las Vegas, where he presented a Triple-A auto club membership card for a discount on a hotel room. From there, he flew to Spain, but some accounts reported that he joined a gym in Del Ray Beach on that same day. According to FBI documents, every hijacker was in at least two different locations at the same time. I found FBI interview statements from a United ticket agent telling of rebooking six hijackers from Phoenix to east coast cities the day before 9/11. However, those details don't match up with the departure cities," Jim explained.

"Could there have been more than one of each of these accused hijackers traveling the world?" Joel asked.

"It is impossible to believe that a one person is in two places at the same time," said Jim.

"Footprints," Max shouted, "it's obvious that these guys were setting the stage so they would be remembered when the FBI showed their photos. That is the only explanation that makes sense for this unexplainable behavior."

"This constant travel of Atta and Marwan in the two months leading up to 9/11 is mind-boggling. Starting in May, the other thirteen accused hijackers began arriving in the United States. They arrived at various airports, Orlando, Newark, JFK, and Miami. How Atta and Marwan found any time to meet and aid these newcomers is never explained, but the FBI claims they did. Most of these summer arrivals landed in Newark. How they found their way to Florida is also unexplained. But that is not the only mystery I discovered with these late arrivals into America. The most suspicious element to this saga is who their realtor was. Somehow, most of these summer arrivals managed to engage the same Jewish realtor to help them settle near Del Ray Beach," Jim explained.

"What? Of all the realtors in Florida, they all chose to deal with the same Jewish realtor?" How does that work? The media is always telling us how Arabs detest Jews. This cannot be explained away as a crazy coincidence," Vera said.

"Not a coincidence, a conspiracy. I am beginning to feel like we have been hoodwinked," Max said.

"Speaking of coincidences, this realtor's husband was the editor of the Sun newspaper in Southern Florida. His offices were targeted in the anthrax scare following 9/11. His photo editor was the first American to die from anthrax exposure. In an online article, the realtor told a reporter that she worked with Marwan for three weeks to find a rental. She mentioned how polite and kind he was. She pointed out how he and his friend escorted her to a bank to deposit their cash down payment. While telling her story to this reporter, she explained that she was Jewish and had she known they were terrorists, she would have driven them off a bridge because neither of them could swim," Jim explained.

"I wonder how she managed to learn they could not swim if they couldn't speak English well?" Rosslyn asked.

"If they couldn't speak English and the realtor didn't speak Arabic, how did they manage to do business?" Ruth Ann questioned.

"If there were multiple people pretending to be these hijackers, maybe some of them did speak English," Max commented.

"Atta and a few others showed up at the Lantana Airport, near Del Ray Beach. This Jewish realtor's husband had been a Civil Air Patrol pilot. She said that Atta asked an instructor there who happened to be fluent in Arabic about crop-dusting planes. Atta was belligerent and obnoxious with a bad attitude which made him memorable. In the month leading up to the attacks, these alleged hijackers were all over Florida, Virginia, Maryland, New Jersey, and Georgia. If they were renting airplanes, cars, and hotel rooms, they had to show identification," Jim explained.

"It's odd that they would use their real identities, which conveniently allowed the FBI to accuse them after the fact. What kind of terrorist would be stupid enough to use their own ID unless they wanted to be discovered?" Max asked.

"Bingo again, Max. They ran completely unnoticed until the FBI presented their passport photos, claiming they hijacked the planes. Several people remembered Atta, but most were uncertain about all the others. Three weeks before 9/11, the Israeli Mossad contacted the CIA to warn them to be on the lookout for five terrorists. These were the same names that Able Danger claimed they uncovered. Remember, Atta, Marwan and Jarrah were in the Hamburg terrorist cell. The CIA's chief of station in Berlin bragged that his team had been surveilling and infiltrated the Hamburg cell."

Max sat straight in his chair, "Wait a darn minute, you are saying that our CIA in Berlin said they had the entire Hamburg cell on their radar, under surveillance and infiltrated them? And then when these terrorists arrive in the United States, they lose all interest? Do I have that correct?"

"Yes, you do. You are beginning to see the pattern. I uncovered information about this joint operation called Able Danger. It started in October 1999 and was created by the Chairman of the Joint Chiefs of Staff, General Hugh Shelton. It was developed as an information campaign against transnational terrorism. That sounds noble enough, does it not? According to some, Able Danger worked with the U.S. Army Land Information Warfare Activity unit and a contractor called Orion Scientific Systems, data mining open-source information on terrorists. All three were abruptly shut down in April of 2000. They had made some startling discoveries. Mixed in with their attempts to find terrorists, they discovered something else more troubling. They uncovered a Chinese spy who was linked to Chinese front companies. He was also connected to Bush's future National Security Advisor, Condoleezza Rice, and the former Defense Secretary William Perry," Jim confirmed.

"How embarrassing," Vera interjected. "Looking for terrorists and finding traitors."

"No kidding. They collected 2.5 terabytes of data. One of the Able Danger members claimed that he found Mohammad Atta living in the United States as far back as 1999, but the official storyline is that Atta arrived in June of 2000. These data miners hit a nerve when they outed this Chinese spy and his connections to Bush. When Orion was shut down, it was raided by Federal agents who confiscated everything. Their government contract was immediately canceled without explanation. The spring of 2000 was six months before the Presidential election of George W. Bush, and Condoleezza Rice was serving as Bush's foreign policy advisor. She gave a speech at the 2000 Republican National Convention where she asserted that ... *America's armed forces are not a global police force. They are not the world's 911,*" Jim explained.

"How prophetic," Ruth Ann commented.

"This connection to the scientist and the Chinese front companies to the Bush administration is alarming. Until Able Danger made this discovery, none of our intelligence agencies made these connections. Able Danger found links to sensitive technologies going to China, and their data mining found patterns which indicated this was not a one-off occasion," Jim said.

"While this transfer of military technologies was happening, the NSA and its ECHELON spy program was hoovering up every electronic transmission, and yet, they somehow missed this very troubling security breach?" Jerry said.

Jim continued, "it appears that some things are not meant to be found. I believe that someone in the Department of Defense was afraid of what would be discovered. They were not concerned about finding terrorists as much as they were about hiding crimes by our own people. After Able Danger was dissolved, they were ignored by the 9/11 Commission staff even though several of the members requested time to explain their findings. They were blocked from sharing their information with the FBI by attorneys from the Pentagon."

"Jim, I must say, you are making this one interesting meeting. I am amazed at how much you have been able to put together," President Sherman commented.

"At the time of 9/11, George Tenet was the director at the CIA. His mentor was David Boren. Boren was a democrat Senator for fifteen years and was President Clinton's original pick for Secretary of Defense, but William Perry was chosen instead. Boren served on the Senate Select Committee on Intelligence. He resigned from the Senate to become the President of the University of Oklahoma in Norman. On the morning of 9/11, Boren was having breakfast with George Tenet in Washington D.C. In the summer leading up to 9/11, Boren asked an old friend of his, David Edger, to join the faculty at the university. Edger joined in August of 2001. He served as the CIA's station chief in Berlin, Germany, from May 1997 until he joined the faculty. According to his statements, his CIA operatives in Berlin infiltrated the Hamburg terrorist cell and directed their activities. Shortly after the attacks of 9/11, he publicly predicted that '*the war on terror would last many years and we'd never be sure when it would end.* He never explained why the CIA stopped paying any attention to Atta once he landed in New Jersey," Jim revealed.

"I see a repetitive pattern, the CIA paid close attention to terrorists in foreign countries, yet when they arrive in America, they lost all interest. There must be a reason for that," Ruth Ann commented.

The room fell silent as heads nodded in agreement. "FBI reports showed Atta and some of the others in Norman, Oklahoma, several times, including in August about the same time Edger arrived. They were spotted at the Wiley Post Airport at Hangar 8. What's interesting about Hangar 8 is that it's the home of Aviation General, owned by the Kuwaiti American Corporation known as Kuw-Am, which was run by Wirt Walker III, President George W. Bush's cousin. Walker was partners with Marvin Bush, George's brother, in a company called Securacom, later renamed Stratesec. Stratesec did security work at the World Trade Center. Securacom received a multi-million-dollar contract following the 1993 bombing at the Twin Towers," Jim said.

"They probably had copies of the blueprints of the towers then," Max added.

"Quite possible, Max. Stratesec was under suspicion for insider trading after 9/11. The shares were bought by Wirt and his wife and doubled in value in the only trading day between September 11th and when the stock market reopened on September 17th. Both the Securities & Exchange Commission and the FBI felt an investigation was in order, but one never occurred. They were both cleared of any wrongdoing because the FBI found they had no ties to terrorism. Wirt Walker worked closely with several CIA operatives, which gave him experience managing CIA front companies.

There are a couple of other interesting characters who were also in Norman around this same time. The man who became famous as the Twentieth Hijacker, Zacharia Moussaoui, arrived in February 2001 to attend flight school. He was arrested in Minnesota in mid-August while taking flight lessons on a 747 simulator. He drew attention to himself for requesting to only learn how to fly, not to take-off or land. From everything I have uncovered about Moussaoui, he was in Norman for six months before his arrest. While riding on a bus in Norman, he sat next to a Jewish student. He noticed the young man had a laptop computer with him, and he asked to borrow it to send an email," Jim explained.

"Wait, this was in 2001?" Ruth Ann asked. "There were no busses equipped with Wi-Fi then, nor were there any laptops that automatically connected to the internet; you had to flip a switch to get the darn thing to search for a signal."

"That's exactly right, Ruth Ann. Not only did he borrow the laptop, but he needed the young man's password to his email account. This information was found when the FBI investigated Moussaoui's computer and discovered the student, Nick Berg's email account and password. It's hard to believe this story. Nick Berg, you may remember, was supposedly beheaded in Iraq, having gone there under the guise of selling his new cell tower design. The war was just getting started when he arrived, and he was not welcomed by either the U.S. or Iraqi military. The Iraqi's were not happy with Berg when they discovered he made a stop in Israel on his way to Iraq. Many people suspected that Berg was working for Israeli intelligence," Jim said.

"Amazing, Jim." Jerry Reitz said as he shook his head in wonder.

"I discovered that intelligence operatives often would use the same online email account and password to communicate using the draft mail option; that way, their communications never go over the internet. This is the connection between Nick and Moussaoui. Berg's email account information indicated that Moussaoui continued using this account long after the bus ride encounter," Jim explained.

"Exactly! Jim, this is a common technique for operatives to communicate," Jerry Reitz confirmed.

"It appears that the FBI was either covering up something or blind to their obvious links. They interviewed Berg, and even though they knew he shared his email account with Moussaoui, they couldn't find a link to terrorism. So, if that email account is not a connection, what else does the FBI need to see? And how is it that Moussaoui is in prison on terrorism charges if he is not a terrorist?" Max questioned.

Ruth Ann interjected, "Similar to the Jewish realtor the accused Arabs found. Here we have another Jew that connects to a terrorist yet; the FBI cannot see Jews."

Jim continued, "Nick Berg worked in the library at the university. The official story claims that several of the tickets for the flights on 9/11 were purchased using the computers in the library. The librarian said that the computer had never been used by any Middle Eastern-looking students but was used by a white kid with a neo-Nazi look. She said he was a temporary library worker. Now, you would think that the FBI would see *that* as a link to terrorists, but nope. They weren't concerned that Nick went to Iraq via Tel Aviv either. The Minnesota FBI tried to get a warrant for Moussaoui's computer but was ignored by their D.C. bosses until after 9/11. When the FBI discovered any connections on Moussaoui's laptop, they were only interested in the Arabs."

"Berg's beheading video was posted online, and there was talk about it being faked and filmed in a Mossad operative's studio. The media claimed that the terrorists beheaded him in retaliation for the abuse of prisoners at Abu Ghraib. I was one of those who questioned the entire story, including the beheading scene. Everything about it was very fake," Max confessed.

"As allied as our FBI and CIA are to the Israeli Mossad, these connections can't be overlooked, unless…" Jerry stopped in mid-sentence as the reality hit him.

Ruth Ann chimed in, "Is our government so politically correct that they are afraid to see a Mossad connection to all of these people? What next? Dare I ask?"

"I have a meeting at 4 o'clock with the budget director. I know it is early, but let's put a lid on this meeting for today and meet again in the morning, there has been a lot to digest, and I encourage you all to do that." President Sherman announced.

"Great idea, Joel," Vera said as she stood up. "I think we can all use a long break."

twenty-nine

Ruth Ann and Rosslyn decided against room service and headed to the lobby bar for a glass of wine. The drive to the hotel was quiet; they were both digesting all the details of the meetings.

"Let's head over to that corner table away from everyone," Ruth Ann pointed.

The women quietly sipped a glass of wine and shared an appetizer tray.

"You see that popcorn machine over there by the bar?" Rosslyn asked.

"Yes, is it calling your name?" Ruth Ann laughed.

"How about I grab us a bag to take to the room, and we can get into our beds and read some more from my dad's diaries?" Rosslyn asked.

"Oh, I like that idea, let's go," Ruth Ann agreed as she placed some cash over the check.

Rosslyn flipped through the pages of the diary they read the night before. As she began reading, a folded paper fell out. "Oh my, Ruth Ann, look what my dad kept in this book!"

"What is it?" Ruth Ann asked, straightening up as if to come to attention.

Rosslyn read in a loud whisper, "*Insider's Plan to Destroy America!*"

Ruth Ann looked shocked, "An insider's plan to destroy America? Who would want to do that?"

Rosslyn nodded, "I don't know, let's see what this is all about; I can't believe my dad would leave me information that he didn't think was useful or important. He wasn't much for frivolous conversation; when he spoke, he had something to say." She continued reading the document: "*The Globalists Take Over of America. Proof that the New World Order was planned with uncanny accuracy back in 1958. There are plans in place by an elite cabal to systemically disassemble the sovereignty of the United States. A part of that plan is to induce the gradual surrender of American sovereignty, step-by-step, to various international organizations — of which the United Nations is the most outstanding, but far from the only example: Here are the globalists aims for the United States:* One, *expand government and be as wasteful as possible.* Two, *higher and much higher taxes. Three, increase and unbalance the budget despite increasingly higher taxes. Four, uncontrollable inflation of our currency. Five, government controls of prices, wages, and materials to combat inflation. Six, increased socialistic controls over every operation of our economy and every activity of our daily lives. This is to be accompanied naturally and automatically by a correspondingly huge increase in the size of our bureaucracy and both the cost and reach of our domestic government. Seven, far more centralization of power in Washington D.C. with the practical elimination of our state lines. Eight, the steady advance of federal aid to control our educational system, leading to complete federalization of our public education. Nine, a constant hammering into the American consciousness of the horror of modern warfare. Extol the beauties and absolute necessities of peace, peace always on communist terms, of course. And then, the constant willingness of the American people to allow the steps of appeasement by our government which amounts to the surrender of the rest of the free world and the United States itself.*"

"Good grief! Those things are all being done now in our country. These globalists want to destroy the last bastion of freedom in the entire world. The only reason they would do this is for total control. When communist dictators reach power, they always disarm the population, leaving them defenseless to their brutality. I remember my grandparents telling how the Nazis used gun confiscation to disarm and repress their political enemies. This allowed the Nazis to be even more ruthless. Look what happened to the Jews in Germany," Ruth Ann explained.

Rosslyn silently read a handwritten page from the diary:

Rosslyn, I had an opportunity to hear this author speak, and shortly thereafter, I saw the corporate media and others destroy his credibility. During my time employed by The Agency, I learned that the author was correct, and the attack he suffered was only a part of the plan they (we) always use to discredit and silence those who were smart enough to figure things out and to speak up about what they found. The author was a genius, and he was very correct. Our government and many of its insiders and their families are the true enemies within. I don't mean to imply that we do not also have foreign enemies. But the most dangerous enemy to our freedoms and way of life are domestic, and they are hidden in plain sight. They like to place things right in front of your eyes. Then they deny the fact that what you are seeing is even there. The Agency has mastered fooling the public. And before my retirement, I discovered that they are among the many enemies within. They, too, are intending and working to destroy America. If you are reading this, I am no longer around to answer your many questions. I have left behind enough information to erase any doubt you may have about our own government. I regret leaving this information to you this way, but it was the only way to protect your and your mother's lives. This is not a crazy conspiracy. It is a true and very real conspiracy, and the conspirators are working for our own government. They are above the laws because they enforce the laws, and they are above investigation because they are the investigators.

Love, Dad.

Rosslyn closed the book, "I think that's enough for tonight, Ruth Ann; maybe we can read some more tomorrow night."

"That's an excellent idea; I'm on information overload, thanks to Jim. What you just read reminded me so much of what my grandparents described of Germany before it turned into a living hell for them. The thought that America is going down that path is more than disturbing to me. I hope we don't have nightmares. Good night, Rosslyn."

"Good night, Ruth Ann."

thirty

The following morning every member of the group was seated and quietly awaiting what else Jim had in store for them.

Jim was the last person to return, "I can see you are all curious as to where this is going to take us."

Tom, who had been silent, finally spoke, "Jim, before you continue, I was skimming through Chip's files, and I came across a document everyone needs to hear. This information was written by an ex-NSA official and published by Wikileaks."

"Let's hear it, Tom. Chip was definitely onto something, and whatever he uncovered could have been the cause of his death," Jim said.

Tom stood up and read, "*Mossad Ran 9/11 Arab Hijacker Terrorist Operation. British intelligence reported that the Israeli Mossad ran the Arab hijacker cells that were blamed for the attacks on 9/11. Prime Minister Tony Blair suppressed this information. Mossad infiltration teams made up of six Israelis, consisting of two cells each with three agents, were involved. One Mossad unit consisting of six Egyptian and Yemeni-born Jews infiltrated the Hamburg cell. They first traveled to Amsterdam, where they submitted to the operational control of the Mossad's Europe Station, which runs out of the El Al Airline complex at Amsterdam's Schiphol International Airport. This Mossad unit then traveled to Hamburg, contacting members who believed they were sent from Osama bin Laden. Ephraim Halevy, the Mossad chief, controlled this operation. The other team flew to New York then onto Florida, where they began their operation. They were in Miami, Vero Beach, West Palm Beach, Del Ray Beach, and Hollywood. Israeli 'art students,' already under investigation by the DEA, lived in the vicinity. In August, the Mossad team* *flew to Boston's Logan International Airport, where security was contracted to Mossad's International Consultants on Targeted Security or ICTS. ICTS's owners were politically connected to the radical Likud Party, particularly the Netanyahu faction and Jerusalem's mayor Ehud Olmert. Olmert interceded with New York Mayor Rudy Giuliani to release five Urban Moving Systems employees from prison, identified as Mossad agents. These five 'Dancing Israelis' were the only suspects arrested on 9/11. The Mossad teams sent regular coded reports on the progress of the 9/11 operation to Tel Aviv via the Israeli embassy in Washington D.C. A Pentagon source conveyed that Americans tied to the media effort to pin 9/11 on Arab hijackers were present in the Israeli embassy on September 10th. Most of these Americans are well-known to cable news television audiences. By mid-August, the Mossad teams reported to Tel Aviv that the final plans for 9/11 were complete. The Florida team documented the enrollment of Arabs in flight schools. Both Mossad units avoided mentioning the World Trade Center or targets in Washington D.C. in their coded messages to Tel Aviv. Halevy covered his tracks by notifying the CIA of a 'general threat of Arab terrorists' to a nuclear plant somewhere on the East Coast of the United States. CIA director George Tenet dismissed Halevy's warning as too non-specific. The FBI ordered no high alert. FBI director Robert Mueller admitted they could not uncover a single piece of paper either in the United States or Afghanistan that mentioned any aspect of the 9/11 plot.*

The Mossad team set up safe houses for the quick exfiltration of the agents from the United States. Intelligence sources reported that two employees of El Al Airlines at JFK airport confirmed that hours after the FAA had grounded all civilian flights, an El Al 747 took off from JFK bound for Tel Aviv's Ben Gurion International Airport. The two El Al employees were not Israeli nationals but legal immigrants from Ecuador. They reported the flight left JFK at 4:11pm, and the U.S. Department of Defense authorized its departure. U.S. military officials were on the scene at JFK and were involved with the air traffic control authorities, who were ordered to clear the flight for take-off. Transportation Secretary Mineta ordered all civilian flights to be grounded at 9:45am that day. The

Mossad teams were listed as El Al employees on the passenger manifest.

These Mossad operatives later infiltrated cells in Syria, where they were arrested by Syrian intelligence. French intelligence figured out that other Jewish Mossad agents infiltrated Yemen and the United Arab Emirates, posing as radical members of the Muslim Brotherhood. They were involved in covert funding for terrorist activities. This Israeli funding for Al Qaeda was fully known to Saudi intelligence. The Mossad's clandestine support of the Taliban and Al Qaeda in Afghanistan, had it been uncovered, could have exposed the Mossad as the mastermind behind 9/11.

For the Israeli Mossad, the successful 9/11 'false flag' operation was a victory beyond expectations. The Bush administration, backed by the Blair government, attacked, and occupied Iraq, deposed Saddam Hussein, and put pressure on Israel's other adversaries, including Iran, Syria, Pakistan, Hamas, and Lebanese Hezbollah.

This document ends with reference to Netanyahu's comment shortly after 9/11 on U.S. television. Netanyahu said: *'It is very good!'* It now appears that Netanyahu, in his zeal, blew Mossad's cover as the masterminds of 9/11."

Silence occupied the room again. The sound of a distant siren could be heard. For a long time, no one spoke until Max said, "Wait a darn minute, Jim, you earlier said that David Edger, CIA station chief in Berlin, bragged that *his* unit infiltrated and controlled the Hamburg cell. Now we have British intelligence saying that the Israeli Mossad infiltrated and was controlling this same Hamburg cell. This is beginning to look like one of the spy versus spy cartoons from Mad magazine." He let out one of his famous belly-laughs, which broke the silence in the Oval Office.

"Well, now, this explains how nearly half of those accused hijackers managed to find the same Jewish realtor in Florida," Ruth Ann commented flatly.

"It also explains why the CIA and the FBI lost interest in these so-called hijackers," Jim said. "Remember, the first two operatives lived with an FBI informant. Atta and Marwan rented a room from a CIA pilot from the Iran-Contra scandal. Three of these guys gave the Pensacola Naval Air Station as their address in the United States on their immigration forms."

"Three of them? That sounds like the Mossad teams this NSA guy was referring to," Ruth Ann added.

"It sounds like these teams were trying to look like Arabs by taking flying lessons," Max mumbled.

Jerry Reitz added, "from my personal experience with the Israelis, this description of how they operate in teams is without question."

"In Israel, there are both Arabs and Jews, and unless they are wearing a yarmulka, it can be very difficult to tell them apart," Ruth Ann said.

thirty-one

Tom continued, "Another leaked document Chip reveals Yemen's former President Saleh's secret phone calls and provides evidence that the CIA's supported the very same terrorists it claimed to be waging war against for nearly two decades.

Two phone calls between President Saleh and CIA Director George Tenet were released following a coup in Yemen. Their authenticity has been confirmed, and the calls took place in 2001. The CIA director can be heard pressuring President Saleh to release a detained individual involved in the bombing of the USS Cole in October of 2000. In one call, Tenet is asked by Saleh's translator for the name of the individual in question. *'I don't want to give his name over the phone,'* Tenet tells him. Saleh noted that the FBI team investigating the USS Cole arrived in Sanaa and asked Tenet if the FBI personnel could meet with him to discuss the matter. Tenet refused, saying, *'this is my person, my problem, and my issue. The man must be released! I have talked to everybody in my government; I told them I would make this call.'*

As Saleh's translator is delivering Tenet's message to him, the CIA director cuts him off and says that the man in question *'must be released within 48 hours.'*"

Vera asked, "If Tenet refused to say the prisoner's name, how did he expect President Saleh to know who he was referring to?"

Tom answered, "The document also claims that the deputy-head of Yemeni Security and Intelligence Service suggested that the person in question could have been dual American-Yemeni citizen Anwar Al-Awlaki. However, Tenet is more likely referring to 9/11 hijacker Khalid Almihdhar, whom Yemen accused of being the mastermind behind the USS Cole bombing."

"Could the claim about Al-Awlaki be CIA disinformation meant to cover up the fact that Tenet was demanding the release of one of the future accused 9/11 hijackers?" Ruth Ann asked.

Tom said, "I think I can explain that. Chip attached an ABC news article dated May 31, 2001, stating the U.S. investigating team moved from the port of Aden to Sanaa. So, the timing indicates it was most likely Khalid Almihdhar that Tenet was referring to since Al Awlaki was the imam at the Mosque in Falls Church, Virginia, at that time.

"That is exactly how the CIA would play the game. They would drop a story claiming Tenet was trying to get Al Awlaki released when it was one of the 9/11 patsies he was referring to. The question I have is, why would Tenet demand this a future accused 9/11 hijacker be released?" Jerry asked.

Jim nodded, "That right there, Jerry explains why there are so many conflicting stories about who did what, when, and what did our intelligence agencies know that caused them to look the other way? The conflicting details of everyone they claim were involved makes this journey very convoluted."

"I followed the USS Cole story closely because one of my old Navy buddies had a son on that destroyer. I was flabbergasted to learn that the U.S. Ambassador to Yemen had a serious personality clash with the lead FBI investigator, John O'Neill. O'Neill and his FBI team were in Yemen less than a month before Ambassador Bodine booted them out. She refused to allow him to re-enter. When young Bush was inaugurated in January 2001, O'Neill was still trying to return to Yemen. He suspected the Cole was struck by a torpedo fired from an Israeli Dolphin submarine. Between the Ambassador and the newly installed Bush administration, O'Neill was never able to return to Yemen. He was still trying as late as the summer of 2001. That played a role in his decision to retire from the FBI in late August. He suspected the CIA and the State Department were preventing him from continuing his investigation for multiple reasons," Jerry Reitz explained.

"This sounds like a cover-up for the USS Cole bombing. The real story of who was responsible was never to see the light of day," Max complained.

"To make matters worse, the CIA and the FBI played good cop bad cop for months. This appears to be a cover-up for an intelligence operation. After 9/11, the FBI claimed the CIA would not share information about the first two hijackers from Kuala Lumpur. Yet, they met a CIA asset and lived with an FBI informant in California. It's well known that the FBI uses informants to infiltrate groups like militias or any group they perceive as a threat to the U.S. government. Considering that Yemen blamed the bombing of the USS Cole on Khalid Al Mihdhar, there is no excuse he was issued a multiple entry visa into the U.S. in June of 2001. If Tenet refused to say the name of who he was referring to, I would bet he was covering up the fact that someone in prison in Yemen was one of his assets," Jerry explained.

"There must be a good reason Tenet refused to say the man's name," Ruth Ann added.

Jerry shrugged his shoulders and tilted his head back, "for all we know, this kid could have been an Israeli General's son and not at all who we were led to believe. Intelligence agents are known for having multiple passports and fake identification. I suspect they had phony U.S. passports to get back into the states."

"A Yemeni General later pointed out that the CIA trained their operatives in Yemen then sent them abroad to conduct terrorist acts for the CIA. The Americans could then blame Yemen," Tom said.

Max interrupted, "This makes sense and explains why the U.S. government later killed Al Awlaki with a drone strike. If he knew that these 9/11 patsies were Tenet's lackeys, he could implicate the entire set-up. This means that everyone in our government, intelligence, and media were either hoodwinked or knowingly played along with this charade. And everyone who knows about this travesty knows that the minute they open their mouths, they sign their own death warrant."

"True, Max," Jerry agreed. "The CIA is famous for silencing anyone, including their own, that becomes a liability."

Vera had been searching the internet, "I know Wikipedia is not the most dependable source, but this says, 'Six days after the 9/11 attacks, Al-Awlaki suggested on the

Islam Online website that Israeli intelligence agents might have been responsible for the 9/11 attacks."

"What else did Chip have in his file?" Jim asked.

"The Yemeni General explained that al-Qaeda and ISIS were not organic, but state-backed organizations. ISIS is armed and funded by the CIA with both weapons and vehicles. The same applies to al-Qaeda, which is supported by intelligence organizations in Washington D.C. and other countries. Anwar al-Awlaki and others were being used as tools by U.S. intelligence agencies," Tom said.

"That describes 9/11 in a nutshell," Max said.

Tom continued reading from a document in Chip's file, "Al-Awlaki's status as a CIA asset explains his relationship with several of the accused 9/11 hijackers. Awlaki's father was a Fulbright Scholar who studied in New Mexico and later worked for the Yemeni government."

"The CIA probably recruited his father at that time," Ruth Ann said.

"Following 9/11, al-Awlaki was one of Washington D.C.'s go-to Muslim sources, considered to be a moderate Islamic voice with positive views toward the West. He did not shy away from publicly condemning Islamic terrorism and the 9/11 attacks. The New York Times, National Public Radio, and The Washington Post, among others, turned to him as their default Muslim voice," Tom added.

Max interrupted, "The deep state always has to have a boogie man, even if they create him themselves, which they no doubt have been doing all along."

Tom continued reading, "Al-Awlaki became the first imam in history to conduct a prayer service in the U.S. Capitol. Months after the 9/11 attacks, Al-Awlaki was a guest at the Pentagon as part of an outreach program to the Muslim community. Declassified documents reveal that Al-Awlaki exchanged emails and voice messages with an FBI agent that same year. An FBI memo shows Al-Awlaki's name in the subject line along with: 'Synopsis: Asset reporting.' In 2010, Al-Awlaki was placed on the U.S. kill list as an individual associated with al-Qaeda. The following year, the CIA liquidated their former asset with a drone strike."

"He became a liability to the deep state," Max added.

Joel Sherman checked his watch, "What do you say we close for the day? Again, this was a great deal of information to digest. I'm sure we all will need some time to think about everything we have heard. Let's meet tomorrow at 10 am."

thirty-two

Joel's mind was filled with details from the meetings. He knew too much, which forced him to do one of two things, depending on the outcome of the upcoming presidential election. His mind ran through a couple of different scenarios. He was confident he held the support of most Americans. Recently he discovered that some retired generals had software that was used to manipulate elections in other countries. They intended to turn their internet influencers on social media against his administration. There was suspicion that they might steal the election using intercepted data packets from the electronic voting machines. Joel knew this evil force fighting against him and recruited professional sports figures and Hollywood stars to speak out against him. He felt the war machine working twenty-four-seven to replace him with a globalist.

The phone on his desk buzzed, "Mr. President, Jerry Reitz is here; he says it's important that he see you for a few moments."

"Send him in, thank you," Joel responded.

"Sir, I'm sorry to drop in so late, but something has surfaced I felt you should know about. Considering everything we have reviewed in our recent meetings; this adds a new dimension to the situation.

"What is it, Jerry?" Joel asked.

"Sir, I was contacted by an NSA analyst earlier this evening. He picked up some chatter, and it concerns you and your upcoming campaign. This information falls into the beyond outrage category. Sir, we may have the makings of a coup d'état. I know men who took part in similar actions in South America, Chile, to be exact. I have read enough history combined with my inside knowledge of how our intelligence agencies work that I can recognize the pattern."

"A coup?" Joel sounded shocked.

"Sir, it appears that is their intention, but they will follow their playbook," Jerry explained.

"They have a coup playbook?" Joel asked.

"Everything they do is methodically planned out. Coup d'états are no exception. They will follow the same process they have used in other countries. With this new intelligence chatter I received, I can see that the process has already begun," Jerry said.

"It has? You mean they have already begun to remove me when I just decided to throw my hat in the ring?" Joel asked.

"Let me explain; the process begins with discrediting and demeaning the target. The media is an extension of the CIA will publicly question your every decision. They will ridicule every personal detail from your speeches. This will begin a constant battering of 'fake news. Through this constant barrage of negative attitudes directed at you and the First Lady, they are convinced they will be able to say anything. Their audience will believe it and vote for your opponent. It is a form of brainwashing, and they have perfected the technique. If they need to pull in fake paper ballots or intercept the data packets from the voting machines, they intend to do whatever it takes to defeat you. Their agenda is to promote socialism, Marxism and to bring on full-blown communism to this country eventually."

"Jerry, what they have done to Vera and me with their sophomoric personal attacks, makes what they did to earlier administrations seem like child's play. I have done everything a president could do to promote success, create new jobs, and reduce government regulations. But still, they create false stories and never report anything positive. If I use an umbrella in the rain or don't use an umbrella in the rain, they mock and ridicule me for days on end until they find something else to nitpick about," Joel complained.

"What you have witnessed is only the beginning. The press is the propaganda arm of your opponents' political party; every channel and newspaper will hammer on you," Jerry said.

"Jerry, are all of our intelligence agencies working for the globalist agenda?" Joel asked. "And what happens if they succeed?"

"If they succeed, the global communist agenda will succeed, and we will have lost our Republic," Jerry said solemnly.

"I am now even more keenly aware of what the CIA is capable of doing. Their history is gruesome. I never imagined they would turn against America," Joel said, then paused. "So, there is a group of global communists that control our intelligence agencies, our State Department, and the mainstream media, and they are so dedicated to their communist cause that they will attempt to overthrow or steal the next election?

"That is exactly right, Mr. President," Jerry affirmed. "These Communists have managed to gain positions of power that might make that coup not only thinkable but possible."

"Are these people willing to enslave their own children and grandchildren into communism without giving a thought to the horrific outcome of their actions?" Joel asked.

"History shows us that the media is always the first to get wiped out when events like this occur. So, the media talking heads probably believe their multi-million-dollar contracts will continue and will save them. This country will need a leader tough enough and strong enough to guide it either from the White House or from the outside," Jerry informed the President.

"Thank you, Jerry, for providing me with this information. I will bring the First Lady in on this information, but I can assure you we have made our decision to run in this election, and we will not back down," President Sherman said as he placed his hand on Jerry's shoulder and looked at him straight in the eye.

thirty-three

"I put a tracking device on agent Smith when we met with him earlier. I figured that was the best way to make sure he was not on the property when we lit it up. No need to kill two government agents unnecessarily," the CIA officer said.

"I have no doubt this will send the intended message to Joel Sherman. His presidency needs to come to an end, or there will be more of this action to follow," the other agent confirmed.

"Pete over at Creech has the drone circling the city. As soon we set the illuminating target on the house, he will launch the hellfire missiles," the first agent laughed. "Coffee, tea, or boom!"

The agents were silent as the inflatable raft traveled toward Alki beach.
Once Vera's house came into view, they slowed the craft to an idle and allowed momentum to draw them onto the beach.

"Kill that motor. The target is set. As soon as I push us back from the beach, signal Pete with the code to let them fly," the officer said.

"Copy that," the other agent said with a nod.

Moments later, the senior officer jumped back into the raft. The agents began paddling as fast as they could.

Jenny woke up to the loudest explosion she had ever heard. She was so startled her hands were shaking. Her first thought was that North Korea launched a nuclear missile, and it hit downtown Seattle. Then, to her left, she noticed an unusual light flickering off the south wall of her bedroom. She sprang to her window and could see Vera's entire house engulfed in flames. "What in the world?" She screamed out loud.

Her first thought was to call 911.

"911, what is your emergency?" The voice answered.

"I would like to report a house fire, it is next door to me, and there are flames everywhere!"

"Do you know if anyone was in the home?" Asked the dispatcher asked.

"No, nobody was home; I know the owner, she is not there," Jenny explained. "Hurry."

Her dog started barking. She ran to the back door to get a leash in case the fire department asked her to evacuate. She grabbed her iPad, cell phone, and purse, then threw on a jogging suit. She remembered an open window upstairs and quickly ran up to close it. The fire trucks were arriving, with their flashing lights strobing through every window. Her house was beginning to fill with smoke. The sound of sirens brought more trucks and police to Vera's house filled the night air. She attached the leash to her dog, "Let's go for a walk."

A red pickup with a Seattle Fire Department logo on the door pulled up next to her as she waited to cross the street. "Are you a fire chief?" She asked the man as he secured his helmet strap under his chin.

"I sure am ma'am, is there something you need?" The chief asked

"I live next door; I woke up to a super loud blast, and then I saw the house was in flames. Something blew up; it had to be a bomb or something," Jenny explained.

"Why would anyone want to bomb your neighbor's house in the middle of the night?" He asked.

"It's not just any old neighbor's house. This is the second home of Vera Sherman," Jenny answered.

"Vera Sherman? Are you referring to the current First Lady of the United States, Vera Sherman?" The chief asked.

"That would be the one," Jenny replied.

"Thank you, ma'am. I'm afraid you are going to have several fire officials and the FBI visiting next door for the next week or so."

"Oh, and you might want to know there is a secret service detail assigned to the house, they don't live in it, but they're not far away.

"Got it," the chief acknowledged as he began walking toward a ladder truck parked nearby.

Jenny and her dog walked away from the commotion and onto the beach. She noticed a small boat in Elliott Bay. It was unusual for anyone to be boating on the Puget Sound at that hour. It was too early for fishermen. She sat on a nearby bench and watched as the small boat met up with a motor yacht. The yacht slowly headed west until its running lights disappeared.

She checked the time; it was still early in D.C.; nevertheless, she typed a text to Vera's cell: "THERE HAS BEEN AN EMERGENCY AT YOUR HOUSE. CALL ME IMMEDIATELY."

Before she could decide where to go next, her phone rang.

"Jenny, what happened? What kind of emergency at the house?" Vera asked.

"Vera, a super loud boom woke me up; when I looked out the window, your house was engulfed in flames. I called the fire department, but your house is destroyed," Jenny explained.

"Vera was in stunned silence. When she finally spoke, she said, "Your house is not damaged, is it?"

"The fire department came quickly and is managing to keep the flames from spreading. I only experienced a little smoke damage, but that can be remedied easy enough," Jenny replied.

"What about the Secret Service agents? They weren't hurt, were they?" Vera asked.

"I met the fire chief and told him about the agents; he was going to keep an eye out for them. I don't think they were on the property when it happened," Jenny said.

"I am relieved your place was not damaged. I will take care of the agents from here. If you happen to get a look when the fire department is in clean-up mode, let me know if anything at all is salvageable," Vera said.

"Will do, Vera."

After hearing the news about her house, Vera ran sobbing to find Joel to convey the news. "What is the matter? Has Kelli died?" Joel asked.

"No, it's worse than that. My house in Seattle has burned to the ground, and everything in it has been destroyed. That house means so much to me," Vera cried.

Joel put his arms around Vera to comfort her as best he could. "I will have Homeland Security investigate this for us. If they smell cordite, we will know it wasn't a group of kids breaking into it in the middle of the night," Joel whispered into her ear.

"Cordite, what makes you think that?" She asked.

"Oh, it's just a hunch, but I will have it thoroughly investigated," Joel assured.

thirty-four

President Sherman welcomed the group back to the Oval Office. "Good morning, everyone. Are you prepared to dive into another day of grueling discovery?"

Everyone looked exhausted, but they all nodded and did their best to look excited to begin. Vera ordered coffee and juice to be delivered with a compliment of cinnamon rolls. The President turned to Jim and said, "please continue with your presentation."

Jim began, "the news media exposed a meeting between the Chairman of the House Permanent Select Committee on Intelligence Porter Goss, Senator Bob Graham and the head of the Pakistani intelligence services, Lt. General Mahmoud Ahmed the morning of September 11th. Ahmed ran a spy agency notoriously close to Osama bin Laden and the Taliban. He wired a hundred thousand dollars to Atta shortly before 9/11."

"Wasn't anyone questioning the involvement of those two congressmen?" Ruth Ann asked.

"Knowing what we know now, the fact that the media never raised questions about this breakfast meeting in D.C. makes a lot more sense," Max added.

"In his junior year at Yale, Porter Goss was recruited by the CIA. He spent ten years in the Directorate of Operations in clandestine services," Jim said.

Max spoke up, "You mean the super spies I call spooks?"

"Goss worked in Latin America and later in Europe, where he recruited and trained foreign agents. He also took part in the Cuban missile crisis in 1962. People claim he was part of the CIA hit squad known as Operation 40, which played a role in the assassination of JFK. Recently uncovered photographs showed members of this assassination team in Mexico City that included Goss, CIA pilot Barry Seal, the body double of Lee Harvey

Oswald, and some of the Watergate burglars. Goss had plenty of connections to the intelligence community," Jim explained.

Max interrupted, "Chip told us how all of these spy agencies work together. Porter Goss's connections to Osama bin Laden are loud and clear."

Jim continued, "It wasn't easy, but I uncovered another wire transfer to the hijackers that took place at a convenience store in Venice, Florida. An additional wire transfer was made to Atta and Marwan at the store owned by a Lebanese man by the last name of Chams. The wire transfer was for seventy thousand dollars, and it was from the United Arab Emirates."

Ruth Ann spoke up, "Excuse me, Jim, that name Chams is a common Lebanese Jewish name. We had neighbors in Chicago by that name. They fled the violence in Beirut and came to America. I remember them because they attended services at our temple."

"Oh, I would not have known that Ruth Ann. That's an interesting detail. I thought it odd that a small corner convenience store would handle such a large money transfer. This Chams fellow was also a partial owner in the *Vegas on Venice* gambling yacht that the D.C. lobbyist Jack Abramoff was involved with. Who else was seen on that gambling yacht?" Jim asked.

"Weren't several of the accused hijackers seen on that yacht with Jack Abramoff?" Ruth Ann asked.

"That's correct, Ruth Ann. Chams' other partners were Ira Goldfarb and Max Burge. To put this all together, Mr. Burge owned several of the planes at Huffman Aviation where it's claimed Atta and Marwan took flying lessons."

"Well, that is an interesting connection, Jimbo," said Max with a chuckle.

"Now that Ruth Ann has recognized Chams as a Jewish name, the association with Ira Goldfarb and Jack Abramoff makes a lot more sense. Some investigators have tried to connect Chams to Islam or the Arab terrorists, but that is not where this takes us. Chams mysteriously closed the convenience store about two weeks after 9/11. The FBI arrived in Venice within hours of the attacks and interviewed a local cab driver who recognized Atta and Marwan's photographs. He told the FBI that they were often hanging around the store and Chams' nearby apartment. However, the FBI was not interested in looking at Chams or interviewing him. I have been unable to find a 302 showing that Chams was ever questioned by the FBI," Jim said.

"That's like how they treated Nick Berg. He had an obvious connection to Moussaoui, but they did not want to see it. The FBI was able to demonize Moussaoui because he wanted to fly the simulator. They assumed he was a hijacker even though they knew he wasn't," Ruth Ann said.

"Reporters tracked down Chams' sister who informed them that he moved to San Diego to help the FBI," Jim added.

"That explains why the FBI didn't interview him, and an official copy of their interview was never found," Max said.

"I guess it does, Max," Jim smiled. "Four years later, when Lockheed Martin was doing their due diligence before a merger with another defense contractor called Titan, Chams' name popped up in a twenty-two-million-dollar wrongful termination lawsuit. The suit was filed not in Lebanon as you might expect but in Saudi Arabia. Titan admitted that Chams had been employed as a contractor, but there is no information on how long he worked there. Nor was I able to learn if he was employed with them while he owned the convenience store. Nevertheless, for some unknown reason, he felt that his work was worth twenty-two million dollars. Titan was the defense contractor that ran the Abu Ghraib prison in Iraq. Several of their employees were charged with rape and torture for mistreatment of the prisoners held there."

"Didn't you say earlier that the death of Nick Berg was blamed on the abuse of the prisoners at Abu Ghraib?" Rosslyn asked.

"Yes, Rosslyn, that was how the story was reported," Jim replied. "Titan also was fined 2.5 million dollars for fixing a presidential election in the small African country of Benin. They settled the lawsuit and paid that amount in 2005 for an election held in March of 2001. Titan had its eye on setting up telecommunication systems in Benin. The president they cheated for was returning to power and had previously become president via a coup."

"Did they really admit they stole a presidential election? That sounds more like the CIA than a private defense company," Max said. "Maybe all of these money-grubbing military-industrial complex joints are running more than just their companies. Eisenhower warned us about this, am I right?"

Jim continued, "He certainly did, Max. Titan's history is interesting; they were absorbed by L3 Communications and briefly partnered with SkyWay Communications. In the spring of 2006, a SkyWay DC-9 aircraft was captured carrying a five-ton load of cocaine. That incident indicates that Titan was acting as an intelligence front company and that they engaged in some serious drug-running out of Central and South America. Most of the upper management from Titan later formed a company called Kratos. Kratos specializes in technologies such as directed-energy weapons, satellite communications, cyber warfare, microwave electronics, and missile defense."

"Let me get this straight in my head, Jim." Max spoke up, "This Lebanese Jewish guy ran a convenience store in Venice, Florida. He handled a seventy-thousand-dollar wire transfer from the Middle East for Atta and Marwan. Atta and Marwan hung around his store and apartment all the time, but when the FBI showed up right after the attacks, they were not interested in interviewing the store owner, but they did interview a local cab driver. His sister said he went to San Diego to help the FBI, and four years later, he sues Titan for wrongful termination. Titan is behind the famous Abu Ghraib prison, and its employees took part in torturing Iraqis. Then one of their subsidiaries gets busted with five tons of cocaine, and nobody in the U.S. government seems concerned. Were you able to find out if Titan settled this lawsuit with him? And what in the world was he doing as a contractor that was worth twenty-two million dollars?" Max shook his head, hoping to make this story make more sense.

"That's correct, Max, and no, I never found out if he was working as a contractor for Titan while he owned the convenience store or went to work for them much later. The lawsuit could have been his way of getting hush money," Jim answered.

"Seventy thousand dollars is a lot of money if you are going to pull off a suicide mission.

Yet, this money came *in* from the Middle East; they were not sending their money home, right? Why did the FBI overlook this convenience store owner? Looking at the people the FBI showed no interest in, they appear to have been working for intelligence agencies," Rosslyn said.

Jerry Reitz chimed in, "I know I have mentioned this before, but I need to reiterate, any money transfers to and from the Middle East would have been captured and logged by the NSA. There is no way that this wire transfer would not have been questioned by our intelligence, unless…" Jerry paused, "unless the intelligence agency was involved."

thirty-five

"Tom, I have not had enough free time to explore Chip's files. Did you have more documents that you wanted to share with us?" Jim asked.

"I do have more information, " Tom explained, "Chip accumulated several articles and excerpts from books about the Joint Chiefs of Staff Chairman, General Hugh Shelton. The General was scheduled to fly to Europe on September 11, 2001. Chip's documents and notes will give you something to think about. General Richard Myers was the acting Chairman of the Joint Chiefs on 9/11. Both Generals and at least one of their aides wrote books about 9/11, so Chip compared their testimonies. According to Shelton's book, his flight left Andrews Air Force base at 7:30 am. He was aboard a modified C-135, the military version of a Boeing 707, nicknamed the Speckled Trout. This was not the plane he would normally fly since it was reserved for the Air Force Chief of Staff and Shelton was Army. Chip managed to find the air traffic control flight strips that showed his plane took off at 7:09 am. Chip was familiar with this aircraft since it was retrofitted and upgraded while he was working at Edwards Air Force base. The Speckled Trout was a flying command and control aircraft. It could command our military, make phone calls around the world, manipulate radar, communicate with fighter jets; you name it, it could do it. Now, here's where Chip's information gets interesting. Shelton's account claimed that one hundred minutes into the flight, which would be one hour and forty minutes or 9:10 am, he was informed of the second strike on the twin towers. However, since we know his flight left at 7:09 am and 100 minutes later would be 8:49 am, the second strike on the towers did not happen until 9:03 am. Shelton claimed he immediately gave the order to turn the aircraft around. He explained, by this time, flights from overseas were not being allowed to enter

U.S. airspace. However, Chip's Freedom of Information Act data showed that flights had not been diverted until at least one hour later, around 9:45 am. General Shelton explains that the FAA denied him entry into U.S. airspace, but at 8:49 am, there had only been one event at the North Tower at 8:46 am. No flights had been diverted or redirected, and initially, the only airport shutdowns were New York and Boston. Washington D.C. area was not affected as flights were both taking off and landing normally. When he learned the Pentagon was struck one hour later, he again ordered the pilot to return to Andrews Air Force Base. He claimed shortly afterward; clearance was granted. He stated that they flew directly over Manhattan and the Twin Towers on returning to Andrews just a few minutes after they collapsed. The plane then vectored directly to Andrews and landed within the hour. Let me set a timeline for you, the towers both collapsed by 10:28 am, so the Speckled Trout would have flown over close to 10:30 am, they would have landed about 11:30 am at Joint Base Andrews," Tom explained.

"That's right, from New York City to Andrews would be about thirty minutes flying time," Jim added.

Tom continued, "Chip has an excerpt from Shelton's book that reads, *'At Andrews, we were met by an entourage of patrol cars and motorcycle cops who escorted us, lights flashing and sirens blaring, through the eerily deserted streets of the city to the Pentagon.'* Upon arrival at the Pentagon, he went to his office and was updated by General Myers and others. He claimed he then examined the damage to the outside of the Pentagon, after which he went to the National Military Command Center inside the Pentagon.

Chip's notes point out serious problems with Shelton's account of his movements. If his plane flew over the towers, as he said, *'just minutes after they collapsed,'* he would have been back at Andrews by 11:30 am, noon at the very latest. That would indicate that air traffic control gave them immediate permission to return to Andrews when first requested. The drive to the Pentagon is twenty-eight minutes without a police escort. Once he landed at Andrews, the duties of Chairman of the Joint Chiefs of Staff would have been restored to him, and he would have been responsible for decisions made from that moment forward.

But General Myers wrote in his book that the exchange of power was not completed until 5:40 pm at the Pentagon. Considering what happened on the ground that morning, it is impossible to believe that Shelton would be out of touch, incognito, or not available for five hours.

The flight strip logs from the air traffic controllers show that Shelton's aircraft landed at Andrews at 4:40 pm. Chip found in a radar file the Trout requested at 2:40 pm a new flight plan from the air to return to Andrews. They requested to fly direct to Andrews, from somewhere near the Canadian border, which is roughly a two-hour flight."

"Why do you suppose he is he lying?" Max asked.

"I don't know for certain Max, but his aide also wrote a book in which she stated that the drive from Andrews to the Pentagon was in *the late afternoon*. In an article dated September 2011, Shelton's flight navigator claimed that the first three hours of the flight went smoothly until the BBC reported on the Twin Tower strikes. That indicated they learned about the event at 10 am.

"So, they learned about the attack from British radio and not from the Pentagon?" Vera asked.

"That is hard to believe since, by the time the South Tower was hit, most of the country thought we were at war," Max commented.

"The navigator reported that the plane did turn, but for the first couple of hours, they didn't have clearance, so they went into a holding pattern near Greenland. According to his story, it was approaching noon, and they were in a holding pattern over the Atlantic. He claimed that it wasn't easy getting security clearance, but the VIP passenger is noted right here on this data file from Boston Center. Notice the A2 designation right here," Tom pointed to his document showing everyone where to look. "I can say from experience, this statement is again untrue, the VIP designation was noted at the time they filed their return flight plan, and every air controller would know exactly what that meant. There is no way they were denied returning to Andrews. By noon, the only aircraft allowed in the air were military or law enforcement," Tom explained.

"That is absolutely correct, Tom," Jim added.

"The General could have phoned the Pentagon, the White House, or Boston Center and been given an immediate clearance," Tom said.

"So, Chip discovered that Shelton and two other people traveling with him all told different stories?" Ruth Ann asked.

"If the General claimed he arrived back at Andrews five hours before he did, why would he be lying?" Vera asked.

Tom answered, "Chip scribbled a note here on the margin of this report that says, *'look deeper into this.'* So, he must have been intending to follow up with answers to those questions."

Since it was the Chairman of the Joint Chiefs of Staff in the sixties, who cooked up Operation Northwoods, you don't suppose he had something to do with what is looking like Northwoods version 2.0, do you? We all know how these freaks love to put things out there, right in your face," Max grumbled.

"Do you think he was coordinating something that didn't make the official story like that US Airways 757 navigating across the Atlantic? The Speckled Trout could have been extremely helpful in keeping their primary radar hidden and giving them the waypoints for navigation to cross the Atlantic," Jim said.

"Chip also noted that General Shelton retired at the end of September 2001, and General Richard Myers was sworn in on Oct. 1, 2001. His final handwritten note at the bottom of this page is *'Cui bono, to who is it a benefit,'*" Tom revealed.

"I want to know why the General was dishonest. He spent a nine-hour day flying in a holding pattern. My flight attendant intuition tells me he was somehow involved in this operation," Vera said.

Tom continued, "Chip had an in-depth biography on twenty-six American and Israeli Jewish men that played some role in 9/11. We need to go over more information at this time, but considering what Max just shared, I am sure you will find their connections to the event intriguing. Chip also found FBI 302 forms from interviews with people who witnessed the now-famous five dancing Israelis. These include interviews with state police and others who encountered Urban Moving System vans in Pennsylvania and between New York City and Boston on 9/11. These five were seen dancing on and around a van that later tested positive for explosives. They were witnessed and photographed celebrating in New Jersey across from where the towers were seen in the distance. The police report said they were all carrying Israeli drivers' licenses and aroused suspicion by their actions. There are several quotes from American Jews who told about an Israeli messaging system that warned them not to go into the World Trade Towers that morning. There is a reason for the star of David on this file cover."

"Didn't you say Chip's wife is Jewish?" Ruth Ann asked.

"Yes, she is. I suppose that could have been one reason why he went down this avenue of discovery. When she gave me the file, she didn't say much other than this was what he was working on in the days before his death. Chip attached a couple more documents to this file, which I will read," Tom explained.

"*President Bush placed Cheney in charge of all federal programs dealing with weapons of mass destruction and their management within the Department of Defense, Health and Human Services, the Departments of Justice and Energy, the EPA, and several other agencies. This placed Cheney in charge of their training and planning. Dick Cheney oversaw everything, including the Office of National Preparedness inside of FEMA.*"

"Cheney must have been the person who rescheduled the war games to be ongoing on that morning. There were at least five war games going on when Boston Center's air traffic controller phoned into the military. There was confusion if the war games were a real hijacking or part of a drill. The war games slowed the military response that morning. I guess now we know why. They needed to delay the military response, or the entire charade would have been stopped." Jim said.

"My inquiring mind has always wondered why Mayor Giuliani did not report to his emergency command post in Building 7. FEMA was set up on Pier 29 for their Tripod II exercise. He even told ABC News that his office was operating out of Building 7 that morning until they were told that the towers were going to collapse," Ruth Ann said.

"So, he was told that the towers were going to collapse? Who would have told him that?" Vera asked.

"There is no way someone guessed that those towers would collapse; someone that the mayor knew well enough to trust had to have told him that. Those towers were designed and constructed to survive a Boeing 707 hitting them," said Jim.

"If Vice President Cheney oversaw all federal training, then he scheduled FEMA to be in New York City that morning. In addition, he arranged for the military drills, some of which included commercial planes flying into buildings. It is impossible to chalk this up to coincidence, Cheney was in complete control, and only a fool would believe that he was not involved in the planning of this disaster," Joel said.

Max could not contain himself any longer, "For years, this horrible event has been blamed on Islamic radicals, the House of Saud, Al-Qaeda, and Muslims in general. However, it has become apparent that our closest ally in the Middle East and our government were far more involved than anyone wants to admit. We have been unwrapping a very different story in these meetings. I don't know about the rest of you, but I don't like being labeled as a lunatic. If I sat and told my barber these details, his eyebrows would be so high on his forehead they may never return to normal."

Max's words caused the room to let out a collective sigh. Varying emotions penetrated each member of the group. They felt anger at the increased government intrusions. They felt resentment at the media for their deception. They felt growing distrust of the government and military for their involvement. They felt an unbearable sadness for the loss of millions of lives in wars fought in the Middle East. Finally, they felt horrified at the truth that had been uncovered. Silence filled the room as the magnitude of what 9/11 was, who was responsible, and the repercussions felt throughout the world bore heavily upon them.

Joel sensed the uneasiness in the Oval Office and suggested they take a two-hour break.

thirty-six

"I cannot help but notice Max has been having a difficult time sitting still since returning from lunch. Max, do you have something you want to add that we have overlooked?" Jim asked.

Max walked over to stand next to President Sherman so he could face the whole group and said, "Oh boy do I, I have felt like a caged animal since I received these two emails. Our website has been a wealth of information, but these two emails tie a bow around our investigation and serve it on a platinum platter. Let me read:

"*Mohamed Atta was in Florida learning to fly. Interestingly one of the last places he was seen on the 7th or 8th of September was at Shuckum's Raw Bar & Grill, a restaurant located on Young Circle in downtown Hollywood, Florida, awfully close to the Hollywood Bread Building, which is central to this account. Twelve hours after the attacks, FBI agents showed up at Shuckum's bar and passed around photographs of the accused hijackers.*

With the 20th anniversary of the 9/11 terrorist attacks on the United States coming up, I decided to write down what I know about what lead up to them. You see, I knew Mohammed Atta. I should have written this down years ago, but I feared for my life and my family's lives for the first years. Once that fear subsided, I just wanted to put it all behind me. I am sure that after 20 years, I might have some details wrong, but the core story is correct.

The Hollywood Bread Building is a 10-story building overlooking Young Circle Park, the central park in Hollywood, Florida. It is currently abandoned, and according to the papers, there are violent 'floor turf wars' being fought inside by the people squatting there. But in 2001, it was filled with many small businesses, including mine. I could see Young Circle from my 9th-floor windows. That's where Shuckum's was, and maybe still is – the oyster bar where the 9/11 hijackers last met to share a meal. It was widely reported that this happened on September 10th, but I believe that the timeline has been revised. I have made the conscious decision not to look up any facts about 9/11 now for fear that it would influence or shape what I remember. I worked together with an employee of mine in these offices on the 9th floor – let's call him Joey (not his real name). As soon as Mohammed Atta was fingered to be the ringleader in the attacks, both Joey and I almost fell out of our seats. "That guy? We know that guy!"

Joey would hang outside the front door a lot because he smoked and wasn't allowed to do it inside the building. So did others from the other floors. Atta was a frequent visitor to our building. What's interesting is who else was renting offices in the building. There was Moishe and the Israeli 'social club' on the 9th floor. They'd come in the late afternoon and stay until all hours of the night, sitting on couches and making phone calls in Hebrew on a speakerphone. I often worked late, sometimes until midnight, and they'd be there with the door open, assuming that all other tenants were long gone.

Then there was the 'trucking company.' They were Americans in a small office on the 9th floor that rented for about $350 a month back then. They started moving racks of computer servers into that office. This intrigued me since we built rack-mounted computers for a living. I was intrigued why a company that was renting a $350 office was moving in what looked like at least $100,000 worth of computer hardware. And what on earth could you need that kind of computing power for if all you were doing was keeping track of a small fleet of trucks? I asked the guy. He had no comment, and ever since that day, they kept their door shut.

And then, there was the 'moving company.' These guys also spoke Hebrew. I remember it as if it were yesterday. I was talking to a young guy who worked for them, outside the door, where they were smoking. I welcomed them to the building and asked what kind of work they did. The young guy didn't seem to know what to say. When he started to say something, an older guy shut him up and said, "we are a moving company." Then he told the young guy to put out his smoke and come inside with him.

What do these three companies have in common? Well, on September 12, 2001, they were all gone! Like they were never there. Offices cleaned out and left without a trace.

And then there was Johnny Cowboy (not his real name). Johnny was an interesting fellow. He functioned as a handyman for the building and offered car washes to people parking in the lot across the street. He never said much, but Joey and I saw him all the time and were friendly with him. He looked like a cowboy out of an old Western. While he scowled at most people, he liked us and spoke to us sometimes.

The 10th floor had been home to the Psychic Friends Network when I first moved in. Later, it became a technical school, and then it was empty. It was different than all the other floors – you couldn't get into the floor without a key. It was off-limits to all, but Johnny Cowboy had the keys. And I think he crashed there from time to time, as well. Meaning, Johnny knew everything that went on in the building at all hours.

One day, I came to work and saw fire trucks outside the building. When I got in the elevator, I noticed that a horrible stench had enveloped the whole building. It turns out someone found Johnny's decomposing body on the 10th floor. There were strange cops in the building, the kind with suits, sunglasses, and earpieces. I asked what happened. "Looks like he drank himself to death. They found a bottle next to his body," a firefighter answered. Joey and I looked at each other, puzzled. So, I said, "uh, Johnny didn't drink." The cop told us that we don't want to go around asking too many questions and told us to move along. Could Johnny have been a recovering alcoholic and had a relapse? Possible. Could he have seen something in that building at night that he wasn't supposed to see? Possible. Joey and I struggled for a while after September 11th, deciding whether we should call the FBI and tell them about Atta hanging out with the Israelis. After a few days, we did. They took our numbers. Nobody ever called us back or followed up. So, there it is, best as I can remember it.

The Israeli social club, the 'trucking' firm with the server banks. The Israeli 'moving company' whose employees didn't seem to know what business they were in – all went poof on September 12th, along with Johnny Cowboy, who drank himself to death or saw something he shouldn't have. Memory is a funny thing, and I'm sure I have mixed some details up. But I wanted to write it down exactly as I remember it, before comparing notes with Joey or researching the internet.

A few months after this happened, I closed my company, sold our house, and went on a multi-year RV trip. I didn't feel comfortable being able to be easily found. Not having an address seemed fine to me. For at least the first year or two, I fully expected that someone would probably find Joey and me either victims of unfortunate accidents or, more likely, with just a single gunshot wound to the back of our heads. I didn't tell anyone about any of this for years out of fear but then decided that if someone saw us as a threat, we would have been long gone. In a sea of conspiracy theories, anything is easily discredited. I don't have a theory – I just know what I saw. I don't claim to know what it all means. Joey and I check in with each other every year on 9/11 to cheer at having made it yet another year. If it was joint CIA/Mossad, then I suspect the CIA mostly supplied the refreshments and directions and left the "wet work" to the experts. The CIA would have botched it worse and sooner, even with the best efforts of their operatives in the media. As it was, the Mossad mob couldn't help themselves getting all over-excited like the dancing Israelis in the carpark in New Jersey who claimed they were sent to document the event.'"

Max stood silent as he scanned the reactions in the room. Most everyone was nodding in agreement. Finally, Ruth Ann spoke, "That certainly cements what we have suspected all along, the Israelis were involved from the beginning, and when the deed was done, they vanished; one thing they do very well is clean up after themselves."

"That's right. When you look at all the Israeli connections we have discovered, all the loose ends have been tied off. No wonder no one in government or the media dares to talk about them. They share this man's fear," Jim said.

"Wait until I read you this next email, I don't think you will have trouble believing it," Max explained and began to read:

"*On September 11, 2001, I watched the events on television with my Israeli brother-in-law in Miami, Florida. He told me that he "had been invited" by his IDF friends to join them in New York several months before. Between 9 am and 6 pm that day, he said, at least six times an hour, "They call this lighting the fuse. It has a double meaning to those guys. I can't believe they went ahead and did it anyway." His older brother, another brother-in-law to me, worked "for the organization that cannot be named" in Israel; around May 2001, he finished a special project for "the organization" using his specific skills as a physicist and mathematician. Within the center of the towers, as you might know, there were hollow vertical shafts for elevators. The "B Project" would have used that "balcony" as a platform for lowering the bomb experts through those elevator shafts to apply specific amounts of "gelatin" to the metal beams at the center. To determine exactly how much gelatin was needed, a physicist/mathematician would have calculated exact amounts in advance. It would then be applied according to specified amounts and locations. A fire ignited on the upper floor would be sufficient to ignite the "fuse" that is attached to the elevator shaft structure and could possibly be ignited from lower-level explosions. Thermite would have been included in the gelatin for the highest possible temperatures. The second meaning is that this event would "lite the fuse" of the global war that continues today."*

"My God, I don't know what to say," Ruth Ann blurted out.

"What can anyone say after that?" Rosslyn responded.

"I think those two emails say it all," Jim said.

"Those emails explain things that never made sense," Jerry commented.

"It certainly does explain how everyone involved in 9/11 had some type of connection to intelligence agencies," Vera said.

"Chip was definitely on the right track; it's too bad he wasn't here to participate in these meetings," Tom added.

Max was still standing when he said, "That explains the five dancing Israelis. This also proves their foreknowledge and whoever sent them to document the event. Our reluctance as a nation to seek the truth is the new world order's green light. Until this mass murder is dealt with and the true kingpins behind it are exposed and apprehended, we will remain in a heap of trouble."

Joel said, "All of this information in the past few days and especially these last two emails have affected me deeply. It will change everything I do as the President of the United States from now on. This knowledge will change the tone of any meeting I have with the Prime Minister of Israel or any of his Arab neighbors. This has been an incredible four days of meetings. I commend Jim for his preparation and presentation and all of you for your contributions. I know I need to decompress, and I am sure each of you do as well, so we will conclude our discussion."

President Sherman shook the hand of each member of the group as he thanked them. He returned to the resolute desk and remained standing. He motioned for Vera to join him and put his arm around her. He cleared his throat to regain his composure and said, "On behalf of myself and the First Lady, I am announcing publicly for the first time that we are running for re-election. It will be an intense campaign, and I am confident we will immerge victoriously. We would like to invite you to the White House to watch the election returns and celebrate with us."

thirty-seven

Following the final day's meeting, Ruth Ann and Rosslyn joined Max and Jim for a steak dinner at the BLT Prime restaurant in the Trump Hotel. The information overload and the repercussions of the meetings left Ruth Ann anxious. It was not so much that the revelations came as a total surprise, but she worried how these disclosures would be presented to the world. As a result, the conversations remained light throughout the dinner. After a round of Bailey's Irish Cream, Ruth Ann was finally able to relax. The mood remained casual, and even Rosslyn felt at ease, laughing and joking with the men. She delighted in Max's retelling of his death and burial experience and how he surprised Jim and Vera at his gravesite.

"So, what is the plan for us to fly back to California?" Asked Ruth Ann.

"Listen, I've got good news and bad news for you ladies. The Gulfstream 650 to LAX will be waiting for you at Dulles. The bad news is the only aircraft I could arrange is leaving at the crack of dawn. It's a beautiful plane though, I have flown on this one a couple of times. I know these last several weeks have been grueling, so I expect you to take some downtime. We will be in touch if any earth-shattering event occurs. Since you must wake up early tomorrow, we had better wrap up this evening and have you scoot back to your hotel," Max instructed.

Rosslyn took one last sip of water and said, "Thank you, Max, and you too, Jim. These meetings have been amazing. I am thrilled to learn that it wasn't just me and my blog readers looking closely into 9/11. Dinner was fabulous, and I am ready to get back to the room and get repacked. There is no problem with an early departure, Max. Early morning departures are one thing I got used to in my first years of flying. But, of course, flying out on a luxurious government Gulfstream with wi-fi and telephones will make it a lot easier to get out of bed."

Ruth Ann and Rosslyn were quiet on the short taxi ride to the hotel. Their room had been turned down, and each pillow displayed a wrapped dark chocolate Godiva heart. They quickly readied for bed after repacking their suitcases.

"I'm exhausted. There is so much on my mind after these meetings that my head is spinning trying to keep all the information in order," Ruth Ann explained.

"I hear you, Ruth Ann," Rosslyn agreed.

"I don't think I can take any more diary reading tonight, but if you read, take notes for me and make sure you pack a couple of diaries for our inflight reading," Ruth Ann said as her head hit the pillow.

"I sure will," Rosslyn whispered as she opened one of her father's diaries and read to herself: *I received classified documents from a White House source. Due to the increase in internet usage, more people are discovering subjects that concern the global elite. They feel they have lost control. There are too many people waking up to the New World Order. Suspicion of Israel grows as more Americans become aware of Zionism, international bankers, and their plan to dominate the entire world. They have lost their influence over the messaging they once had. When it was only a few television networks, books, and magazines, control was easy. The internet grew so rapidly that they lost their control. Now, they intend to use it as a weapon.*

Israel funded and promoted gatekeeper channels on the internet, which allows them to watch the content and comments. These shill channels are used to gather and identify open-minded people investigating the New World Order and its connection to Zionism. The purpose is to attract people to these truth movement channels to tag, track, and identify them. If people are informed and awake about the New World Order and Zionism, Israel wants to know exactly who they are, so they track people's IP addresses.

They will launch two projects; the first one uses YouTube and other social media channels. Some hosts are paid to espouse truthful information to attract an audience that can be tagged, tracked, and identified. We have had the technology for a long time to do this. There will be no escaping if anyone is informed and educated about their master plan because they will be considered a threat.

During the second stage, they're going to exterminate people. I saw two sets of numbers, one said 15%, and the other said 7% of Americans will die. People will be tagged for anti-Semitic speech, hate crimes, or misinformation. These documents expose guillotine use as described in the Noahide laws signed by both President Bush and his son. They will use targeted viral attacks to eliminate people without suspicion. They want to infect certain people with a virus that imitates the flu.

There will be power outages along with this purge. They're going to take people out of their homes and place them into camps. It will be a massive operation. It will occur under the cover of darkness during a planned electrical blackout. The blackouts will be blamed on everything from Iran to climate change. It has not happened yet because the tagging, tracking, and identifying are not complete. Once the elite knows who they are and where they live, they will be eliminated.

This goes beyond banning speech, which they're already doing, but not aggressively. If people stand in the way of their agenda, they will be gone. Unfortunately, too many people are waking up and influencing the conversation online, which is distressing Israel and the elite.

People considered to be high-value targets will be picked up. Lower value targets will be given viruses that activate in their bodies either immediately or later. The virus may be followed by a vaccine that frequencies will manipulate. Suddenly, several Americans become sick. Official stories in the news media of a flu outbreak will function as a cover, which shows this will begin in the winter. The authorities want a one-world government, and they will not tolerate any opposition. Eventually, they plan to dissolve the United States of America. World leaders and the media will endorse crazy ideas. In addition to the United States, other countries will be disbanded by creating a financial collapse. The total financial meltdown will be the reason governments claim we have to come together, create a new currency, and form a world government. It will be six months of financial chaos, food shortages, and crime.

Rosslyn read until she fell asleep.

Thirty-eight

Joel and Vera sat quietly over their dinner plates. The White House chef prepared one of their favorite meals, but neither had much of an appetite. The recent meetings with Jim Bowman and the others exposing the truth about 9/11 left them physically and emotionally exhausted. Moreover, the meetings presented them with a new challenge to continue with Joel's presidential campaign. They both pondered the ramifications of the whole 9/11 truth. The campaign would require them to be exposed to large gatherings of supporters. The threat of assassination to either of them was daunting and beyond comprehension.

"What do you say we give up on dinner and retire to the residence, have some dessert delivered and just talk?" Joel asked as he pushed his dinner plate away.

"Joel, I have so many thoughts and feelings about how to manage all of this new information; I'm not sure I can even eat my favorite dessert at this point. But a slice of either white cake or fresh apple pie might be easier to swallow," Vera said, "and maybe a few Godiva chocolates."

"The Godiva are no problem; I have a private stash you don't even know about," Joel admitted as he stood and winked.

"You do? You have hidden chocolates?" Vera asked. "Where?"

Joel raised his eyebrows, "I'll never tell you, but I will show you. I know how you love your chocolates."

After giving instructions to the staff, the two left the dining room and rode the elevator up to the residence. In less than five minutes, Mike tapped quietly on the door, "Sir, it's Mike with your dessert tray."

"Come in, Mike. You can set the tray just inside the door," Joel instructed. Vera was changing into her pajamas and robe in the dressing room, so Joel placed the gold box of Godiva chocolates on the tray.

"Oh, Joel! You are the sweetest," Vera said as she pulled the cellophane wrapping from the box.

"Looks like you confused the kitchen staff; they sent the white cake, apple pie, and a platter of fruit and cheese. They must know we are about to have an important conversation," Joel explained.

Vera made herself comfortable on the end of the sofa closest to the dessert tray. "Joel, as much as I knew that we had been lied to on 9/11, putting all these pieces of the puzzle together the way we have has cemented the awful reality in my mind. That reality is much more horrific than what they told us. It is much worse. What do we do with this knowledge? Is the truth about that day going to be hidden like the UFO files? How do we deal with this?"

Joel placed a slice of apple pie next to Vera as she spoke. He slowly shook his head, "Vera, I know exactly what you are feeling. Believe me; I have been considering the political fallout from exposing this truth to the public. If I did, I can't imagine what the generals at the Pentagon would do or say. Some of them must know this was an intelligence operation. I recall the Pentagon budget was about to be slashed until 9/11. They were given an unlimited budget beginning the afternoon of September 11th. Many of these generals became extraordinarily wealthy promoting the wars that followed and the false story of weapons of mass destruction in Iraq."

"I remember the Secretary of State at the time, on television promoting that theory. Didn't they claim that Mohammad Atta met with a son of Saddam Hussein in Prague?" Vera asked.

"Vera, your memory is correct. I must wonder how many of those generals and intelligence operatives demonizing Saddam Hussein knew that there were no hijackers on those planes? Not long ago, I read a book about how the Central Intelligence Agency trains its recruits. They set up fake scenarios, much like those faked hijackings," Joel's voice slowed.

"Joel, when I think about that event, I play every scenario out in my mind over and over," Vera admitted.

"Millions of people have been killed and injured throughout the Middle East. We have been destroying countries with weapons that will prevent them from farming their land for decades. Can you imagine being the parent of a soldier who lost his life in Iraq or Afghanistan and then twenty years later finding out that the war your son fought was the result of a staged event? We have destroyed people and families on both sides of these conflicts," Joel said as his face became red with anger.

"Joel, what about all those hundreds of Middle Eastern men we have picked up and thrown into Gitmo? Our intelligence agents tortured hundreds of men until they admitted to whatever they were accused of doing. If the truth were to come out, the entire world would react but not in a good way," Vera lamented.

"No kidding. I can only imagine what would happen if we revealed what we have learned over the past few days," Joel paused.

"Do you think presidents and politicians who preceded you have known the truth all along?" Vera asked as she felt a wave of nausea.

"It's difficult to say who knew what or when. My gut tells me that most likely both Clinton and Bush and their cabinets knew, as well as the top Generals in the Pentagon," Joel's said as he contemplated how the system was supposed to work. "The CIA is supposed to take direction from the President. It is possible that they were acting without his knowledge. The Director at the time served for several years under both administrations."

Vera leaned forward and grabbed her iPad off the coffee table. Her fingers quickly typed on the attached keyboard. "Before Tenet was the Deputy Director of the CIA, he spent his entire career working in intelligence. Ha! Joel, listen to this: *'Tenet appealed to the original mission of the agency, which was to 'prevent another Pearl Harbor'.*"

Joel was shocked, "Does it really say that?"

"Right here in his Wikipedia, under CIA Career, the last paragraph," Vera held the iPad toward Joel to show him.

"Unbelievable yet, that is exactly how they referred to that day, and the Project for a New American Century also refers to a need for a New Pearl Harbor!" Joel exclaimed.

Vera's iPad chimed with an incoming email. She read it to herself and then said, "It is from Jenny. I will read it to you. "*Vera, I hope this note finds you and Joel well. I felt I needed to share this information with you, and I hope you have time to read it. My brother brought this to my attention. I have noticed the state and city governments here in the other Washington using terminology from the documents provided. It is like a code or something. The city of Seattle has a self-admitted full-blown communist on the City Council. This is very frightening, and even my brother, who is not usually interested in political things, is concerned. After reading these documents, I am also questioning what happened to our country? This new cancel culture and insane political correctness are destroying people's careers and our once-great nation. Wishing you both success in the upcoming election season. Love, Jenny.*"

Vera sent Jenny's documents entitled Agenda 21 and Agenda 30 to the printer. She was thankful Jenny had highlighted some of the details and had included personal notes of concern. Kelli, their golden retriever, laid at Joel's feet, staring at him until he scratched her behind her ears.

"These are United Nations documents. These might help explain what Jenny was talking about. Are you aware of these United Nations manifestos they call 'A recipe for Global Socialism?'" Vera asked.

"I recall hearing about their proposals when I was the Speaker, but since the UN doesn't make our laws, I didn't give them much thought," Joel admitted. "Our founding fathers established our system of government so that we have a representative republic. Unfortunately, the media in this country often prefers socialism and the UN in control to replace our system of government," Joel said.

"Let me tell you why Jenny is so concerned about what is happening on the west coast. This UN plan is designed to empower a global one-world government within fifteen years."

"That sounds like a biblical prediction from Revelations, a one-world government. Is there anything in there about the mark of the beast?" Joel chuckled.

"Joel, I don't think this is at all funny. This looks like their roadmap to socialism and corporate fascism. They plan to redistribute the world's wealth, and they intend to destroy the middle class. The UN has been infiltrated by communists, which means we need to keep our eyes and ears open every talking head and political hack. It's a serious plan, and the survival of our republic is not part of it."

"Well, that middle class they want to destroy makes a huge contribution to our tax base. If they destroy the middle class, there will only be the wealthy and the poor, and that will destroy our country," Joel said.

"It looks like this group of globalists at the UN is planning to take away our freedom to eat red meat or use frozen and convenience foods. In addition, they want to do away with private ownership of motor vehicles, some electrical appliances and restrict the use of air conditioning. By claiming that these things are 'not sustainable,' they will control everything," Vera said.

"Who do you suppose will be making the judgment if something is sustainable or not?" Joel asked. "Will there be a global king, or do they think they can control every human action on the planet from a committee at the UN?"

"I haven't figured that out yet, but it looks like they have an end-times plan. This plan sounds dark and gloomy. These globalists have even adopted the communist party chairman Mao Tse-tung's motto, 'Next Leap Forward'!" Vera exclaimed.

"That motto didn't work out for fifty million Chinese who were either worked, starved, or beaten to death. He was one brutal dictator. Why would anyone want that for our country or, worse yet, for *every* country?" Joel questioned.

"They intend to dissolve our country, our history, and our national pride. This is a plot to re-engineer civilization. They want to do away with borders so there will be no nations, no national pride, and ultimately no freedom. The population will be slaves to the elite leaders. It explains why these same people want to open our borders to foreigners. Could that be the reason so many on the other side of the aisle fight against the border wall?" Vera asked.

"Perhaps."

Vera placed the printed documents in front of Joel, "This is their game plan, and I think we better figure out how to save our country. They also plan to control our healthcare, which has always been a keystone of socialism," Vera added.

"We must hit the campaign trail hard in the next several months. If I win the election and stay in office, we will expose and subvert this agenda. I know the polls show us ahead, but we cannot take anything for granted, Vera. If these communist sympathizers take over the Congress, the Senate, and the White House, we will find ourselves on the fast track to destruction," Joel warned.

thirty-nine

It was still dark when Ruth Ann and Rosslyn arrived at Dulles airport to board the jet to take them to California. They quickly stowed their carry-on luggage and nestled into the plush leather seats.

Ruth Ann found two pillows and a blanket and set them on her lap. "Between your father's diaries and all the information Jim shared, this certainly has been an interesting trip."

"You can say that again," Rosslyn said as she pulled a small diary from her purse. "I am not ready to quit. I plan to read more!"

"Let me know if you find anything I need to know about. Wake me if I fall asleep. I am going to rest my eyes and listen to some Vivaldi for a while," Ruth Ann said.

The pilot's voice came over the intercom, "We are ready for takeoff. Make sure your seatbelts are fastened. We will be at LAX before you know it."

"Sleep if you must but be ready for me to wake you. You know how interesting this diary material can be," Rosslyn laughed as she cracked open the small book and began to read.

Rosslyn tapped Ruth Ann's shoulder.

Ruth Ann pulled her headset off, "What is it?"

"This is mind-blowing. It's entitled 'The Illuminati and the Council on Foreign Relations,' it's a speech given by Myron Fagan in 1967."

Ruth Ann said, "let's hear it."

Rosslyn began to read from the diary: " '*The question of how and why the United Nations is the crux of a great conspiracy to destroy the sovereignty of the United States and enslave the American people within a UN one-world dictatorship is an unknown mystery to the vast majority Americans. The reason is simple. The masterminds behind this great conspiracy have absolute control of all our mass-communications media, especially television, the radio, the press, and Hollywood.*

We all know that our State Department, the Pentagon, and the White House have brazenly proclaimed that they have the right to manage the news, not tell the truth, but what they want us to believe. The aim is to brainwash the people into accepting the phony peace bait to transform the United States into a one-world government.

Bear in mind that the UN police action in Korea killed 150,000 of our sons. It was part of the plot, just as the undeclared war in Vietnam is part of the plot; just as the plot against Rhodesia and South Africa is part of the UN plot. However, the vitally important thing for all Americans to know is that our so-called leaders in Washington, who we elected to safeguard our nation and our Constitution, are the betrayers, and behind them are a small group of men whose sole objective is to enslave the whole world in their satanic-plot of a one-world government.

To give you a clear picture of this satanic plot, I will go back to the middle of the 18th century and name the men who put this plot into action and then bring you down to the present. Let me clarify the meaning of the expression 'he is a liberal.' The one-world conspirators have seized upon the word "liberal" as a cover-up for their activities. It sounds so innocent to be liberal. Make sure that the person who calls himself a liberal or is described as a liberal is not, in truth, a 'red.''"

"By 'red,' I understand he is referring to communists," Ruth Ann questioned, "Is that it? Has our history lesson ended?"

"Looks like we are in luck; there is more," said Rosslyn as she continued to read: "*'This satanic plot was launched back in the 1760s when it first came into existence under the name Illuminati. This Illuminati was organized by Adam Weishaupt, born a Jew who was converted to Catholicism and became a Catholic priest. At the behest of the then newly organized House of Rothschild, defected and organized the Illuminati. Naturally, the*

Rothschilds financed the operation and every war since then, beginning with the French Revolution.

After the Illuminati was exposed and became notorious, Weishaupt and his co-conspirators began to operate under various other names. In the United States, immediately after World War I, they set up the Council on Foreign Relations, commonly called the CFR. The masterminds in control of the original Illuminati conspirators were foreigners, but to conceal that fact, most of them changed their original family names to American-sounding names.

Immediately after the Napoleonic wars, the Illuminati assumed that all the nations were so destitute and weary of wars that they'd be glad for any solution, so the Rothschilds set up what they called the Congress in Vienna and tried to create the first League of Nations. But the Czar of Russia caught the stench of the plot and completely torpedoed it. The enraged Nathan Rothschild, then the head of the dynasty, vowed that someday he or his descendants would destroy the Czar and his entire family, which they carried out in 1917.

At this point, the Illuminati was not set up to operate on a short-range basis. Normally a conspirator of any type enters a conspiracy with the expectation of achieving his aim during his own lifetime. But that is not the case with the Illuminati. True, they hoped to conduct their aim during their lifetime, but paraphrasing 'The show must go on,' the Illuminati operates on a very long-range basis. Whether it will take scores of years or even centuries, they have dedicated their descendants to keep the pot boiling until they see the conspiracy is achieved.'"

Ruth Ann was spellbound, "Is there more? This is fascinating."

Rosslyn turned the page, "Yes, there is more, and continued reading, "*Adam Weishaupt was a Jesuit-trained professor of canon law, teaching at Engelstock University when he defected from Christianity to embrace the Luciferian conspiracy. The House of Rothschild retained him to revise and modernize the age-old protocols of Zionism, which from the outset, was designed to give the 'Synagogue of Satan,' (so named by Jesus Christ: 'and who are 'them which say they are Jews and are not' - Revelation 2:9) ultimate world-*

domination so they could impose the Luciferian ideology upon the human race. Weishaupt completed his task on May 1, 1776. Now you know why May 1st is the great day with all communist nations. Once Weishaupt completed his plan and officially organized the Illuminati, he put the plan into execution. The plan required the destruction of all existing governments and religions.

The aim was to be reached by dividing the masses of people, whom Weishaupt termed: goyism, nationalism, or human cattle, into opposing camps based on political, social, economic, and other issues - the very conditions we have in our country today. The opposing sides would then be armed, and manufactured events would cause them to fight and weaken themselves until gradually they would destroy national governments and religious institutions."

Rosslyn asked, "Shall we continue?"

Ruth Ann quickly nodded her head in anticipation as she took a sip of water.

Rosslyn read: "*Why did the conspirators choose the word 'Illuminati' for their satanic organization? Weishaupt himself said that the word is derived from Lucifer and means 'holder of the light.' In short, using the words: 'peace on earth' is bait, the same bait as 'peace' was used by the 1945 conspirators to force the creation of the United Nations. Weishaupt recruited some 2,000 paid followers. These included the most intelligent men in the field of arts and letters, education, the sciences, finance, and industry. He then established Lodges of the Grand Orient and Masonic Lodges to be their secret headquarters. The Weishaupt plan of operation required his Illuminati to do the following things to carry out their purpose: Use monetary and sex bribery to obtain control of men already in high places. Once influential persons fell for the lies, deceits, and temptations of the Illuminati, they were held in bondage by application of political and other forms of blackmail, such as threats of financial ruin, public exposure, or fiscal harm. Even death to themselves or beloved members of their families was not out of the question. Do you realize how many top officials in our government are controlled in just that way by the CFR? Do you realize how many homosexuals in our State Department, the Pentagon, all federal agencies, and even the White House are controlled that way?*

Illuminati and the faculties of colleges and universities were to cultivate students with exceptional mental ability belonging to well-bred families with international leanings and recommend them for special training in this internationalism. Such training was to be provided by granting scholarships to those selected by the Illuminati. That should give you an idea of what a "Rhodes' Scholarship" means. It means indoctrination into accepting the idea that only a one-world government can put an end to recurring wars and strife. That's how the United Nations was sold to the American people. One of the most notable Rhodes Scholars in our country is Senator William J. Fulbright, sometimes referred to as half-bright. His voting record spells Illuminati.

All influential people trapped into coming under the control of the Illuminati, plus the students who had been specially educated and trained were to be used as agents and placed behind the scenes in governments as experts and specialists so they would advise top executives to adopt policies which would serve the secret plans of the Illuminati.

The most crucial directive in Weishaupt's plan was to obtain absolute control of the press so that all news and information could be slanted to convince the masses that a one-world government is the only solution to solving problems. '"

Rosslyn looked at Ruth Ann, "this is all taking place today. No wonder they tell the same story and always take the side of the democrat party or those who call themselves liberals. It's starting to make sense to me now; they are communists."

Rosslyn continued, reading: "*In 1785, the Bavarian government outlawed the Illuminati and closed the Lodges of the Grand Orient. In 1786, they published all the details of the conspiracy. The English title of that publication is: 'The Original Writings of the Order and the Sect of the Illuminati.' Copies of the entire conspiracy were sent to all the heads of church and state in Europe. But the power of the Illuminati, which was the power of the Rothschilds, was so great that this warning was ignored.*

Nevertheless, the Illuminati became a dirty word, and it went underground. At the same time, Weishaupt ordered Illuminists to infiltrate the Lodges of 'Blue Masonry,' where they formed their own secret societies. Only Masons who proved themselves internationalists and whose conduct proved they had defected from God were initiated into the Illuminati. Thenceforth, the conspirators donned a cloak of philanthropy and humanitarianism to conceal their revolutionary and subversive activities.

Now here is something that will stun and likely outrage many who hear this, but there is documentary proof that our own Thomas Jefferson and Alexander Hamilton became students of Weishaupt. Jefferson was one of Weishaupt's strongest defenders when his government outlawed him, and it was Jefferson who infiltrated the Illuminati into the then newly organized lodges of the Scottish Rite in New England. Here is the proof: In 1789; John Robison warned all Masonic leaders in America that the Illuminati had infiltrated into their lodges, and on July 19, 1789, David Papen, President of Harvard University, issued the same warning to the graduating class and lectured them on how the influence of Illuminism was acquitting on American politics and religion, and to top it off, John Quincy Adams, issued his warnings. He wrote three letters to Colonel William L. Stone, a top Mason, in which he exposed how Jefferson was using Masonic lodges for subversive Illuminati purposes. Those three letters are at this very time in the Whittenburg Square Library in Philadelphia.

In short, Jefferson, founder of the Democratic Party, was a member of the Illuminati, which accounts for the condition of the party currently. Through the infiltration of the Republican Party, we have very few loyal Americanism today. The disastrous rebuff at the Congress of Vienna created by the Czar of Russia did not destroy the Illuminati conspiracy. It merely forced them to adopt a new strategy realizing that the one-world idea was, for the moment, killed. The Rothschilds decided to keep the plot alive. They would have to do it by heightening their control of the money system of the European nations.

In 1826, Captain William Morgan decided it was his duty to inform all Masons and the public about the Illuminati, their secret plans, intended aims, and to reveal the identities of the masterminds of the conspiracy. The Illuminati tried Morgan in absentia and convicted him of treason. They ordered Richard Howard, an English Illuminist, to carry out their sentence of execution. Morgan was warned, and he tried to escape to Canada, but Howard caught up with him near the border, near the Niagara Gorge, and murdered him.

This was verified in a sworn statement made in New York by Avery Allen that he heard Howard give his report of the execution in a meeting of Knights Templars in St. John's Hall in New York. He also said that arrangements had been made to ship Howard back to England. That Allen declaration of facts is on record in the New York City Archives. Copies of the minutes of that meeting are still in existence in safe hands

Weishaupt died in 1830, but prior to his death, he prepared a revised version of the age-old conspiracy titled, The Illuminati, which was to organize, finance, direct, and control all international organizations and groups by working their agents into executive positions of power. In the United States, we have Woodrow Wilson, Franklin Roosevelt, Jack Kennedy, Lyndon Johnson, Dean Rusk, Robert McNamara, William Fulbright, George Bush, etc., as prime examples. While Karl Marx was writing the Communist Manifesto under the direction of one group of Illuminists, Professor Karl Ritter of the Frankfurt University was writing its antithesis under the direction of another group."

Ruth Ann interrupted, "That sounds like the Hegelian Dialectic, problem, reaction, solution."

Rosslyn agreed, "It sure does."

"Max has mentioned something he called The Octopus and the New World Order, so I have heard of it. I am thinking that what you are reading here is the background for that," Ruth Ann explained. "Please, continue."

Rosslyn read: "*The idea was to use the differences in those two ideologies to enable them to divide larger and larger numbers of humans into opposing camps so that they could be armed and then brainwashed into fighting and destroying each other. Which, in turn, would destroy all political and religious institutions. The work Ritter started continued after his death and was completed by the German philosopher Friedrich Wilhelm Nietzsche who founded Nietzscheanism. Nietzscheanism later evolved into Fascism and then into Nazism which was used to foment World War I and II.*

World War II was fomented by using the controversies between Fascists and Political Zionists. Hitler was financed by Krupp, the Warburg's, the Rothschilds, and other internationalist bankers. The slaughter of six million Jews by Hitler didn't bother the Jewish internationalist bankers at all. It was necessary to create worldwide hatred of the German people and thus bring about war against them. In short, the Second World War was fought to destroy Nazism and increase the power of political Zionism so that the state of Israel could be established in Palestine.

During World War II, international communism was built up until it equaled the strength of united Christendom. When it reached that point, it was to be contained and kept in check until required for the final social cataclysm. As we know now, Roosevelt, Churchill, and Stalin put that exact policy into effect, and Truman, Eisenhower, Kennedy, and Johnson, continued that same policy.

World War III will be fomented, using controversies by the Illuminati that are now being stored up between the political Zionists and the leaders of the Muslim world. That war is to be directed in such a manner that all of Islam and political Zionism (Israelis) will destroy each other, while at the same time, the remaining nations, once more divided, will be forced to fight themselves into a state of exhaustion; physically, mentally, spiritually, and economically.

Can a thinking person doubt that the intrigue in the Middle and the Far East is designed to conduct that satanic aim? Albert Pike himself foretold all this in a statement he made to Mazzini on August 15, 1871. After World War III ended, Pike said that those who will aspire to undisputed world-domination will provoke the greatest social cataclysm the world has ever known. Quoting his own words taken from the letter he wrote to Mazzini and which letter is now cataloged in the British Museum in London, England, he said: 'We shall unleash the nihilists and the atheists, and we shall provoke a great social cataclysm which in all its horror will show clearly to all nations the effect of absolute atheism. The people will be forced to defend themselves against the minority of world revolutionaries and exterminate those destroyers of civilization and the multitudes disillusioned with

Christianity. A manifestation that will result from a general reactionary movement will follow the destruction of Christianity and Atheism; both conquered and exterminated at the same time.'

During his term of office as the President of the United States, Jack Kennedy became a true Christian. In his attempt to repent, he tried to inform the people of this Nation at least twice that the Illuminati and CFR were manipulating the Office of the President of the United States. At the same time, he put a stop to the borrowing of Federal Reserve Notes and began issuing United States Notes, which were interest-free, on the credit of the United States. It was the issuing of these United States Notes that caused Jack Kennedy to be assassinated."

"Oh, my, that is one history lesson," Ruth Ann said solemnly. "Didn't you say this was from a lecture given in 1967?"

"Yes, that's correct," Rosslyn answered.

Ruth Ann had an internet search open on her iPad, "Myron Fagan died in 1972. It is amazing to think that he wrote this nearly sixty years ago and look at the mess our government is in now. Several years back, anyone who mentioned the Council on Foreign Relations, or the Trilateral Commission would have been labeled a conspiracy theorist. Now, the mainstream media openly talks about them all the time. Our nation must be at a turning point in history, and Joel Sherman's chance placement in the White House was not what these globalists had in mind. Their plans must have been slowed down, and we better pray that he is re-elected in the upcoming election, or we could see this horrific master plan play out. I know what happened in Europe a hundred years ago, and it is hard to imagine that could happen here in America. Still, as this Mr. Fagan said, these communists are evil, and there is no limit to the horrors that a one-world communist government could bring. Imagine if America fell to communism; as President Reagan said, we are the last bastion of hope in the world. If we fall to communism, the entire world will lose hope."

"You're right, Ruth Ann; we better pray that President Sherman is re-elected and that he can fight this global monster whose mission is to destroy our nation and our freedom.

Didn't Nikita Khrushchev say to a group of Western ambassadors in 1956, 'We will bury you' and then years later he clarified that statement by saying, 'Of course we will not bury you with a shovel, your own working class will bury you.' That sounds to me like he was saying your enemy is from within," Rosslyn opined.

"Khrushchev did say those things, and they have certainly come to pass. I wonder if we should copy those pages from your father's diary and send them to Joel and Vera," Ruth Ann suggested.

Rosslyn was busy searching through the diary for more documents. "We probably should do just that, Ruth Ann, that's a good idea. What will happen if these globalists that want to destroy our country manage to steal the election from Joel? I know his poll numbers are super great, and the people love what he has done for our country while he's been in the White House, but what if they find a way to rig the electronic voting machines or, heaven forbid, something happens to Joel and Vera. What if they install a globalist or communist, and they begin to rapidly dismantle our borders and constitution?"

"When we get to Randall's house, we need to scan and email these notes to Jim and Max. They will get them to Joel. Max wants to keep tabs on us for the next few months just in case the explosion at Vera's house was suspicious," Ruth Ann said.

"Good idea. Ruth Ann, the warning my dad left in his diaries, is that he believed this cabal is real and their plan to destroy America is real. As I read that last page, I remembered him mentioning America's destiny, but he would never tell me more. This must be what he was referring to. I am feeling sick to my stomach after reading those pages. I know now that our meeting at the spa that day and your connection to the First Lady and the President was not a chance meeting. We were destined to be a part of this mission to wake up the people of this country to the threat to our land."

"Rosslyn, I need to close my eyes for a few minutes; how much flight time is left before we land in California?" Ruth Ann asked.

"We have a little under two hours to go; get some sleep, Ruth Ann. You know Randall will be full of questions, and after dinner, we will be filling him in on everything we learned in the meetings. I know he adores President Sherman, so he will be excited to hear every detail," Rosslyn said.

She closed the book and placed it back inside her tote bag. She felt deceived by the corporate media, and she began to question how much of this dastardly plot others were aware of. Why would someone want to destroy a nation that offered hope to so many people around the world? It all seemed too Satanic and evil. She decided to close her eyes, too, and rest her mind for the duration of the flight. She was excited to be reunited with her cat, Dizzy Bear, and wondered if he would be happy to see her. She and Ruth Ann were planning to tour throughout the southwest; she had always wanted to experience Sedona, Arizona.

"Disguise is only a tool...

Before you use any tradecraft tool,

you have to set up the operation for the deception."

~ Tony Mendez, Former CIA, 'Master of Disguise'

A FINAL WORD

You are probably asking, what next? And I keep writing 'this is the last book in the series,' at the end of every book. But, this time, I will say, I intend to write one more book in this series. Although the next book may not have the same level of discovery about 9/11, it will hopefully explain why 9/11 happened and how we might manage and maneuver through all the changes that resulted from that event.

As I write this note, we are approaching the twentieth anniversary of 9/11. The current U.S. government is now working with the Taliban of Afghanistan, the proclaimed enemy and the reason for the war following 9/11. Unfortunately, history has a way of repeating itself, especially if we are too busy to recognize the patterns. There is nothing new under the sun, but we must be knowledgeable about our history to avoid past mistakes and vulnerabilities.

In closing, I would like to invite you to join my membership webpage: www.behindthegalleycurtain.com. You will find 9/11 information, a daily news broadcast, and more. I do not associate with any sponsors, so I have the freedom to say what I see on matters of daily events and worldwide news. I can be contacted at the membership site or via the website: www.readroth.com

CPSIA information can be obtained
at www.ICGtesting.com
Printed in the USA
LVHW021646280921
698930LV00003B/389

9 780997 645767